THE ROAD HOME

MALISSA CHAPIN

IVORY KEYS PRESS LLC

To Eva Bonner
My beautiful mother, who met her precious Jesus April 10, 2020.
You always believed I would write a book. I wish you were here to
read it.

'Tis so sweet to trust in Jesus,
Just to take Him at His word,
Just to rest upon His promise,
Just to know, "Thus saith the Lord."
Jesus, Jesus, how I trust Him!
How I've proved Him o'er and o'er!
Jesus, Jesus, precious Jesus!
O for grace to trust Him more!
—Louisa M. R. Stead

CHAPTER 1

D *eercrest, Wisconsin*

The second time Audra changed her name was a disaster. The first? Well, she had wiped it from her memory. But you know what they say about the third time. She hoped never to change her name again or need to disappear at midnight. Audra smiled in the mirror and checked her teeth for bits of breakfast.

"Good morning, Cadence," she said to her reflection.

She tied her brown hair into a messy bun low on her neck and rubbed moisturizer onto her pale, freckled cheeks.

While escaping the mess from name change number two, Audra stopped in the tiny Northwoods town of Deercrest, Wisconsin. She planned to move on, but the "for rent" sign on the little white cottage changed her mind. Deercrest offered her a fresh start, so if it helped her blend in, she would live a dull, quiet life.

The little white house reminded her of the last place she belonged—Grandmother's. She loved everything about the cottage: the crooked gate, the flower beds, and the feeling of safety. She filled it with vintage treasures she found on her trips to the thrift store and made it her home.

In Deercrest, Audra was Cadence—the quiet barista and thrift store queen. She knew her quirkiness made people scratch their heads, but she must blend in. So her past—and her name—remained secret.

Her phone rang. "Cadence, can you come in for the Cowcrest Festival? I know you do your antique shopping on Saturday, but I need you for the noon shift."

"Of course, Laura. I'll come right over." She had just enough time to run through her favorite antique store before work if she hurried.

"Morning, Cadence."

Cadence scooped up a shopping basket. "Gotta hurry today. Laura needs me at the café for the festival."

The clerk nodded, "New stuff at the top of the stairs."

Cadence took a deep breath. Dust and age—mmm, her favorite.

Who knows what I'll find?

She touched laces and linens and scanned book titles. She checked a set of old china for chips and flipped through bins of old photos.

Oh. You poor people. You're like me—unwanted.

She grabbed a photo of three children. A pudgy boy with a mischievous grin stood in front of his siblings. His round tummy strained the jacket buttons. Cadence laughed out loud at his sweet expression. "You're going home with me, little guy. I want you even if no one else does."

She spied a red metal box labeled "Recipes." Cadence popped the lid open and held her breath.

Bingo! Handwritten recipe cards.

She flipped through the cards and whispered the titles: "'Salmon Salad Surprise,' 'Republican Dessert,' 'Apple Stack Cake,' 'Kilt Lettuce,' 'Biscuits,' 'Kentucky Blue-Ribbon Pie,' and a bunch of those awful mayonnaise gelatin salads. Poor box."

Why do people discard things so easily?

She grabbed a pair of naughty Christmas choir boy figurines at the checkout counter. Both wore white choir robes with red bows tied under their chins. One sported a black eye, and the other one's pocket held a slingshot. She chuckled while the cashier totaled her purchases.

City officials change highway and road signs for the two-day festival. "Welcome to Cowcrest" and "You are leaving Cowcrest" signs greet tourists and locals as they enter or exit town on Highway 10.

The two-day festival features a genuine Wisconsin kickoff for June Dairy Month. Grab your favorite dairy treats and enjoy a family-friendly day in Cowcrest. Bring your best moo for the cow calling contest or enter to win the best cow costume prize. Plenty to do for all ages at Cowcrest Days.

—Deercrest Daily Digest

Deercrest's streets buzzed with traffic. Cows hung from the light poles, and cows or cow print curtains hung in every window along Main Street. A teenager in a cow costume took selfies with children. Music drifted from the park where food trucks sold dairy treats. Cadence sniffed the air for deep-fried cheese curds—she would grab some after her shift.

Chalk drawings of cows and barns covered the sidewalks. Children with painted cow-print faces licked large cones of frozen custard. Wisconsin loved dairy, and Deercrest loved June Dairy Month. The town became Cowcrest for the weekend festival, and people came from all over to celebrate.

Cadence smelled coffee and vanilla when she opened the door of the busy café. "Sorry I'm late!" she hollered.

"Did you stop at the antique store?" Laura called from the cash register.

She shrugged. "Sorry. Couldn't help it."

"No worries," Laura said, laughing. "Grab an apron and get me another tray of cream puff bars."

Laura's cream puff bars won an award from a local travel magazine, and every customer purchased one with their coffee or took several to go. Cadence and Laura baked hundreds of bars every day last week. The freezer racks held trays of cream puff bars ready to top with rich honey-sweetened cream.

Laura's daughter, Allie, waved her spatula when Cadence hurried past. "Morning, Cadence. Mom stuck me on whip cream duty today."

"You're doing great. I love your cows in the window."

"Chalk marker!" Allie hollered over the noisy mixer. "Did you find cool stuff this morning?"

"A recipe box."

"I'll peek at it whenever Mom lets me take a break, okay?"

"Sure. I'll leave it on the desk."

The hours flew by while Cadence served guests. She pulled bars from the freezer, cleaned tables, and chatted with customers. Her feet ached, but her heart was happy.

She loved Cowcrest Days, but she wanted to get home to clean out the weeds in her garden and practice her knitting lesson. She whistled while washing dishes and swept the back room.

"Cadence," Allie called. "I Googled the name in that recipe box for you. The woman's daughter lives in town, so I wrote her address on a card. Wonder if there's a reward if we return it." Allie raised her eyebrows and made a silly face. "*The Case of the Missing Recipe Box* sounds like a good mystery novel, doesn't it?"

Cadence smiled. "Definitely. You write it, and I'll read it."

"Will you try to return the box?"

Cadence shrugged. "Maybe."

Allie fancied herself an Internet sleuth, so when Cadence found labeled vintage items, Allie searched for family members. She and Cadence worked together to return the treasures to the families. Cadence wondered if people viewed her hobby as strange, but it brought her joy.

I hope someone sends me a message when they find something of Grandmother Miggs's.

Cadence cleaned the bakery area and clocked out. She hummed a cheerful tune, excited for the evening ahead when a woman's voice drifted to the back room.

"I'll take a caramel latte, half-caff, soy milk, no whip, extra drizzle. Not too hot. Hurry up."

"No!" Cadence's stomach knotted, and her hands shook. She leaned on the counter to gulp air. "No. No. No. Why is she here?"

Chapter 2

Indianapolis, June 1940

Ida Bealle Evans raced to answer the door before her father got to Bud. "I'm ready." She slipped out the door and tried to close it before Daddy cornered him.

"Excuse me, son. Where are you off to with my daughter?"

"To the festival, Mr. Evans. I'll have her home by 10."

Father didn't like Bud, but for the life of her she didn't understand why. Bud was simply a dream.

When her father nodded, Ida Bealle gripped Bud's hand and followed him to the car. "I'm sorry, Bud. Daddy's too strict. I hope he doesn't scare you."

"Your father loves you, Miss Ida Bealle, and I respect him. He wants to keep you safe." Bud smiled, and she wanted to swoon.

Music from a calliope drifted across the fairgrounds and children ran to buy tickets, followed by mothers carrying tired babies.

Bud and Ida Bealle strolled through the festival and stopped to pet animals. Bud won a teddy bear in an Uncle Sam game. He threw five balls into the open mouth and never hit the flag-striped box underneath. When the bell rang, Ida Bealle clapped her hands and hugged the bear.

Bud laughed and reached for her hand. "You know, I thought your name was Ida *Bell* until I heard your mother call you to the car after church one Sunday. She said, 'Ida Bealle Evans, march!' Aha! It's *Bealle*—like *wheel*. I went home and repeated your name ten times a day while I worked up the courage to ask you on a date. I didn't want to embarrass myself and say your name wrong." His blue eyes twinkled when he smiled. "How about a ride on the Ferris wheel, Miss Ida Bealle?"

She hated heights but loved Bud, so she nodded and followed him through the maze of people.

The Ferris wheel took them high above the festival at sunset. "Oh, it's so beautiful up here!" She gripped Bud's strong hand, worried about the tall ride, but the evening sky and Bud's strength eased her mind.

"It's only beautiful because *you're* here, Miss Ida Bealle."

She giggled. "Bud, you make me blush." She turned away from the festival lights, and her heart raced at the look in Bud's eyes.

He squeezed her hand and whispered, "Will you marry me?"

Did my brain trick me? He did not say . . .

She jerked back to look at him, "Bud, did you say . . ."

He nodded and held out a small box, his eyes bright.

"Marry me, Miss Ida Bealle?"

She took the red velvet box and touched the ring—a thin gold band and small square diamond. "Bud?"

He leaned over and pulled the ring from the box. "Look inside."

"To IBE from BH 1940"

"Oh, Bud—what about the war? What if you have to go away? I . . . "

Bud took her hand and slid the ring onto her finger. Their seat rocked when he leaned closely to her. "I'm a seminary student."

"After seminary?"

"Ministerial deferment, Miss Ida Bealle."

She nodded, "Yes, yes, of course, Bud Horne. I'll marry you and spend every day with you for the rest of my life."

A smile spread across his handsome face, and someone below whooped, "Kiss her!"

He leaned over and kissed her to the applause of the other Ferris wheel passengers.

Ida Bealle blushed and rubbed her finger across the ring. Peace filled her heart. She tried filing away every detail of this perfect moment. She never wanted to forget the night Bud Horne's heart became her home.

<h1 style="text-align:center">Chapter 3</h1>

*H*ome. *I have to get out of here without Taylor noticing me. Get home.*

Cadence's head pounded, and her stomach ached. She leaned over the counter and gulped air to calm herself. Her mind raced. It would only take Taylor Nash a few seconds to place a coffee order and destroy Cadence's life.

Cadence loved to run out and greet customers, but not this time. She would not walk out there and allow Taylor to expose her identity. Cadence gritted her teeth and held the counter. She filled her lungs with air.

Calm down.

While she waited for her heart to slow, she rehearsed all the ways Taylor had wounded her. Her head pounded, and her queasy stomach rumbled.

How will I sneak out of here? Laura will wonder why I didn't greet the customer, but I can't go out there. If I leave, Taylor will see me walk home. Too risky.

She struggled to breathe, and her stomach twisted. When she focused her eyes, her head hurt. She leaned on the counter for a moment, then tiptoed to the doorway. Taylor walked through the front door, her red hair tumbling down her back in tight corkscrew curls. Adult Taylor appeared the same as teenage Taylor—stylish, confident, and beautiful.

Ugg. Why are you here now? I'm happy. At least I was happy.

Cadence leaned on the counter to get her breath under control.

Think fast, Cadence, or you're about to be Audra on the run again.

"Cadence. Honey, are you okay? Are you sick?" Laura hurried over. "What happened? You were fine a minute ago."

Laura's concern made her heart lurch. She bit her lip to stop the tears.

Pull it together, Cadence, before you ruin everything.

Laura leaned down and checked Cadence's eyes. "Oh, sweetheart, you are positively green. Come. Sit down. Put your head between your knees. Do you need a trash can? Is your stomach sick?"

Laura moved her to the chair and laid a cool cloth on her head. Laura rubbed Cadence's back in small circles the way her grandmother used to do.

Oh, Laura, please don't be sweet. I can't hold it together if you're kind.

"You okay?"

Cadence nodded. "It's okay. I need to get home." She stood and swayed. The floor moved in circles, and everything waved.

"I'll call Thatcher. I saw his cruiser go by a minute ago." Laura hurried to her office, leaving Cadence alone with her nausea.

Not good. Thatcher Stevens is the last person who needs to see me.

"Thatcher's on his way, but he said it will take several minutes." Laura called from the office, "I haven't heard of any tummy bugs around here. I hope it wasn't food you ate."

Cadence sat with her eyes closed and breathed in and out.

Focus.

The bells over the front door jingled. "Thatcher's here," Laura said.

Cadence put her head in her hands. *Why is my life out of control again?* White-hot rage forced tears down her cheeks. *Good. No one has to know it's anger. They'll assume I'm sick.*

"Cadence, what happened? Let's get you home." Thatcher's deep voice sounded near her ear. His hand under her elbow guided her to the door. His muscular arms held her up when her knees buckled. "Whoa —I got you."

"You rest," Laura said. "Don't worry about tomorrow—we're okay. If you want to work Monday, call me. Otherwise, take care of yourself."

Cadence nodded and waved a weak goodbye. Thatcher herded her out the backdoor and settled her into the front seat of the police cruiser. "Put you in the front—the back is for bad guys." He grinned.

She nodded, thankful for his thoughtfulness.

"Should I stop for crackers or tea?"

"No, thanks, Thatcher. I'll feel fine when I rest. No need for you to go out of your way."

"It's no trouble, Cadence. I'm happy to help."

"I'm good."

Pressure built behind her eyes, and she bit the inside of her cheek. She took several deep breaths.

Me in a police car—ironic. What will I do? Breathe, Cadence. Breathe.

Do not cry. Do not sweat. Don't cops look for nervousness? He'll suspect me if I sweat.

Cadence wanted to get home and slam her door shut on the outside world, to cocoon inside her cottage, where she was safe, to curl up in bed under the soft covers until the cold fear in her belly left, and then wash her face and move on—as she did last time, and the time before.

She leaned her head on the cool window and thought about her friendship with Thatcher. Before their bowling date last week, he had come in while she was cleaning the kitchen. She offered him a pickle from her first attempt at canning. Thatcher hopped up onto her counter and crunched his way through a whole jar, complimenting her on her canning success. When he left her at her front door, he gave her a chaste kiss on the cheek and begged for more pickles. If her life wasn't such a mess, she imagined him as "the one". He was so fine in his uniform, but now—he can't find out. *I can't afford to let him find out about Audra. No police officer for me.*

"Home," Thatcher said. "Here—let me help you inside."

"No, Thatcher. I'll get myself in." She stumbled over her words and hopped out of the car. Her hand shook when she tried unlocking the door.

Get inside, and this nightmare is gone. You worked too hard this week. Get in bed and forget Taylor. Forget your problems. Survive 'til this blows over.

Cadence slipped inside the dark entryway and set her bag and the recipe box on a shelf. She blew out a heavy sigh and swallowed hard. "A cup of tea, a blanket, and a quiet evening. I'm fine. Everything is fine. Tea in my cozy kitchen will settle these nerves. I'll brew chamomile. Yes, that should do it."

She reached for the kitchen light and gasped. Her nausea returned, and she grabbed the doorframe before her legs gave out.

No.

CHAPTER 4

Indianapolis, September 1940

Ida Bealle Evans sat in the corner and listened while the church ladies chatted and knit. She focused on the pattern and her stitches. If she messed up, she would have to start over—again.

Fingers flew and knitting needles clicked while balls of pink and blue yarn rolled across the floor. This month the members of the Ladies' Missionary Society were knitting baby blankets for a hospital in Brazil. Ida Bealle enjoyed knitting, but these ladies speed-knit, talking and laughing, never looking at the pattern.

The happy voices stilled when a little girl stepped up to Ida Bealle with a large box wrapped in brown paper.

"Oh, thank you, Elsie." Ida Bealle read the attached card. "This is from everyone. Thank you."

A red-and-white quilt sewn in exquisite detail rested inside the box. Ida Bealle pulled it out and gasped. "What a beautiful treasure!"

She reached for Mother's hand and glanced around the room at the ladies. Tears spilled down her cheeks, and Mother pressed a handkerchief into her hand.

"No tears, Ida Bealle. It's a happy occasion." Mrs. Ray smiled from the other corner of the room. "We know you aren't moving to a foreign land, Ida Bealle. But I told the ladies you're going to Who-Knows-Where, Kentucky, and you deserve a quilt too."

Ida Bealle smiled. "I'm thankful for this beautiful treasure." She patted her eyes with the handkerchief. The church ladies had known her since her birth. Mother helped found the missionary society and had dragged Ida Bealle to a meeting when she was three weeks old. She spent many childhood hours at meetings while the church ladies worked. They liked reminding her of her foolish shenanigans. They helped her grow up—an extension of her mother. They scolded when necessary and hugged often. Their opinions and bossiness annoyed her at times, but she loved them.

I'll miss this circle of women surrounding me in my next chapter of life.

"You can start a missionary circle down in Kentucky!" someone called from the back corner of the living room. "You're the pastor's wife—no one can say no!" The women chuckled.

"Imagine our Ida Bealle, a pastor's wife." The women sighed, and a few pulled out a handkerchief and wiped teary eyes.

"Speaking of pastor's wife . . ." the women turned to Mrs. Elliot.

A petite lady waved and hurried through the maze of women and chairs, stepping over purses and toes. "We have one more gift for you, Ida Bealle." Mrs. Elliot held out a bright red box with pictures of little jars across the front—a letter on each jar spelled out *Recipes*. "Recipes from each of us." Mrs. Elliot smiled. "A word of advice, you never want a hungry pastor."

The women laughed, and Ida Bealle smiled through her tears.

Thank you, God, for these dear women. Thank you for their support and encouragement while I grew.

"Let's pray for our sweet girl, ladies." Mrs. Elliot rested a hand on Ida Bealle's shoulder, and the women gathered around. Surrounded by a circle of love and prayer, she bowed her head as the women's prayers filled her soul with peace.

Ida Bealle sat in her bare room surrounded by trunks. She held the quilt in her arms; the vibrant red fabric made the white pieces stand out and showed off the quilt pattern. The ladies had spent many hours sewing the quilt, and when she found their names embroidered in a corner, she smiled and ran her finger over the stitches.

I'll never feel this spoiled again.

The daughters of John Evans, the banker, enjoyed many perks—Father spoiled them and gave them everything they wanted. Her parents' community service and generous donations gave their daughters prominence in their city. But now she was leaving—off to Kentucky—to marry the "fool-headed boy," as Father called him.

Ida Bealle smiled. Tomorrow she would marry Bud, and while she knew he would always cherish her, she knew he would never attain wealth. She enjoyed life with a housekeeper and cook in their big comfortable home. Ida Bealle liked Father's money—a lot.

Mother knocked and peeked around the door. "May I join you?"

"Come in, Momma."

Mother sat on the bed and hugged Ida Bealle. "Ida Bealle Evans, why are you up here sighing?" her mother whispered while kissing the top of her head. Mother's signature scent, "Joy," enveloped Ida Bealle in a familiar cloud of jasmine and roses. "Tomorrow is your big day, so dry your eyes. Prince Charming will arrive for dinner in twenty minutes."

"I'm not sad, Mother. Not exactly."

Mother nodded. "I know, baby girl. I cried for weeks before your father and I got married. It's nerves and goodbyes and all the unknowns. But you're happy. I can see it in your eyes."

"Father says he's foolish."

"Bud Horne isn't foolish. If he were, I'd lock you up and keep you here. He loves you, and most importantly, he loves God. He'll take you on a crazy adventure, and you'll love it."

"Why does life always change?"

Her mother nudged her, and she sat up straight. "You can't go from the city banker's daughter to the country preacher's wife without change, dear heart." Her mother giggled and took Ida Bealle's chin in her hands. "Look at me, baby girl. God loves you, and so do I. You've always wrapped your father around your little finger, and that young man adores you. Someday you'll take the road home to visit and bring a carload of grandchildren that I'll spoil. We'll write long newsy letters, and I'll visit and see where Bud took you. You are happy, and you will have so much to do—you'll hardly miss us. Now freshen up before Bud gets here." Mother kissed her cheek and left. Ida Bealle folded the quilt and tucked it in her trunk.

She picked up the recipe box and scanned the recipe titles. "Salmon Salad Surprise. Jell-O Mold. Ham Loaf. Olive Spread. Oh, my—I'll never make some of these awful recipes." She laughed and tucked the red box into a fold of the quilt. She twisted the key to lock the trunk and went down to meet her love.

Chapter 5

Cadence turned on the kitchen light and gasped when she saw Taylor Nash. Her dirty sandals rested on Cadence's favorite vintage tablecloth. Cadence's heart pounded, and her head ached. Her breath came in gasps, and her shaky knees gave out. "What are you doing here?"

Taylor smiled a smug victor's smile and swung her feet off the table. "Come on—what do you *think* I'm doing here? A little Mayberry in this town, huh, sweetie? You don't lock your back door?" She leaned forward, her chin on her hand, and pointed at a chair with her other hand. "Sit."

Cadence shook her head and forced her eyes to focus. Heat and a chill raced through her body.

What a nightmare!

"Oh, I'm right here, *Cadence*," Taylor said, emphasizing the fake name. "I'm here to see my dear friend Audra March. A clever little twist on your real name. Cadence . . . March . . . good one. Come. Sit. Time to catch up." Taylor patted the chair.

Cadence turned the burner on underneath her kettle—small defiance. Taylor always called the shots and got her way.

Taylor kicked the chair out from under the table. "I said sit."

Cadence sat, her hands twisting in her lap. "What do you want, Taylor?" she whispered.

"I stopped to talk about the good old days. We've been friends for ages, right?" Taylor smiled, but it didn't reach her green eyes. "We haven't chatted lately. Have we?"

A chill shook her, but Cadence would not shiver in front of Taylor. Taylor would smell weakness, like a wolf. "It's been a while, but that's not why you're here."

Taylor laughed. "Always the smart one, aren't you? Okay, I'll cut to the chase. It's like this, *Cadence.*" She made air quotes with her fingers. "My husband doesn't make much money. We're the typical Americans—two kids, a house, bills. You know, the regular." Taylor shrugged. "Our anniversary is next month, and I need a cruise. The husband maxed out our credit cards, and he's too lazy to pick up hours." She snorted, the sound a mix of laughter and a cackle.

Cadence shifted in the chair and turned away from Taylor. "I don't understand how I'm involved.

"Anyway," Taylor cleared her throat, "as I was saying before you rudely interrupted me, my girlfriends and I packed up for this podunk Cowcrest festival. We took a road trip weekend and stayed at a bed and breakfast up the street—nice place, by the way. I soaked away my stress in the tub and searched for a decent cup of coffee in this backwoods town. Lo and behold, whose picture did I see on the page for The Muddy Cup Café? My good friend Audra—oh, excuse me, 'Cadence,'" She rolled her eyes.

"I hopped out of the tub and danced across the floor. 'Cruise time!' I yelled. And voila, here I am." Taylor flipped her hair and raised her hands; her diamond earrings shimmered in the light.

"How does my picture on the café page pay for your cruise, Taylor?" Cadence stared Taylor in the eye, pretending she didn't know the answer.

Taylor stared at Cadence—her icy green eyes widened.

How does she do this? I blinked. Why did I look away? Why do I always give in?

"Oh, honey, you know exactly how I'll pay for my cruise. Go to your bank, withdraw $10,000, and I go on a nice little cruise." Taylor held her palms up in the air and shrugged.

Cadence whispered, "I don't have that kind of money, Taylor. Even if I did—"

"Even if you did, what? If you did, you wouldn't give it to me? That's where you're wrong. You *will* give me the money, and you will do it a week from Tuesday. Wonder what that Barney Fife who brought you home like such a gentleman would think about Audra March?" Taylor tapped her finger on her lips and raised her eyebrows.

Her stare made Cadence shiver. Taylor didn't issue idle threats. Cadence scraped the money together the last two times, but this obscene demand was impossible.

Last time, Cadence left town without care, but the idea of leaving Deercrest hurt. She loved this tiny, boring town. She enjoyed her job, her boss, Laura, and her every-other-Friday-night bowling date with the hunky police officer. She even loved the silly cow festival.

Her little white cottage and her quiet life in Deercrest brought her joy.

Why do you ruin everything, Taylor?

Taylor walked around the kitchen, "It's a regular museum in here. What's with all the old junk?" she laughed while filching through Cadence's cupboards.

She tossed dishes and ingredients onto counters. "Audra, all this stuff is old. What are you doing? Who reads cookbooks from a hundred years ago?" She rifled through drawers and cupboards and made snide comments. "You living in the past?"

Taylor pawed through her vintage treasures, and dread slithered through Cadence's belly. She shook, and her brain turned to ice-cold mush.

No, I'm not living in the past. I like technology. I just like when my stuff has a history.

Taylor peeked into cans and moved dishes. "You hide money in here like Grandma? That's it!" She snapped her fingers and rushed to the table, leaning over to stare. "You're decorating your house like your grandma, aren't you? What's her name? The one you always talked about? Is it the old, fat broad in that picture?"

Cadence's fury rose. "Get out, Taylor Nash. No one insults my grandmother. Get out of my house."

Taylor grabbed her purse and smacked her gum, "Oh, I'll get out, 'Cadence,' but next Tuesday you'll have the cash ready. It would seem such a shame if your little Mayberry here ran you out of town." She raised her eyebrows and winked.

Taylor grabbed the door handle, "It was sooo nice to see you, girl. See you in ten days," her voice high and fake.

Cadence glanced out the kitchen window. Taylor stopped to pick up the neighbor's kitten and nuzzled the little cat with her cheek. When she rubbed its head, a beautiful smile transformed her face. She set the kitten down and waved ten fingers—an unmistakable message.

Cadence grabbed a ball of wool from the basket and jabbed knitting needles into it until her heartbeat stopped thumping in her ears.

CHAPTER 6

C adence dragged the recipe box across the table to check the address Allie had found. Her cozy kitchen, a cup of tea, and knitting practice soothed her nerves most nights, but tonight she couldn't sit still and her mind raced. She studied the treasures that reminded her of Grandmother Miggs. A white Hoosier cabinet held vintage cookbooks. A row of white milk glass spice jars with cherry labels lined the counter, and vintage gingham aprons hung from a peg near the stove. The red-and-white porcelain-top table sat in the middle of the kitchen, covered in a vintage tablecloth. Her kitchen reminded her of happier days—when she belonged.

Cadence opened the box and read the note Allie had left on top of the recipe cards.

"Ida Bealle Horne of Norris Creek, Ky., joined her husband in heaven on April 25, 2015. Ida Bealle is survived by one daughter, Fredonia Addison of Deercrest, Wisconsin."

Cadence pulled the recipe cards from the box and wondered about the woman who owned them first. A folded envelope with a penciled note on the front fell from the stack—the letters written in the shaky hand of an older woman.

"Fredonia, find my tin. It has all the answers. I've always loved you."

"Wonder what that means?" Cadence opened the envelope. "Hmm .. . empty. Why didn't you keep your mother's recipes, Fredonia?"

She pulled the cards out of the recipe box and searched for other clues. "Nothing." She flipped through the cards but found only other disgusting recipes.

"Hmm, Ida Bealle Horne. Your recipes sound awful, but I bet your story is interesting. What does your little note here mean? What tin? Where? What is your secret?" She sighed and paced. She needed to solve her problems, not this Ida Bealle woman's problems.

"Why did Taylor give me ten days? It doesn't make sense." She paced but stopped to jab knitting needles into the yarn several times. She straightened the mess Taylor had made when she pulled things from the cupboards. Her head swam.

I can't leave Deercrest. It's my home.

She would lose too much if Taylor outed her. Cadence plopped onto the vinyl chair, sorting the puzzle.

Describing the scent of the number five is easier than making sense of Taylor Nash. I give up.

Taylor wouldn't hesitate to call Thatcher, and he would arrest Cadence. No more peaceful days in Deercrest.

Flirting with a police officer wasn't her brightest idea. But she loved men in uniform and enjoyed Thatcher's friendship. His dark hair and muscular build made her heart sing, but she kept walls up.

Get too close to Thatcher, and my freedom is gone.

When she met Taylor in high school, Taylor's curly hair and freckles, her expensive clothes, and fancy gifts dazzled Audra. Taylor Nash possessed all the things Audra did not.

Taylor Nash lived in an expensive house on the nice side of town.

Audra lived wherever social services placed her and placed her and placed her.

Taylor Nash lived with two married parents.

Audra lived with various foster parents.

Taylor Nash—rich.

Audra March—poor.

Taylor Nash—friends and groupies.

Audra—alone.

Taylor Nash needed a pushover.

Gullible Audra fell for bribery.

The first time Taylor made her steal, Audra said no. Taylor grabbed a notebook from Audra's hands, and the last picture she owned of Grandmother tumbled to the ground. Taylor swooped down and shredded the photo. Audra gasped, reaching for the pieces, but Taylor pinched the back of her arm.

"I said take the candy. Now." Her fingers dug in and left red marks.

Audra glanced around. When the clerk turned to a customer, Audra slipped a candy bar into her pocket and met Taylor in the parking lot.

Taylor hugged Audra's shoulders and smiled. "You're my best friend. We'll have so much fun together." She snatched the candy from Audra's hand and popped it into her mouth, tossing the wrapper on the pavement. "Pick that up."

Taylor destroyed everything Audra valued. A foster kid with no family and desperate for a friend, Audra did anything to fit in. Taylor's demands escalated, and Audra never said no.

Who cares what I do? No one expects big things or success from me.

Beautiful Taylor Nash was constant in her life—always there. She pulled Audra into her circle and gave her expensive gifts—purses, jeans, makeup. The presents made Audra feel special, but the excitement and belonging kept Audra unaware of the trap ready to spring.

At first the demands were innocent.

Get this.

Do that.

Buy gum for me.

Friends help each other, right? I don't mind.

The gifts became more extravagant when the demands grew. Audra ignored her conscience and her sick stomach. She followed Taylor's orders—no questions.

Taylor commanded her to run errands, steal, and drop brown bags at houses around town. She made Audra tease overweight girls and flirt with awkward, pimple-faced boys.

Taylor stood in the shadows to watch and laughed at the hurt faces. Audra hated that part—the pain in their eyes. She longed to fit in, and Taylor always reminded her that she didn't.

"Hey, Taylor, please. I don't want to tease them; it's not nice. That girl is friendly. She helps that boy in the wheelchair every day, and she gave me her pencil for a test."

Audra trailed off when Taylor mocked, "It's not *nice.*" Taylor stretched out the word *nice* and tossed her red curly hair. She hissed in Audra's face. "*Nice* isn't the goal. Doing what I say is the goal. Understand?"

She nodded but wished for courage. She wanted the good times, the group, and the gifts. Audra would never say no.

Cadence paced and sighed. *I graduated from high school twelve years ago, and here I am, back to square one. Following Taylor's commands.*

Chapter 7

Church bells chimed Sunday morning; Cadence ground her teeth at the cheerful sound. She burrowed under her bumpy chenille blanket and cried. She remembered going to church with her grandmother. Once upon a time she loved Sunday school and believed in God. But life changed, and now she was agnostic.

"God, if you're real, I hate you," she yelled. "I hate that you won't stop her. I hate that you took my grandmother, and I hate that I'm alone. This isn't a prayer either, in case you're wondering."

White-hot anger churned in her stomach, and her muddled brain hurt. Her dreams didn't produce any brilliant ideas to escape Taylor's threats. She grabbed her phone and checked her bank app.

"Hey, God, any chance you can fill my bank account magically? How about you magically make Taylor disappear? Oh, look—four hundred dollars." She threw her phone at the wall.

She hugged her pillow and sobbed. She gulped a deep breath of air and adjusted the soggy pillow under her head. She stared at the ceiling and replayed yesterday. She smiled at the memory of tourists, cow costumes, and mounds of cream puff bars. The fun atmosphere added to her thankfulness for Deercrest, but Taylor's arrival had ruined her evening plans. Taylor's blackmail threatened destruction. Her peaceful, happy days in Deercrest might end soon, but Cadence planned to fight this time.

"This is too much," she cried. "I can't do this again, Taylor Nash. Why don't you leave me alone?"

She punched her pillow and fell into a fitful sleep.

When Taylor had dropped hints that Audra didn't fit in the group anymore, she panicked. If Audra wasn't an in-girl, Taylor would tease and decimate her with rumors leaving her nowhere to belong. She didn't want to drift alone. Audra poured her energy into pleasing Taylor. She planned ways to prove her importance to the circle—ways to keep Taylor happy.

One night she remembered a former foster home with jewelry and cash taped under dresser drawers. She mentioned it to Taylor, and her stomach twisted at the betrayal of the Boyds.

They didn't keep me; why should I feel guilty?

Taylor smiled and hugged her. "I knew we kept you around for a reason."

Audra's sick stomach eased—relief.

Several weeks later, Taylor held up her wrist. A diamond tennis bracelet sparkled as brightly as Taylor's smile.

"Good tip—they found five thousand bucks hidden under those drawers." Taylor hugged her. "What would I do without you?" She laughed and wiggled her wrist; the diamonds glittered in the light. "She'll miss this beauty. Couldn't have done it without you."

Audra smiled, glad she had pleased Taylor, but Taylor's laugh made her uncomfortable. When she understood that Taylor enjoyed her betrayal of the Boyds, Audra realized Taylor's world demanded a cost. Her demands were endless.

She pulled away from Taylor and the group. She pretended busyness when Taylor called or forgot errands Taylor demanded—small rebellions.

One night Taylor invited her out for dinner. "I'll pay. Order whatever you want."

Audra ordered her favorite chicken salad croissant and pink bubble tea. The girls talked about school, graduation, and Taylor's party. They laughed about mutual friends, and Taylor pointed out the fashion faux pas of a middle-aged woman at the counter.

When the creamy raspberry cheesecake came, Audra savored each bite. She had never ordered dessert before. She licked the last bite of cheesecake from her fork and leaned her head on the booth.

How did I get this lucky?

Taylor leaned over the table and motioned. Audra leaned in, excited at what Taylor might say. Taylor smiled, and the heaviness in her heart lifted.

It's good news. I hope she asks me to help with her graduation party or ride to the prom in her limo. Please say, 'Ride with you to the dance.'

"You were eighteen when you told me where they hid the money and jewelry. It wasn't me, you know. Someone must have overheard you and robbed those people. Unfortunately, you're an accessory now. The crime is aiding and abetting." Taylor smiled and lowered her voice. "Don't make me unhappy. What a shame if anyone ever heard what you did!"

She slid out of the booth, leaving Audra with the bill.

The threats and blackmail began after graduation until Audra escaped town. But Taylor found her. Taylor always found her. She demanded money and threatened to expose Audra. At first Taylor demanded small amounts of money, but over the years her demands grew. Now ten years later, she was dealing with another ridiculous Taylor demand.

Cadence sat up and swung her legs over the side of the bed.

Dizzy.

She took deep breaths and glanced around her bedroom. She had painted the walls a pale lilac—Grandmother Miggs's favorite color. The glow of sunshine on the purple walls brought peace most mornings, but not today. She managed to stand after several tries, but her head swam and her stomach lurched.

She stumbled downstairs. A mug of peppermint tea would settle her stomach and calm her mind and aching body. She rested her head on the table and waited for the whistle of the tea kettle.

She needed a plan—any plan. Taylor would return and get what she wanted—she always did. Taylor would expose her and enjoy Cadence's destruction. She had worked way too hard to carve out a spot as Cadence in this little town. She had found people who cared for her here. Well, they cared for the person they believed they knew. She loved her little house and this small town. *No, Taylor, you won't destroy me again.*

She tried concentrating, but the cobwebs in her mind kept her from thinking. Words and ideas wove back and forth, confusing her. She tried making sense of the words, but everything hurt, and she was so tired.

"Insurance!" She pushed her feet into her fuzzy pink slippers and searched the kitchen. "Where is that renter's policy?" She opened a cupboard and scanned file folders. "Think. It's important. Where is it?"

The tea kettle whistled a cheery screech while she wracked her brain. "Bookshelf." She grabbed the folder and read the legalese. She swallowed a bubble of laughter and grinned. Her policy covered household items at twenty-five thousand dollars.

"An unfortunate fire solves the Taylor problem," she whispered. "But that leaves me homeless."

Her home reminded her of Grandmother Miggs; love and acceptance.

Can I do it?

She sipped the hot tea and weighed her options. "My options are to start an unfortunate fire and use the insurance money to pay Taylor or disappear again. So basically both my choices stink. What else?"

Defeat. None of the ideas lifted the burden from her shoulders. She should quit.

Taylor wins.

Cadence rested her head on the table and fell asleep.

Chapter 8

Indianapolis, October 5, 1940

Ida Bealle woke when her sisters slammed open the door and jumped on her bed.

"Wedding day! Wedding day!" They sang with too much cheer for early morning. They burrowed under her blanket and snuggled.

She groaned. "Girls, I'm sleeping." She rubbed her eyes and stretched.

"How can you sleep on your wedding day?" Anna sat up and jabbed her in the side.

Ella popped out from under the covers. "I expected to come in here and find you awake in your gown already."

They snuggled until a sob escaped from Ida Bealle.

"Why are you crying?" Her sister Ella popped her head out of the blanket.

"I'll miss you."

From underneath the blanket, her sister Anna hugged her. "You won't miss us. All you think of is Bud. Bud this. Bud that." She mocked in a sing-song voice.

"Hey." Ida Bealle protested. "That's not how I sound."

"Yes, you do!" Both sisters yelled and burst into giggles.

"It's okay. We like Bud. Not as much as *you* like Bud, but he's okay," Anna said.

"We'll visit you." Ella hugged her and kissed her cheek. "You better get up before Momma hollers at us. She sent us to wake you for breakfast. Everyone's at the table."

Ida Bealle crawled over her sisters and grabbed her robe. "I'm not sure I can eat a bite, but we better hurry if Daddy's already at the table."

Her sisters rolled out of bed, and they linked arms in front of the mirror. Ida Bealle smiled at their reflection. Their trio would shrink after Ida Bealle became Mrs. Horne.

Anna sighed and squeezed her sister.

Ida Bealle's tears threatened, but Momma's sharp call sent them scurrying downstairs.

The strains of "Here Comes the Bride" floated upstairs, where Ida Bealle held her father's arm. She gripped a lavish bouquet of red roses and trailing ivy and glanced into the mirror one last time. Her ivory dress, remade with fabric from Momma's wedding gown, touched the floor in a loose drape. The tulle skirt and lace veil added enough daintiness for her taste.

"Ready?" Daddy asked. "You can still change your mind."

"Daddy," she whispered.

He squeezed her hand and kissed her forehead, his voice husky. "You're beautiful, sweetheart."

He walked her down the stairs and up the aisle. Ida Bealle concentrated on the smile on Bud's face. She wanted to memorize his joy and tuck it in her heart for the days when they were old and gray. His joy told her she would never regret the day she married Bud Horne.

A man in uniform sat near the aisle, and Ida Bealle frowned—her happiness wavered for a moment. Wedding plans kept her busy with dresses, flowers, and cake. The wedding pushed the worry of war far away from her busy mind. War wouldn't touch their family as it would many others—no boys, Father too old, and Bud, a minister. Ida Bealle smiled at Bud and whispered a quick prayer.

God, remind me that he didn't get drafted if I ever complain about his call to minister.

Daddy kissed her cheek and answered the minister's question: "Her mother and I do."

She smiled at Bud through her veil and reached for his strong hand. He held her hand and all her tomorrows.

Chapter 9

"I can't work tomorrow." Cadence lifted her head from the table. "I'm so groggy. I should get a cat so the neighbors don't wonder if I'm talking to myself." She chuckled and pushed down the anxiety before it overwhelmed her.

She flipped through the recipe box and read Allie's note. Before she talked herself out of it, she slipped on her shoes and grabbed her purse and the recipe box. "Let's get you home," she said, patting the little red box.

Cadence punched the address into her maps app and imagined a small run-down home on the edge of town—a ramshackle house near the railroad tracks. She grabbed the wheel of her ten-year-old Honda Civic and scanned street signs as she drove.

When she turned on Frey Lane, the houses got bigger and statelier—not one ramshackle house.

"Whoa—I must have taken a wrong turn." She checked the app and Allie's note.

Did I enter the wrong address?

"You have arrived at your destination," the app said in a mechanical voice.

Cadence stared down the driveway and let out a low whistle. Instead of the run-down house she had imagined, a three-story brick mansion worthy of a magazine cover sat at the end of the driveway. Cadence pulled into the lane and checked for a security guard.

They'll send me away. I'm underdressed, out of place, and poor. What am I doing?

Cadence parked her beat-up car at the end of the lane near a shiny, bright red Jaguar and scooped up the box. She smoothed her skirt and stepped onto a porch larger than her house.

Oh, man! Her hands shook, and she wanted to run away. She bit her tongue to stop herself from laughing.

I do not need the giggles. Does this Fredonia lady work here—cook? Chef?

Cadence pushed the button. The doorbell chimed, sounding like the church bells that had woken her this morning.

Imagine so much money you can afford church bells.

She smirked and rolled her eyes, and the door opened.

A small woman dressed in white linen pants, a pink shell, and several strands of pearls stood inside the door. Her fashionable haircut showed gray streaks, and pink lipstick pulled her look together. She stared at Cadence.

How old is she? Sixty? Fifty-five?

"I'm here for Fredonia, please." Cadence smiled.

Housekeeper? Secretary?

"Did you have an appointment?" The woman glanced at her watch and frowned.

"Umm . . ." *Oh, I should have stayed home.* "I don't have an appointment. Sorry. I have something for her."

The lady's eyes widened. "What do you have for Fredonia?"

Cadence swallowed; heat rose in her cheeks. "I'll wait for her. Would you call her, please?"

The woman raised an eyebrow. "Follow me."

The woman hurried down the hall, her heels clicking on the marble floor. Cadence jogged to keep up.

How does she walk so fast in those heels? I'd break my neck.

Cadence gasped for breath but hurried after the woman down a long maze of halls that ended at a large, sunny room; the lady pointed to a floral couch.

"Sit."

Cadence plopped onto the couch, too stunned to disobey. She glanced around the comfortable room. The furnishings displayed the owner's wealth. Fluffy, cream-colored rugs scattered over the wood floor added warmth. She scanned the bookcases lining the walls and imagined herself curled up in the corner of the soft couch with a good book.

A black concert grand piano sat in the middle of the room, a piece of sheet music on top, the shiny finish spotless—not a fingerprint. Cadence stared out the windows. Another garden with rows of blue hydrangeas and a large pool sat in the middle of the yard, surrounded by a deck and white wicker furniture. She imagined a pool party packed with rich snobby women who avoided the water by lounging in the sun on the patio.

Cadence pulled her gaze from the room and beautiful yard when the woman asked, "What did you have for Fredonia?"

Cadence stammered, "I—I—well, I will wait for Fredonia."

"*I* am Fredonia. I said, state your business."

Cadence let out a long breath and then sat up straight. She pasted on a perky grin and hoped it hid her nervousness.

"Well, I found an item of your mother's and wondered if you'd like it back." She grabbed the box, but Fredonia interrupted.

"How do you know about my mother?

Cadence regretted her mission as words tumbled out. "Well, I love shopping at the antique store. I shop for treasures and unusual items— old things. I love them; they feel homey. I don't know why people get rid of such wonderful stuff."

The woman cleared her throat.

"Oh. Here. I found this" Cadence grabbed the recipe box and held it out. "It's full of recipes, and several cards say, 'From the kitchen of Ida Bealle Horne.'"

"Stop." The woman held out her hand and shook her head. "You found a box, and you say it was my mother's, but explain how you found *me*."

Cadence grimaced and whispered, "We searched for you on the Internet."

The woman glared. Cadence shrank back on the plush cushions, her mouth dry and her stomach twisted.

"The Internet? You searched for me on the Internet?"

"Well, I can't help it because I like old stuff, and I guess I'm weird. I imagine the people and their stories. Who owned it, and why did they get rid of it?" Cadence shrugged. "So my friend and I searched for Ida Bealle Horne and found her obituary and your name." She trailed off and pasted on her sweet, innocent face, worried that Fredonia might consider her an ax murderer.

Allie will laugh at this insane story. Wish she were here.

Fredonia took the recipe box, flipped through the cards for a moment, and snapped the lid shut. "Yes, this was my mother's, but I donated it last week. I cannot understand why you brought it here."

Fredonia handed the box back to her. "What did you say your name was?"

"Cadence Audley." She stood and extended her hand.

Fredonia ignored Cadence's hand and left the room. She stopped at the door. "Follow me."

Cadence grabbed the box and followed the woman through the hallways. She chattered in a nervous stream: "What an impressive hall. Is this natural marble? How do you keep it clean—special cleaners?" She hurried behind the older woman.

Fredonia stopped and gestured outside.

"I hope my interruption doesn't get you in trouble with your boss," Cadence said.

Fredonia stared for a moment. "I'm fine."

The door clicked shut in Cadence's face, and she blushed. She blew out her breath and replayed the conversation, groaning at her stream of babble.

She'll think I'm crazy.

Her Honda parked near the shiny, red Jaguar screamed, "You're broke, girl!" Cadence shook her head and pretended she wasn't jealous of the beautiful car—or all the wealth.

"Excuse me, young lady," Fredonia called from the door.

Oh, no—here it comes. What did I do wrong?

The lady stood inside the door with an odd look on her face. "You like old things?"

"Definitely," Cadence said with a smile. "Vintage and I are besties."

The lady raised her brows again. "Well, that's sad, but to each their own, I guess. I wonder if it's lucky you showed up uninvited tonight. I'm emptying my mother's home and need help. I planned to leave tomorrow morning. If you help me, you can keep some of Mother's items—save me the trouble of disposal in Kentucky. I'll pay you, of course. I'm certain there are many items like that recipe box if you enjoy that type of thing."

Cadence hesitated. Travel with a stranger didn't sound rational, but Taylor's threats weren't rational. A road trip with a stranger would give her time to figure out the mess.

"I'll go," she said before common sense kicked in.

"Write your address." Fredonia held out a paper and pen. "I'll pick you up at six tomorrow morning. Make sure you're ready."

Cadence scribbled her address. "I'll have my bags packed and the coffee brewed." She smiled, but Fredonia shooed her away and shut the door.

Cadence sighed and slid behind the wheel of her car.

What have I done?

CHAPTER 10

Norris Creek, Kentucky, November 1940

"What have I done?" Ida Bealle muttered when she pulled the liquid-y cobbler from the oven. The fruit hadn't set, and it was a mess. "Can't serve my preacher boy a runny cobbler." She sighed and shut the oven door. She hoped more time in the oven would cure the cobbler's ills.

The screen door slammed.

"Bud, that you?" She stepped into the living room, wiping her hands on a red gingham apron.

Her husband held a pumpkin. "For my bride." He smiled and held his arms out. She leaned into his chest with a contented sigh and rested her head on his shoulder. "Marriage isn't all bad, is it, love?" he whispered against her hair.

Ida Bealle whispered, "No, Bud, it's not. It's all good." She leaned against him for several moments, delighting in his closeness and his bristly beard on her cheek. "Three weeks in, I'd say we're experts at it."

He laughed and kissed her. "What smells so good?" He shrugged out of his coat and followed his nose.

"Chicken pie, with berry cobbler for dessert. Don't you have a meeting tonight?"

"I have a meeting, but I also have enough time to gobble my dinner and kiss my bride." His smile made her stomach flutter, and she hoped the butterflies never left.

Ida Bealle had spent the first three weeks of their marriage unpacking and decorating the parsonage. The white two-story house sat across the lawn from the church—small but roomy enough for two. When God blessed them with a few babies, they would figure it out. The church owned the home, but the Hornes would live in it as long as Bud was the pastor. When Ida Bealle sat on the porch in her rocker, she saw Bud's office. Sometimes she whistled, and he opened the window, waved, and blew her a kiss. Bud's kisses left her weak. The fire inside him surprised her, but she enjoyed it and matched it with a blaze of her own. They were a good fit. Marriage had changed her, and she loved every moment of her new life.

She checked the cobbler and leaned on the counter. She twisted a curl around her finger and tilted her head, "I'm sorry, Mr. Horne, but I didn't expect you so soon. Your dinner's not ready." She touched her lips and raised her eyebrows. "But, if you'd rather have dessert first?"

He jumped from his chair, tugging off his suit jacket and tie. "Why, Mrs. Horne, what would the church ladies say?" He tugged her hand, and she followed him up the stairs with a giggle.

<h1 style="text-align:center">CHAPTER 11</h1>

Cadence rushed home laughing. She didn't know how to get out of this mess, but she would not wait for Taylor to extract her pound of flesh.

She parked the car and locked every door and window in the garage. She made a list of to-dos while chamomile tea brewed, and she laughed at the turn of events.

I just might outwit Taylor, but if I don't stop this laughter, I'll break out in hysteria.

She had held her emotions in check for so long. She took several deep breaths and sipped the hot tea.

"Okay, get yourself packed."

The afternoon passed in a blur as she threw clothes into her red Samsonite suitcase. She packed toiletries in a matching train case she had found at an antique store. She tossed in casual pieces for dirty work but threw in a dressy outfit—just in case. Who knew what they would do down there.

Where is "down there"?

She threw in an old vintage homemaker book and her yarn and knitting needles in case there was free time. Zipping the overstuffed luggage made her short of breath, and she laughed. She danced around her room. The thought of leaving Taylor in the dust lifted her spirits.

Cadence walked through each room and pulled shades, locked windows, and unplugged appliances as Grandmother always did. She checked the locks on the basement windows. When Taylor came back, she would find the empty house locked tight.

"She will rage." Cadence grinned and wiped her hands. She rehearsed her to-do list and checked for forgotten items. She sent a quick text message.

—Laura, I need a little leave of absence from the café. I'll get in touch as soon as possible. I need rest.

Deserting the café meant the end of her job, but she would deal with Laura later.

Cadence fell into bed, her heart full of relief and hope. Things would get better for her someday. She had spent many years letting life happen to her—big mistake. Time for action and ending Taylor's tyranny—never mind that she planned to run away. It was a step in the right direction.

—ele—

Her alarm rang at 4 a.m., and in the gray light she doubted her sanity. Her bleary eyes and tired mind reminded her of her insecurities and shortcomings.

I'm crazy. I shouldn't have agreed, but I can't stay and let Taylor win. I need time and a strategy.

Her phone pinged.

—Of course, Cadence. A couple of weeks or months? Can I take care of you? I'm worried.

She hated her lies.

——Don't worry about me. A couple weeks—I'll let you know. Thanks.

Cadence turned off the lights and peered through the front door while she waited for Fredonia. All the emotions churned—excitement, worry, hope, and terror.

She had run from Taylor before, but this time Taylor wasn't calling the shots.

I'm leaving before Taylor gets her way. She's out of my life soon.

A funny horn beeped, and Cadence ran out. Fredonia stepped out of a pink Cadillac convertible and grabbed Cadence's bag. "Come on—get in. Time's wasting."

Cadence plopped into the passenger seat, her laughter bubbled. "This is my dream car, Fredonia. What is it, a '58?" She patted the pink leather seat and ran her hand across the smooth dashboard.

"'59. Here—tie this on." Fredonia handed her a pink chiffon scarf.

Cadence tied it around her head. "My grandmother wore these."

"Keeps the hair out of your eyes. Shut the door. Time to hit the road."

Cadence noticed her pink rose bushes in the front garden and glanced at her little house. The street signs at the corner caught her attention—Bliss Street and Paradise Avenue.

When I get Taylor out of my life, it will indeed feel like bliss and paradise.

Cadence kept her gaze straight ahead while Fredonia drove out of town. She didn't want to find Taylor hiding in the shadows.

"Will we ride in this car the whole way?"

Fredonia's brow furrowed. "What do you suggest? Switch cars in Indiana?"

"What if it rains?"

"Full of questions, aren't you? Top goes up."

Cadence nodded. "Where did you get this car?"

Fredonia patted the dashboard and smiled. "She's a beaut, isn't she? Cici here was my husband's pet project. He finished her right before . . ." She trailed off.

The smells and sights of a beautiful Wisconsin morning helped calm Cadence's mind. They drove past fields of young corn planted in rows of green ribbons.

"'Knee-high by the Fourth of July,'" Fredonia said. "You ever hear that one? My mother used to call pleasant mornings like this 'glad mornings' and sing to me."

Cadence shrugged. "Let's hear it."

Fredonia laughed. "Not a chance—my singing will make you cry."

Cadence smiled and turned to watch the scenery. She gasped when the Cadillac crested a hill. A bright red barn surrounded by Holstein cows sat in the middle of the rolling hills in the valley below. The sun shone behind the barn. "I'd like that for a calendar photo—so pretty."

"It's so Wisconsin," said Fredonia, and they grinned. "I love it when the fields look like a quilt."

"Pretty enough to paint." Cadence sighed as the black-and-white calves ran around their mother.

I hope the trip turns out okay. Better than Taylor's threats. Fredonia seems decent. Someone at the mansion must have run a background check. Right?

The sound of tires on the road lulled Cadence to sleep. She dozed for several miles but popped her eyes open. "Fredonia, how did you end up in Wisconsin?"

"Oh, it's a story for later—after I rest and shower."

Cadence counted the miles between her and Deercrest as they traveled. Every mile meant distance from Taylor. For the first time in years, she was hopeful—her tension lessened as the countryside rolled past. The combination of the car and her relief from Taylor's imminent threats made her sleepy. She leaned her head back on the seat and slept until Fredonia shook her.

"Hope you don't mind if we share a room tonight. I need rest." Fredonia raised the top on the Cadillac.

Cadence stretched and yawned. "Perfect. A comfortable bed sounds wonderful right now."

"You slept the whole way," Fredonia said, teasing.

Cadence shrugged and grabbed her suitcase. "I didn't sleep well last night."

"Excited to set out across the country with a stranger, huh?"

Cadence followed her into the small hotel.

I hope this woman isn't a psycho.

"As far as I know, there are no ax murderers named Fredonia," she whispered.

"What?" Fredonia asked.

"I said I'm on my way." Cadence hurried down the hall. Her energy flagged, and she worried how she would keep up with this woman. If today indicated her activity level, she was in for a long week. She was ready for bed, and Fredonia sprinted down the hall fresh as a daisy.

She sighed, "It's better than Taylor."

CHAPTER 12

Norris Creek, Kentucky, May 1941

Ida Bealle slid her recipe box across the table and grabbed a notepad to write a grocery list for Bud's shopping trip in town. The small grocer in Norris Creek carried a few items—butter, eggs, and produce.

She settled on a recipe called "Super Sandwiches." When she made the "Salmon Salad Surprise" last week, Bud pushed his plate away after one taste.

Ida Bealle bit back a sharp comment, offended that he wouldn't eat her food. She took a huge bite and said, "Mmm . . . "

He laughed when she spit it into the trash. They chuckled together several times over the past week, and she promised she would never cook "Salmon Salad Surprise" again. She scanned the ingredients and hoped he would find the items. They pinched pennies and stretched their budget, thankful for a rent-free parsonage. She wrote Bud's list, tore off a sheet of paper, and wrote a letter to her mother.

Dear Momma,

Bud and I are well. The parsonage is quite tiny, but it's cozy. It's a pretty white house with a big porch, and I love sitting out there. Bud found a rocking chair perfect for me. I sit and knit. The birds chirp and swoop in and out of the trees and keep me company. We have a big oak tree in the yard—much bigger than the trees back home. The church built the parsonage for their second pastor in 1890. We heard they ran their first pastor out of town in the middle of the night, but Bud hasn't figured out why. He searched church documents, but no one knows the details. We also can't figure out why they named the church Turkey Creek Baptist Church when the town name is Norris Creek. Bud tried to find the information but didn't find anything in the records.

The kitchen is small, but I'm getting good at cooking since the church bought me a brand-new Hardwick stove. It came with a built-in clock and light, which is perfect for nighttime. I can see the time and avoid stubbed toes in the dark. The oven is big enough for baking eight loaves of bread at once, but of course, Bud and I don't need eight loaves. I'm pretty good at baking the two we need each week— whenever we have babies, all that oven space will help. You'd be proud of me, Momma; most of the time when I cook, it's good. I still laugh at Bud's face when he took a bite of Mrs. Ray's "Salmon Salad Surprise." It was so awful we scraped it into the trash. We don't waste food, but we refused to eat it. I kept the recipe card because Mrs. Ray is so dear, and I know she prays for us, but we can't eat her recipes. Wonder how her family survives? Someday my children will inherit this box and laugh at their crazy momma for eating this food. I should take her cards out of the box and use them for bookmarks. Bud said he's not sure he can trust my cooking anymore, but he's teasing.

I better close so I can get this to the post office. It's a two-mile walk, and I enjoy the scenery. It gives me time for daydreaming, and I often see church members. Norris Creek is in a narrow valley between the mountains. It looks like the buildings touch the mountains on both sides of the street. We live out of town in a holler—both the church and parsonage. We can see the mountains all around; it's so different than home.

I love you. Please write soon.
Mrs. Bud Horne

CHAPTER 13

A rustle on the other side of the hotel room woke Cadence. Fredonia touched her toes and reached up. Cadence adjusted her head on the pillows and wrapped the blanket around her shoulders; she sighed and scrunched her eyes closed—one more minute.

"How old are you, Fredonia?"

Fredonia stopped mid-toe touch and gaped. "You don't ask a lady how old she is. Didn't your mother teach you any better?"

Cadence cringed when Fredonia scolded.

My mother taught me nothing, Fredonia.

"I'm sorry," she said, "It's the first thing that came to mind when I saw you working out over there."

Fredonia nodded and continued her toe touches, then jogged in place. She huffed. "I'll swim laps before we grab breakfast and hit the road. Join me?" She disappeared behind the bathroom door and came out in her swimsuit and cap. Cadence hopped out of bed and changed into her suit, hurrying down the hall behind Fredonia.

The lap swim refreshed Cadence. Although she never worked out at home, she enjoyed the morning exercise—a perfect start for the day. Fredonia sat in the hot tub, and Cadence joined her as two other women sat down. Fredonia leaned her head back on the side. The women chattered like magpies, their voices loud and fast. They scooted near Cadence and included her in the conversation.

"I saw an ad for a cat, and we hopped in the car. Right in the car— we didn't stop to think. Right in the car. Isn't that what we did, Sally?"

"Yep, that's what we did—didn't even think for a second. Tee told me there's a cat for free, and she picked me up in half an hour, and we drove all day, and here we are. Do you like cats?" They turned their expectant gaze on Cadence.

"Sometimes."

"Oh, we love cats. I have five, and Tee here has ten. We love 'em. Everything about them, right, Tee?"

"Yep. We love cats. I couldn't just leave this cat when I saw the ad. No way. We had to rescue it. We're rescuing it, right, Sally?"

"Rescuing cats is what we do." They laughed, scooted closer, squishing her between the handrail and Fredonia.

They turned to Cadence, their eyes bugging out. "Allen!" They yelled in unison.

Cadence glanced around the pool area for him, but no one looked like an Allen.

"Allen's surgery the other day—gall bladder. It was full of infection and—"

Fredonia shot out of the water and climbed the stairs.

The women stared at her open-mouthed for a second, then turned back. "Like I said, infected. Totally infected—the doctor said it was a good thing they got it out on time. What would have happened to his cats if he died? Oh, the poor cats." Both women shook their heads, eyes damp with tears.

Cadence tried standing, but the ladies scooted closer. They continued the saga of Allen's cats and medical woes.

"Ladies," Fredonia interrupted, "Please excuse us. We're off schedule." She held her hand out, and Cadence grabbed it.

"Enjoy your cats," Cadence said and hurried down the hall behind Fredonia.

In the hallway Fredonia turned and laughed. "I never knew I'd meet the crazy cat ladies in a hotel pool." She held her side and gasped for breath.

Cadence giggled at Fredonia's amusement and replayed the ridiculous scene.

"They squished me into the stair rail," she said with a laugh. "And when they started on Allen and his gallbladder."

Fredonia grimaced. "That isn't a conversation I'll have with strangers."

They giggled and repeated lines from the crazy cat ladies while they dressed. Cadence enjoyed the comfortable ease between them.

Does this mean she likes me? I hope it means we'll get along for the rest of the trip.

Fredonia handed her a new purple scarf. Cadence wrapped her hair in the wispy chiffon scarf and tied a neat knot under her chin.

"We look like Easter eggs with the scarves and this pink car." Cadence giggled.

She took a deep breath of the fresh air. The crisp morning air meant perfect weather for driving with the top down.

"Do you have family in Deercrest, Fredonia?" Cadence waited for an answer but decided she wouldn't ask again. She knew a couple of things about Fredonia. One, Fredonia didn't discuss medical ailments with strangers, and two, she didn't talk about her personal life.

"You see," Fredonia said after a long silence, "it's a difficult story for me, and we don't know each other. But on the other hand, the drive is hundreds of miles."

Cadence smiled and waited, but when Fredonia kept silent, Cadence rolled her shoulders and leaned her head back, trying to stay awake.

CHAPTER 14

Norris Creek, Kentucky, October 1944

Ida Bealle rolled her hair in a victory roll and carefully pinned it into place. She smoothed the skirt of her day dress. Her sister Ellie had sent the beautiful green dot crepe fabric. Ida Bealle sewed it, using a new pattern Bud had brought from town. She tucked a warm loaf of bread and a jar of pawpaw jam into her basket and grabbed her hat.

Her friend, Lolly Preece, had received a telegram last night, "Othel declared MIA." Bud sat with the family through the night, offering prayer and comfort. Right before dawn, he came home exhausted and fell into bed beside her. "Go see her," he said and fell asleep.

Ida Bealle walked into town. Her mind swirled, and she whispered a prayer for strength.

Help me here, Lord. I don't know what to say. Please don't let me hurt her with stupid platitudes.

Othel and Lolly's tiny house sat on a corner at the edge of town, the street already lined with cars. Ida Bealle took a deep breath before she opened the door. She went inside prepared to comfort her friend.

Lolly's mother hurried back and forth in the tiny house. She grabbed Ida Bealle's basket and nodded toward the dark front room.

Ida Bealle slipped in and found a chair. Lolly's red-rimmed eyes tugged at Ida Bealle's heart, and she wanted to cry with her friend. Lolly twisted a handkerchief between her white-knuckled fingers and sobbed.

"I'm so sorry, Lolly. What can I do for you?"

Lolly shook her head and closed her eyes. The sound of Lolly's sobs broke Ida Bealle's heart, and she whispered a prayer for wisdom. She held Lolly's hand and wished that her concern was enough to bring Othel home.

"Why'd she come?" A voice drifted from the kitchen.

"She's the preacher's wife—she's tryin' to be kind."

"People who don't have boys over there don't know what it's like. She shouldn't have come."

"Hush. Don't let her hear ya. You'll hurt her feelings."

"I'm supposed to care about the feelings of slackers?"

"Shh . . . she brought bread and jam. Leave her be."

Ida Bealle's cheeks burned. She wanted to set the person straight. Bud served this community—worked hard. He gave up sleep to pray with Lolly and Othel's family. Exemption from the draft didn't mean he lived an easy life. Bud fought battles every day for the people of Norris Creek—if they only knew. Lolly's stare startled her, but she turned away.

She wanted to storm into the kitchen and stick up for Bud. But a preacher's wife didn't march into kitchens and set people straight. Instead, she stood and nodded at the women in the room. "I best get home. Let me know if I can help, Lolly."

She left out the front door avoiding the kitchen and the faceless voices. She didn't want to know who had spoken such terrible words.

Chapter 15

Fredonia mulled over her life story, wondering how much to tell this stranger. There were parts of her story that she had never shared with anyone.

Is keeping it secret a good thing? I should have talked to someone before now. But, no. I stuffed it inside and soldiered on—stiff upper lip, no feelings.

Her position in the town as one of the Addisons prevented her from familiarity with others. Her mother-in-law's constant watchful eyes kept her on script.

She wanted friends, but Mother Addison kept a tight rein on the family. If Fredonia toed the line, she kept Phillip's wealth. This drive home—to her roots—behind the wheel of Phillip's dream car made her wonder if staying in Deercrest was worth it.

Did I give up too much of myself holding on to memories of Phillip?

The emotions churning in her heart surprised Fredonia. She had lived a no-nonsense, all-business life for so long—no feelings. She wondered if unloading her story on a stranger—a young stranger—was wise.

Why does it matter? I doubt I'll see her when we get back to Deercrest. Why not tell her?

"You don't have to tell me, Fredonia. I'm too nosy. I just wondered how you got from Kentucky to Wisconsin. Ignore me. I shouldn't have asked."

Fredonia laughed. "Thank you. I appreciate that. Let me tell you about Norris Creek before you see the town. Sorry I didn't tell you before we left, but I worried you'd say no."

Cadence frowned.

"It's just that Norris Creek is . . ."

"Fredonia, you're scaring me."

"Cadence, no—nothing bad. Relax. It's a tiny community."

"Like Deercrest?" Cadence interrupted.

"Ah . . . no. Deercrest is a metropolis compared to Norris Creek."

"Whoa . . ." She let out a small whistle." I've never lived anywhere smaller than Deercrest. Cities come *smaller*?"

"Norris Creek isn't a city. It's a village in the eastern Kentucky mountains way out in coal mine country. The town has a few businesses and houses, a church or two. There's a tiny store for a few conveniences, a gas station, and the courthouses."

"Courthouses?"

"Long crazy story. Norris Creek's population is three hundred. Many more live in the hollers and valleys outside of town and up in the mountains."

"It sounds beautiful."

"The scenery is beautiful. Yes. But there's a lot of poverty and a lack of resources. The people have a long, proud heritage, but life isn't easy.

"Is that why you left?"

Fredonia shook her head. "No . . . yes."

Cadence chuckled. "I get it."

Fredonia smiled, wondering about the girl's story. "Where did you live before Deercrest, Cadence?"

Cadence mumbled a few words too low for Fredonia to hear, but she didn't press.

She won't share her story either, but I've held mine in so long. It's time.

Fredonia took a deep breath and blurted out, "I'll start at the beginning."

Cadence raised her eyebrows.

"Sorry—some parts are hard."

"Oh, please, don't worry. I understand. You don't owe me your story —I'm only a helper for your job. It's not like we're friends or anything."

An odd hitch in her heart pinched Fredonia at the "we're not friends or anything." She missed time with friends, and it sounded crazy, but she wanted this girl's approval.

"I've kept so much of it in—it's time. I'm fifty-seven, by the way." She trailed off and took a deep breath. "I was born in Norris Creek, Kentucky, to Preacher Bud and Ida Bealle Horne."

Cadence interrupted. "It's not 'Bell'? I like 'Bealle'."

Fredonia sighed. "The road home is fourteen hours of driving, Cadence. I'll never finish my story if you interrupt."

Cadence raised her hand like a schoolchild, "One more question? What was your father's real name?"

"Bud. His Momma called him 'Buddy' 'til the day she died, but his legal name was Bud Horne."

Cadence pretended to zip her lips.

"I grew up the only child of two well-respected people—one of them the preacher. The preacher's kid in a tiny community carried a heavy responsibility. My parents enforced strict rules. My friends participated in many more activities than I did, and I chafed at the rules now and then. But life was good because Momma and Daddy loved me so much. My parents were in their forties—surprise baby." She winked.

"I know they had given up on having babies and had made peace with childlessness. Momma told me I was the best surprise ever. Polite ladies didn't talk about birth in those days, so she never told me what she went through while waiting so long. But she showed how much she loved me with her actions and the time she spent caring for me.

"My mom loved kids—she baked and shared treats with kids on the way home from school. They'd swarm the porch and devour her cookies or muffins. She talked with each one of them and gave each a hug before they left—even the dirty ones." Fredonia chuckled.

"And the naughty ones—like the Crum boys." She rolled her eyes. "The Crum boys still wreak havoc around town, but that's a story for another day. I often wondered why my parents didn't have more children, but I suspect Momma experienced a hard birth because of her age."

Fredonia smiled and struggled against a lump in her throat. "Anyway, I grew up happy and loved—spoiled, if I'm honest. But I always wanted more than small-town life. I knew my roots were somewhere other than in Norris Creek. I don't know why, and I never told my Momma. When I read books about exotic places and adventures and handsome heroes, I wanted the same. I knew my handsome hero didn't live in Norris Creek because boys fit for the preacher's girl were in short supply. Mother and Daddy didn't mind if I married a local boy—Daddy was a local boy after all. But boys my age didn't have enough bravery to ask the preacher for permission to court his daughter." Fredonia winked. "I never met a gentler or more loving soul than my Daddy, but boys feared him. I suppose it ended up all right for me.

"I read my books and dreamed of adventures and worked hard in school. I attended high school up the road because Norris Creek has only an elementary school and junior high school. Even town boys weren't brave enough to ask Preacher Bud for permission to date me. I went on a couple of dates, but Daddy prohibited me from dances— Baptist preacher's girls didn't dance. We didn't smoke or chew or wear trousers either." She winked.

"Oh, the rules. Lots and lots of rules. Most of the time I survived, but oh, how I dreamed of the dances! I wanted a pretty dress and lipstick."

"Did you have a job?" Cadence asked.

"When I turned seventeen, Daddy let me work at the restaurant off the highway right up the road from school. I walked down after classes a couple of days a week and helped with the supper rush. Daddy picked me up after work and brought me a candy bar for the ride home.

"One afternoon I was wiping down the counter and stools when a man sat in front of me. He was so handsome in his suit and tie and oh, his smile.

"He said, 'Afternoon, Miss. Aren't you a sight for sore eyes? I drove for three hours through the mountains, my stomach begging for food. Your café sign is the best sight I've ever seen. But when I came in and saw a beautiful angel, I wondered if I'd gone straight to heaven.' He winked at me and held out his hand. 'Phillip Addison, and I guess your name is Angel?' My ears turned bright red, and I blushed and mumbled my name.

"The funny thing is that he talked the whole time he ate, and I sat and stared. I loved his beautiful eyes, and his smile lit up the room." Fredonia shook her head. "Well, enough. No one wants to hear an old lady ramble on."

"I love your story," Cadence said. "Tell me all about him."

Fredonia drove for miles thinking of Phillip Addison and his dazzling eyes. Tears threatened, but a loud pop scared her before she fell apart. The car lurched.

"Tire." She pulled the Cadillac onto the shoulder of the highway and sighed.

Chapter 16

Norris Creek, Kentucky, October 1957

Ida Bealle sighed, wondering how years flew by so quickly. She spent her days in a flurry of activity. Bud needed help typing his sermons and letters, and the ladies wanted her help cleaning the church before services. Children stopped by for cookies or chats about their day. Life in Norris Creek settled into a predictable but busy pattern. Her activities changed with the seasons, but her life centered around the church, the community, and Bud.

She sat in the empty sanctuary and prayed while she worked. She prayed for the church people and the requests Bud shared from mountain folk. She prayed for their marriage and poured out her heart before God for her husband and his ministry.

When she polished the pews in the hallway—set there for mothers of young children—tears flowed. "Jesus, I don't know why you haven't given us a child yet. Bud says to wait and trust, but my heart hurts. We've waited seventeen years. Isn't that long enough? I want a baby, Lord. I'm old. Can't you please send us a baby soon? Bud tells me you know best, and I know you do, but I don't understand. I'd be such a good momma, Lord. I know you can trust me with a baby. When I see Bud with the church babies, I fight tears. He'd be such a good poppa too. Why, Lord?"

She wiped her eyes, put away the feather duster, and pushed her heart's desire out of mind. She stayed busy during the week, but the lump in her throat returned every time she polished the oak pews in the hall. She wrestled with her desire for a child all over again.

Ida Bealle loved serving as the preacher's wife, even if it meant scrutiny and comments. Some ladies critiqued her housekeeping skills and money habits. She learned to bite her tongue, pray for them, and release it to God. She enjoyed special friendships in Norris Creek— Lolly Preece especially. She counted her blessings and poured love and kindness on the others. She knew Bud supported her. He ignored her housekeeping mistakes and meal failures.

Life in the parsonage meant blessings. It meant gifts left on the porch—eggs, meat, vegetables, pies, cookies, and cakes. It meant everyone recognized her and loved her husband. It meant Sunday school and enthusiastic children whose little eyes lit up at the truth of the gospel.

The Ladies' Missionary Society didn't take root, although Ida Bealle used her mother's tips and project ideas. Participation wasn't enthusiastic, but she hoped to find an inspirational project soon. She wished they understood the joy of service, so she tried again.

She hung out the laundry when the sun rose and waited for the breeze to work its magic. She folded the red-and-white quilt inhaling the scent of crisp mountain air. She ran a finger over the names embroidered on the corner square and prayed for each woman. "And dear Lord, bless dear Mrs. Ray and bless poor Bud for the times he eats her awful recipes."

Mother's Ladies' Missionary Society adopted her and Bud for their main project. Packages arrived, often stuffed with gifts for her and Bud and items for the church or the Norris Creek community. Just yesterday, Bud had lugged home a large box that contained storybooks for the Sunday school children and twenty dollars for her and Bud.

She smoothed the quilt over their bed and updated the ladies at home.

October 6, 1957

Dear Ladies' Missionary Society,

Bud and I received your gift yesterday, and it made us smile. Your gift is an answer to our prayers. Bud's truck—he calls it George—needs new tires. The mountain roads wear them out fast, and he takes so many trips up there. I won't worry about him so much if he drives on safe tires.

What he sees in the mountains breaks our hearts. We do the best we can to help the families. Bud can't stand seeing needs go unfulfilled if he can help. He often comes home with a list of items he wants to share with some family--clothes, food, and blankets are things he takes most often. Bud meets their physical needs and then tells them about Jesus. You should see him when he shares truth from the Scripture. His eyes light up, and love pours out of him, but I worry he'll get burned out. The need is so great. He tells me God fills him up and helps him, and when someone trusts the Lord for a burden or turns their life over to God, it keeps him energized.

The books you sent will make the Sunday school children happy. Bud will take the colorful alphabet book for a little girl who lives on the mountain. He says she loves his stories and asks about Jesus.

Your gifts and prayers mean so much. We are thankful to know others pray for our church and ministry. Please join us in prayer for opportunities to show the love of God to those in our community.

In his love,

Bud and Ida Bealle Horne

Turkey Creek Baptist Church, Norris Creek, Kentucky.

She slid the letter into the envelope and checked the clock—enough time to pop Bud's favorite "Super Sandwiches" under the broiler if she hurried.

CHAPTER 17

*H*ighway 51, Indiana

"Flat tire?" Cadence jumped out of the car. "Want help?"

"No, you stay put. We don't need two of us out on the road." Fredonia popped the trunk and muttered. Something thumped and banged and the car shook.

I like her. She seems proper and no-nonsense, but she's fun underneath all that.

Fredonia's story about the handsome stranger with dazzling eyes made her sigh. She glanced in the mirror at a loud rumble—several motorcycles parked behind the car revving their motors.

Oh, no.

Cadence hopped out of the car and hovered near Fredonia on the side of the highway. She imagined all the ways this encounter could end badly.

"You ladies all right?" a beefy man hollered from his bike. A tiny woman sat behind him, her arms wrapped around his large middle.

"Yes!" Cadence called.

"No, we're in a bit of a pickle—flat tire!" Fredonia said at the same time.

Three men hopped off their bikes—their chains jingled. One flashed Cadence a grin and winked. A cold chill crawled up her spine when she imagined the headlines: *Police discover two bodies in the trunk of a 1959 Cadillac on the side of the road in Somewhere, Indiana.*

She shivered and rubbed her arms. Her scared heart needed calm.

Fredonia smiled and shook the biker's hands. The biker who winked at Cadence grabbed the tire iron and spare. "Whitewalls. What year? '56?"

"Nah, Joe, the '56 didn't have fins like this. She's a '59, right, ma'am?" The short one removed his leather cap and nodded in Fredonia's direction.

"You know your Caddys. How fun!" Fredonia smiled.

"Where you girls off to tonight?" asked the short one. Tattoos covered his arms from wrist to shoulder. Cadence noticed a gun under his vest and glanced in the direction of the bikes. A woman stared—her cold gaze a threat.

I'd rather deal with biker chicks and Shorty's gun than Taylor.

"Cadence and I are traveling to Kentucky. I'm emptying my mother's home. She passed a while ago, but I've not made the trip."

"Sorry, ma'am," the big one called Joe said. "Almost done." He wrenched the tire iron while the girls stared at Cadence.

Fredonia grabbed her purse, "Gentlemen, let me offer you payment for your trouble."

"No, ma'am—put your money away. Happy to help you ladies, and workin' on this beautiful car is all the pay we need. Right, boys?" He turned to the boys and wiped greasy hands onto the leg of his jeans. They nodded, and big Joe called out, "Night, ladies! You stay safe!"

The bikers pulled onto the highway, the bikes rumbling. Cadence's eardrums shook.

"All good." Fredonia slid behind the chrome steering wheel. "You know I call her 'Cici'?" She patted the dashboard and pulled onto the highway. "Let's find a place to lay our heads, and please, God—no crazy cat ladies in the pool tonight." She chuckled, and Cadence laughed too.

Sun peeked through the clouds, and a soft mist hung over the earth in the morning. Fredonia exercised the night before to save time. They hit the road early.

"We should be there shortly after lunch." Fredonia opened the convertible and handed Cadence another chiffon scarf.

"Where did you find so many scarves?" Cadence wrapped hers around her brown hair and tied a loose knot under her chin.

"When you help me sort mom's things, you'll understand." Fredonia laughed.

Cadence sipped her coffee and planned ways to outwit Taylor.

I can stay in Kentucky.

I can come up with another name and find a new town.

I can turn myself in.

I can curl up and die.

I can light my house on fire and pay her with insurance money.

No good options for the Taylor problem. The stress threatened—a black hole of depression.

Take your mind off Taylor, quickly.

"Tell me the rest of your story."

Fredonia glanced over. "You don't want to hear an old woman's story. It's old news."

"At least tell me about the handsome stranger," Cadence begged. "You can't leave me in suspense."

A small smile pulled at the corners of Fredonia's mouth. "Weeks passed before he came back. I'd hold my breath and hope he'd come through the door while I worked. I picked up extra shifts, worried I'd miss him. I dreamed about him constantly.

"Momma said, 'Are you sick?' and Daddy asked, 'Are you dating a town boy without permission?' I didn't want to let them know I pined away over a stranger. I did less 'moonin', as Momma said. My heartsick mind worried—*What if I never saw him again?*

"Momma wanted me to work less, but I burst into tears when she told Daddy I needed more rest and time at home. Daddy and I made a bargain: if I kept my grades up and didn't worry Momma, he didn't mind if I worked as much as I wanted.

"My boss told me to quit flitting around and looked at me funny. I worked hard, but every time the door opened, I jumped and stared.

After all the 'moonin' and jumpiness, I was washing dishes in the kitchen, my hair a damp mess from the heat, when I heard him. 'Where's Angel?'

"I ran out front, and when Phillip saw me, he got the biggest smile. 'Angel. You're here.'

"Hello, Mr. Addison. Can I take your order? Did you hear our special of the day? He said, 'No, Angel—tell me all about you.' He leaned on the counter and smiled, and I wanted to throw up." Fredonia chuckled.

When Fredonia talked about Phillip, she was beautiful. Her prim formality softened, and her cheeks blushed a soft pink. Cadence was amazed at the transformation. She wanted to hear more.

CHAPTER 18

After several miles of silence, Cadence gave up on Fredonia's story. The fields and hills slowed her racing mind. As they passed cornfields and small towns, she worked on a plan to outsmart Taylor.

"We talked for hours."

"Hmm?"

"Phillip and I, we talked for hours. I hustled around and helped other customers, but between customers, we talked and laughed. I fell hard. It sounds silly, I know, but it's true. He shared which day he'd stop and asked when I worked. You better believe I found a way to work a shift if he said he'd stop."

"On one of my days off, I plopped onto the stool at the counter and ordered an orange Coke. I wore my prettiest dress with my hair down. I waited with a pit in my stomach and wondered whether he chatted with me because I waitressed at the diner or because he liked me.

"He tapped my shoulder. 'Angel? You're off today?' He sat down on the next stool. 'I guess we'll eat together this time.' He paid for my orange Coke, and we talked for hours.

"His father owned a lumber mill up north, and Phillip was their salesman. His dad sent him all over the country selling their products.

He told me he loved his drives through our small towns and the people he met, but his favorite stop was our café. He wanted every detail about me, but how many details does a high school kid have to share?"

Fredonia smiled; tears glistened in her eyes. "We talked for hours every time he stopped. On days I didn't work, we ate and took a walk. I remember the first time he held my hand." She sighed. "Over time we grew close and talked each other's ears off. We never ran out of topics for discussion. When he'd leave, he'd hand me a stack of letters. He wrote one every night and saved them 'til he came.

"I never shared anything about Phillip with my parents. What would I say? By the way, I've fallen in love with a tall, handsome stranger from the north. I know little about him, but he's nice. They would have locked me in the closet under the stairs to save me from myself." She chuckled.

"After four or five months of once-a-week stops at the diner, he told me he wanted to marry me someday. Between our talks and the letters, we knew each other. Oh, how he wrote—those letters were . . . " She trailed off, and a rosy-red blush crept up her cheeks.

"I asked, 'Why wait?' But my parents. His parents. My age. The 'cons' list was a mile long, but I loved him." She shrugged her shoulders and smiled. "I said, 'Take me along with you.' He said no. I know it sounds like he was dishonorable, but he wasn't, Cadence. Phillip was impeccable about honor. He didn't even kiss my cheek. He was twenty-one, and my eighteenth birthday was a few months away.

"It seems crazy when I look back, but at the time it all made sense— at least to me. He was so handsome, sweet, and gentle. His life up north sounded fabulous. I imagined his daddy's business operated like those around us in the small towns and mountains. He was an only child and wanted a big family. Of course, I grew up as a Baptist preacher's only child, so thinking of so many children made me blush. But when he put his arms around me and whispered, 'I love you,' in my ear, I fell hard. It's a fitting description—totally gone.

"The next time he came, I put my foot down. I told him that when I turned eighteen—in May—we would marry. He chuckled and said no, but when he left he put his forehead on mine and whispered, 'Okay, we'll figure it out.'

"I walked on clouds, no care about my family or his family or if I'd fit in up north. I intended to marry Phillip. On the day I turned eighteen, I tucked a few items into my school bag. I was afraid that Momma might see it and keep me home that morning.

"I regret that I didn't tell my parents. I can't explain because I know it sounds like I escaped a hard life or acted foolishly, but it's not true. I wanted Phillip. I can look back now and see how it appeared or imagine how I scared my parents. I simply chose the man I loved. He never talked me into it. He tried talking me out of it, but I made him take me."

Cadence held her breath. It sounded romantic—eloping and starting a new life with a handsome stranger.

If there were any handsome strangers handy, I'd elope and run somewhere far from Taylor.

Cadence ignored the knot in her belly. She needed to focus and create a plan.

If you exist, God, now's an excellent time to send a handsome stranger to rescue me. I can use a break right about now.

Chapter 19

Norris Creek, Kentucky, August 1959

Ida Bealle stared at the mess in the kitchen and took a deep breath. Canning season—so much to do. A bushel of cucumbers sat in the corner for pickling. She wanted to try a new recipe for refrigerator pickles, but she planned to can several quarts of Bud's favorite dills. A pot of apple butter simmered on the stove, and she inhaled a deep breath of the spicy mixture while she stirred.

So much to do and so little time.

She hummed while she stirred. She had hummed it all week since the baptism last Sunday.

> *'Tis so sweet to trust in Jesus,*
> *Just to take Him at His word,*
> *Just to rest upon His promise,*
> *Just to know, "Thus saith the Lord."*
> *Jesus, Jesus, how I trust Him!*
> *How I've proved Him o'er and o'er!*
> *Jesus, Jesus, precious Jesus!*
> *O for grace to trust Him more!*

She heard talk of mountain women birthing babies far into their forties. She wasn't that old—yet. Hope lived in the secret corners of her heart, and until she was too old, she prayed. She didn't talk about babies to Bud anymore. When she mentioned her ache, Bud's eyes dimmed and he would point her to Scripture. She loved his devotion to God and his love of Scripture, but she wanted him to cry with her.

She tucked away her baby wishes and attacked the counter with a cloth. "That apple butter gets sticky," she muttered. She gave the pot of apple butter a final stir. When the canner water boiled, she poured the apple butter into jars to boil.

The cucumbers will wait 'til tomorrow.

"Miss Ida Bealle! Miss Ida Bealle!" a boy called through the screen. It sounded like a herd of buffalo on the porch.

"Just a minute!" she called. She double-checked that the apple butter was off the flame and hurried to the door.

Wilbur Crum and three other boys stared and Wilbur waved a newspaper clipping in the air when she opened the screen. The boys talked at once.

"Hold on!" Ida Bealle talked over them. "I can't hear you!"

"The fair."

"The contest."

"Cake."

"Help us."

Ida Bealle held up her hand, "Boys, slow down. I'm gonna sit for a spell in my rocker, and you tell me one at a time."

They gathered around her rocker. The smiles on their little-boy faces made her feel empty spots in her heart. How different their lives were without children—quieter, that's for sure!

"Okay, tell me what yer hollerin' about," she said, smiling at the boys and waiting as they poked and prodded each other.

Lolly's youngest boy, Robert, stepped forward, the spitting image of his daddy, Othel. The months spent waiting for news of Othel's return —or death—flashed through her mind. A missing soldier seemed a cruel trial for a family to endure.

Poor Lolly. Thank you, Lord, for bringing Othel home from the war.

Robert cleared his throat, "Miss Ida Bealle, the fair is next week, and we're needin' yer help 'cause we wanna win."

"Win what?"

"The contest." Wilbur waved the clipping toward her.

"Oh, this *is* exciting. What's your plan?" she asked.

They all shouted plans while she shook her head and laughed. "Boys, I can't hear you all at once. You tell me." She pointed to the boy hidden behind the others.

He smiled. "We want to make the biggest cake. The paper says the cake with the most layers wins a prize."

"Is that so? How much?"

"Twenty dollars!" they yelled.

"Why do you need *my* help?"

"Cause you're the best cook around. Least my momma says so," Robert said.

She hugged him and tousled his hair. "Well, flattery is certainly one way to get me to help."

They grinned, and Robert pulled out of her hug, making a face.

Ida Bealle rocked, enjoying the cool air on the porch. Canning season heated her kitchen far beyond comfort. "What about a stack cake?" she asked, thinking of the apple butter cooling on her stove.

"My momma only makes stack cake at Christmas," Wilbur said.

Ida Bealle nodded her head. "Yep, it's a lot of work. But if you boys help me, I'll help you. I'll give you the apple butter, but you raise the money for ingredients."

"What if we asked people to pay for a layer, and we can buy the ingredients with the money?" Robert asked.

"Aw, come on—no one's gonna pay us to make a cake!"

"We can try."

Ida Bealle laughed. "It's brilliant. You boys go on and sell the layers, and I'll help you make the cake. We don't have much time because stack cake needs to sit for a couple days. Get movin'."

The boys scrambled off her porch.

"I'm glad they asked," she whispered, her eyes shining. The boys' laughter drifted back to her as they ran down the road.

Banging on the screen door interrupted her canning. "Miss Ida Bealle, we're back!"

"What did you boys figure out?"

Wilbur held up a bag with coins and bills. "We got $56, Miss Ida Bealle."

"Whoa, you didn't steal it, did you?" She stared each of them in the eye with a scowl.

"No. No, Miss Ida Bealle. We told everyone we wanted to win and were selling layers for $2, and we sold $56 worth."

"Wait a minute—that's . . ."

"Twenty-eight layers!" Robert yelled, a huge grin on his face.

Ida Bealle's eyes widened and she shook her head. "Boys, stack cakes aren't twenty-eight layers. I don't think we can do it."

"But we sold 'em already. We *gotta* do it!"

She fanned herself with her apron. "Give me a minute. We'll think of a plan."

"Let's ask Preacher," they said and ran to the church.

"How are we gonna get a twenty-eight-layer stack cake to the fairgrounds?" she said, laughing. "I'd better make more apple butter."

Chapter 20

*H*ighway 645, Kentucky

Cadence enjoyed the breeze whipping her hair. The chiffon scarf kept most of it out of her face, but the loose strands flew around. The long hours on the road lulled her into believing that outwitting Taylor was possible. The sound of the wheels on the road gave Cadence an idea. If she backed over Taylor with Fredonia's car, Cici, the threats ended once and for all. She smiled, wishing it weren't an impossible dream.

I can't murder her. I just want her gone.

She dozed off and dreamt of pink Cadillacs and disastrous accidents until Fredonia's question woke her.

"What's *your* story?"

"Oh no, Fredonia," she said as she sat up and yawned. "You have to finish *your* story first. Don't leave me hanging."

What do you want to know, Fredonia? I don't have a family. My obnoxious nemesis wants an obscene amount of money to keep my secrets. I'm tired and angry. I'm the kind of person you don't bring into your life. If only you knew, Fredonia.

Fredonia chuckled, "What do you want to know?"

"Ummm . . . hello? Did it work out? What did your parents say? His parents? Where did you live? Were you happy?"

"Yes, it worked out. My parents were not happy—they were hurt. His parents were livid. They despised me—still do. We lived in Deercrest in the house I live in now."

"Where is your house?"

Fredonia turned to Cadence with an odd expression. "Cadence, you came to my house a few days ago. What do you mean, where is my house?"

Cadence slid down in her seat. "You live in the mansion?"

Fredonia laughed. "What did you *think* I was doing there?"

"Well—I—I thought you *worked* there." Cadence covered her eyes and blushed.

Fredonia burst into a belly laugh.

"Oh, Cadence, I haven't worked a real job in forty years. You're funny. Nope. The mansion is my beautiful house."

"I'm so sorry."

"No need to apologize. When you see Norris Creek, you'll understand what moving north meant for me. Culture shock in so many ways. Momma and Daddy didn't have that kind of money. We didn't know anyone with money like that. Even the rich guys in town didn't compare to Addison money."

"His parents weren't happy you married?"

"'Not happy' is an understatement. Phillip's parents had chosen the local judge's daughter. She came from money, and she was classy and stylish—the right connections. He wasn't in love with her, and I'm proud he stood up to his parents—well, his mother. She tried to make us miserable but failed. Phillip and I were so happy in our beautiful dream."

"*Were*?" Cadence asked.

Fredonia bit her lip, and a tear rolled down her cheek.

"I'm sorry. I didn't mean to make you cry." Cadence wanted to comfort Fredonia, but Fredonia didn't look like a hugger, and patting her arm seemed awkward.

Fredonia let out a deep breath. "Yes, Cadence, I was happy. Happy and in love with a perfect marriage. I'm not exaggerating. We knew very little about each other, and it seemed a recipe for disaster, but it was a beautiful dream come true. Our only problem was Mother Addison."

"What happened?" Cadence asked.

Fredonia straightened her shoulders and tapped the pink steering wheel. "That's a story for another day."

Cadence stopped the questions, remembering her secrets.

It's not like I share my *gritty details.*

The mountains and winding highway mesmerized Cadence. They were so different than Wisconsin's hills and lush green landscape. It took little time before she focused on Taylor's threats. Cadence knew they weren't idle. Taylor would come to collect in a few days.

And I'm far away.

She pictured Taylor finding an empty house next week and smiled.

I've never told you no, Taylor Nash, and you have ruined my life. You've taken everything from me, but I won't let you do it again. You can rot in hell for all I care. I hate you.

Cadence's heart pounded and heat flushed her face—anger at Taylor's threats, her losses, and her stupidity, anger at her mother for dropping her at Grandma Miggs's and never returning, anger at God for letting Grandma die.

Will I fall apart if I let go of this anger? What if it's all that holds me together? How can I get Taylor out of my life?

She didn't condone violence, but something needed to change. Cadence leaned her head back and fell asleep, dreaming of a happy world free of Taylor Nash.

CHAPTER 21

Ida Bealle checked on the commotion. Loud little-boy voices and her favorite deep voice chattered on the porch. The boys surrounded Bud, talking at once. He winked at her above their heads.

"Miss Ida Bealle, these boys tell me you agreed to help them win the cake contest at the fair. That right?"

"I did agree, Preacher Bud, but they sold twenty-eight layers. I don't know how we're gonna get it to the fair."

Bud leaned back his head and roared with laughter. "Boys, you outdid yourselves." He wiped his eyes and sighed. "Let's sit down and figure out a strategy."

The boys plopped onto the steps, and Bud sat between them. Ida Bealle sat in her rocker and listened to their brainstorming session.

"We can tote it in our wagon."

"How 'bout Preacher's truck?"

"How's it gonna stay together?"

Bud held up his hand. "I'm thinkin' we should use the church kitchen. Good idea, Miss Ida Bealle?"

She nodded. "Good idea—more room."

"We can use my truck, but we'll have to think of a way to keep the cake from smashing on the way."

The boys groaned.

"No complaining, now," Bud said. "Let's put our heads together and decide on a plan."

Half an hour later, Bud and the boys left in his pickup truck to gather lumber for a box in which to transport the cake.

Ida Bealle calculated the ingredients for a twenty-eight-layer stack cake. She shook her head and chuckled. "How did I get mixed up in this?"

On baking day the church kitchen buzzed with excitement. Noisy boys chattered, ignoring Ida Bealle's pleas to wash their hands. She cornered each boy, tying one of her colorful aprons around his small waist and checking his hands.

The boys mixed and stirred, following Ida Bealle's orders. The scent of cinnamon and nutmeg filled the kitchen, and the boys stopped their work to say, "Mmmm!"

"Can I lick the spoon, Miss Ida Bealle?" Robert Preece asked.

"No, it'll take all day to bake these layers. No licking anything—especially your fingers."

The boys nodded and turned back to stirring and measuring. Bud slid cakes into the large church oven and set the timer. He came to report to Ida Bealle. "We're at twelve layers. What are we doing with them?"

"Spread them on the counters and cover with a clean cloth. Have the boys do it. It's their project—right, boys?"

Wilbur ran to help Bud. Ida Bealle sighed at the commotion and cheerful faces. She pushed down her wish for motherhood and forced herself to pay attention to the project at hand.

"You okay?" Bud called from across the kitchen.

She nodded. "Gonna' sit for a spell." She pulled out a chair and took a cool drink of water. "This kitchen is hot."

"Should we prop the door open, Miss Ida Bealle?"

"No way—flies."

The boys spilled flour and smeared molasses across the kitchen, but the day progressed smoothly. Bud pulled the last layer from the oven. "Boys, count those layers, and let's make sure we got 'em all."

They ran around the kitchen, "Twenty-eight!" they said, cheering. "We did it!"

"Yes, you did," said Ida Bealle, "and now you're gonna clean up."

They groaned, but she handed them brooms and cloths. "Hurry up now, 'cause you and Preacher Bud need to build the platform for the cake before you leave."

They cleaned the messy kitchen and hurried outside to find Bud. The buzz of Bud's saw and the boys' excited voices filled the church yard. An hour later, the boys followed Bud, carrying a large box.

"Wipe it down and cover it in foil," Ida Bealle directed.

The boys listened to Ida Bealle's orders, and cake construction began. They spread apple butter between each layer and stacked the cooled cake layers.

"The layers will get nice and soft when they sit for two days—jest in time for judging at the fair," Ida Bealle said.

Their eyes bugged out, and the kitchen filled with laughter as the cake's height grew. Bud shook his head. "Boys, I don't know how we're gonna get this to the fair."

"Maybe Daddy will help," Robert said.

"Good idea. You boys ask your daddies to come to church the morning of the fair, and we'll figure it out."

The boys ran out of the church kitchen, laughing and hollering. Bud gathered his wife in his arms. "How do you get me into these crazy situations, Mrs. Horne?"

"Oh, shoo, Preacher Bud! You loved every minute of it."

Bud laughed and leaned down to kiss her. "Every minute I'm with you, Mrs. Horne."

Ida Bealle walked to church in the morning with a mug of coffee in her hand. The thick haze settled around the church, pretty as a postcard. Ida Bealle smiled. She loved Norris Creek.

When she opened the door to the church kitchen, she raised her eyebrows at the noise level. The boys and dads tried to decide the best way to transport the cake while Bud filled the back of his old blue pickup with blankets and quilts.

"Boys, sit down so you don't run into us. Dads, grab a corner, and let's move slow." Bud directed the effort, and the cake was on the move.

Ida Bealle sat with the boys. All of them held their breaths, and Robert Preece whispered a prayer.

"It's in!" Bud called, and they followed him to the truck. The cake sat in the middle of the pickup, the box surrounded by soft blankets. Ida Bealle breathed a sigh of relief.

"Let's say a prayer, folks," Othel said. The men took off their hats, and Othel prayed. "Dear Lord, these boys worked hard—purt near a week. Help Preacher Bud git to the fair with this cake in one piece."

"And let us win," Wilbur interrupted, and the adults laughed.

Bud hopped into the truck, and the boys walked alongside. Ida Bealle whispered a prayer, "God, I don't know if you care about apple stack cake, but I know you love those boys. Please let Bud get there with the cake in one piece." When they were out of sight, she tidied up the kitchen and went home to wait for news.

The sights and sounds of the fair filled citizens of Martin County with wonder this past week. But nothing prepared us for the spectacular twenty-eight-layer apple stack cake made by four local boys with the help of Mrs. Ida Bealle Horne.

The spicy spectacle made judges and spectators gasp. Between the layers, spicy brown apple butter oozed down the sides. The judges gave the boys a blue ribbon and declared their cake the winner of the layer cake contest and the entire fair.

The boys will split a twenty-dollar prize.

When interviewed, Wilbur Crum, age ten, said, "Preacher Bud didn't go no more than five miles an hour the whole way here. We was worried we'd crash and ruin it, but we said a prayer 'fore we left."

The layer cakes from the contest sold at auction, but the bidding war for the apple stack cake was fierce. Hub Cassady won, paying

forty dollars for the mammoth cake. He said, "Come on over to the hardware store and get a slice for two bucks. I'll make coffee."
—The Norris Creek Gazette

Prize-Winning Apple Stack Cake

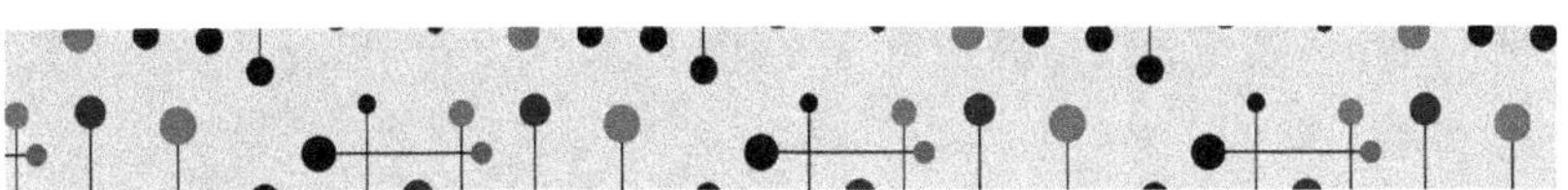

5 c. all-purpose flour, plus more as needed
1 tsp. baking soda
1 tsp. baking powder
1 tsp. salt
⅔ c. vegetable shortening
1 c. granulated sugar
1 c. sorghum molasses
2 eggs, lightly beaten
1 c. buttermilk
5 c. apple butter

Cake layers:
Preheat oven to 350°. Grease and flour a well-seasoned cast-iron skillet to bake layers one at a time.

Whisk together the flour, baking soda, baking powder, and salt in a large bowl.

In another large bowl, beat the shortening, sugar, and molasses with a mixer on medium. Beat until the mixture is smooth.

Add eggs one at a time, beating well after each addition.

Add the flour mixture in thirds, alternating with half of the buttermilk. Dough will be thick like a cookie. You can knead if it works better. Add a bit more flour as needed.

Pat out dough on a floured surface. Divide into six pieces and wrap each piece to keep soft. Use lightly floured hands to pat a piece of dough into the bottom of the prepared skillet—about ½ inch thick.

Lightly prick the dough with a fork, making a pattern. Bake until the layers are firm when lightly pressed—fifteen minutes. The dough won't rise as it bakes.

Turn out the first baked layer on a large cake plate. Spread warm layer with 1 c. apple butter. Bake, stack, and top the warm layers. Don't put apple butter on the top layer.

Cover cake, or store in an airtight cake carrier. Allow cake to rest at room temperature for at least two days before serving.

CHAPTER 22

*N*orris Creek, Kentucky
Cadence dozed the rest of the way into Norris Creek. She drifted in and out of sleep and plotted Taylor's demise. Everyone would talk. Laura . . . well . . .

Laura will never speak to me again. I can see the headlines: Police Officer's Former Friday Night Date Arrested for Murder. *Who cares? If Taylor turns me in, I'll go to prison. What difference does it make why I'm there?*

Cadence mulled over ways to rid her life of Taylor.

Which ones can I manage? Nothing bloody or messy. Her earlier idea of a catastrophic accident between Taylor and Fredonia's pink Cadillac might work. She opened her eyes, "Fredonia, how much would you sell Cici for?"

"I won't sell Cici, Cadence."

"Come on. How much is she worth?"

Fredonia sighed. "Last time I checked, this model sold for thirty thousand. I'd sell her to you for thirty-five." Fredonia winked and patted the steering wheel. She leaned forward and stage whispered, "Don't worry, Cici. I won't sell you."

Cadence whistled.

Well, I can't afford Cici. I'll borrow her.

Murdering another human—a mother—bothered Cadence deep in her soul. Somehow the battle with Taylor needed to end.

Taylor's life has always been easy—parents, money, friends. It's my turn to have a break. One of us has to go.

The changing scenery calmed her, and she took a deep breath.

What kind of psycho dreams of murdering someone?

"Mountain air is good for you—makes you healthy." Fredonia smiled.

The hum of tires lulled Cadence to sleep until Fredonia interrupted. "I haven't told you much about Norris Creek. It's . . . I don't know how to explain. It's small." She shrugged.

"Oh, I'm used to small. We live in Deercrest." Cadence smiled.

"I guess you'll see. We'll stay at my parents' house. No room-sharing this time, and as far as I know, no crazy cat ladies." She smirked.

Cadence laughed. "Crazy cat ladies in the pool. What a riot!"

Fredonia laughed.

"How long have you been away?"

"I visited Momma and Daddy when Daddy was sick about five years ago. I came for Momma's service, of course, but didn't pack up the parsonage. The church told me to take my time."

"Parsonage?"

"The church owns the preacher's house, right next door to the Turkey Creek Baptist Church."

"Wait. The church is 'Turkey Creek' and the town is 'Norris Creek'?"

Fredonia laughed. "Cadence, my new friend, it's one of the great mysteries of life. No one knows why, so we roll with it." Fredonia shrugged.

"If the preacher's house belongs to the church, why did they let you leave your mother's things for so long?"

"The new preacher has a home, and he's not in a hurry to move. The church used the space for meetings and visiting preachers, so it was good to have furniture."

Cadence nodded. "Makes sense."

Fredonia slowed the car at the "Welcome to Norris Creek" sign.

"Word to the wise," Fredonia said. "Never speed through Norris Creek. Speed trap."

They entered a deep narrow valley with a winding road cut through the middle of the town. Buildings rested their backs against the mountain.

Cadence tried to look everywhere. The old buildings stood near the road, some dilapidated, others with roofs caving in. A faded Coca-Cola mural on the side of a building made Cadence smile. The houses and businesses sat next to each other, unlike Deercrest, with homes and businesses in neat, separate areas. Sadness settled over Cadence when she imagined living here.

"There must be more I don't see?" she asked Fredonia.

"A little bit, but most people live up in the mountains. Norris Creek is tiny, and it's worsened over the years. The town was in better shape when I was a kid. Even twenty years ago, the town was in better shape than this."

They drove past an elementary school. The swing set needed paint. The asphalt under the play equipment sprouted tall weeds.

"That play equipment looks dangerous," Cadence said.

"Norris Creek parents don't bubble wrap their kids."

They drove past a small white store also in need of paint.

Cadence sat up. "Fredonia, did that road sign say 'Hog Liver Road'?" She cranked her neck around to read the sign.

Fredonia laughed. "Welcome to small-town Kentucky, Cadence. Hog Liver Road is two roads before church. We're home." She parked Cici under a mammoth oak tree. Sunlight filtered through the leaves, dappling the car.

Cadence sat for a moment and listened to birds chirping and breezes rustling the leaves.

Peaceful.

Fredonia hopped out and closed the convertible's roof.

The house sat farther back from the road than the church—an afterthought. Both buildings needed paint.

They look tired.

A porch hugged three sides of the house, and a rocking chair by the front door beckoned to Cadence, the perfect spot for a book and a glass of lemonade.

I doubt I'll have time to relax.

Fredonia popped the trunk to grab suitcases, and the screen door slammed open. A short woman with round cheeks and a rounder belly stepped out. Her gray hair piled high atop her head streaked with flour. She wiped her hands onto a towel and squinted in their direction.

"Freddie Mae? That you?" she hollered.

"It's me, Miss Ollie!" Fredonia smiled. "I'm home."

The lady hurried off the porch and threw her arms around Fredonia.

"Oh, Freddie, it's so good to see you. How was your trip? The car run good?" The woman patted Cici's tail fin.

Cadence stepped out of the car while the woman called "Miss Ollie" fired questions at Fredonia. The woman turned to Cadence, and her mouth gaped. She glanced back and forth between Fredonia and Cadence, frowning.

"You didn't say nothin' about guests," Miss Ollie said, chiding Fredonia.

"She's not a guest. I hired her to help. Besides, Miss Ollie, did you want me driving down here alone?"

Fredonia patted Miss Ollie's arm and grabbed the suitcases. She motioned for Cadence to follow.

"I just weren't expecting her—that's all." She inspected Cadence from head to toe. The look on her face told Cadence that Miss Ollie disapproved. Cadence smoothed her blouse and patted her scarf-protected hair.

When she stepped onto the porch, the smell of chocolate wafted through the screen door.

"Got your momma's cake in the oven for dessert tonight. You hungry? I can warm up some beans."

"We're fine, Miss Ollie. We'll unpack and get to work."

Fredonia led the way up a narrow wooden staircase. Cadence glanced at pictures on the wall, a smiling little girl in most of them. Fredonia's childhood smiles made Cadence grin, but a jealous ache formed under her heart.

Why can't I have a family? If I grew up with a happy family, I wouldn't have to run from a maniac.

Fredonia pointed to a room at the top of the stairs. "You can have this one. The bathroom is downstairs off the kitchen if you need to freshen up." She disappeared, leaving Cadence alone with swirling thoughts.

CHAPTER 23

*N*orris Creek, Kentucky, 1961

Ida Bealle buried her swirling grief in busyness. Housekeeping chores around the parsonage consumed most of her days. There was always plenty of work for the preacher's wife. She sang while she hung laundry on the clothesline.

> *'Tis so sweet to trust in Jesus,*
> *Just to take Him at His word,*
> *Just to rest upon His promise,*
> *Just to know, "Thus saith the Lord."*
> *Jesus, Jesus, how I trust Him!*
> *How I've proved Him o'er and o'er!*
> *Jesus, Jesus, precious Jesus!*
> *O for grace to trust Him more!*

She hummed and sang as she worked, tucking grief into the secret corners of her heart. Keeping the parsonage spotless kept her busy, but she found time to serve in the community.

The women of Turkey Creek Baptist Church loved Ida Bealle, and she loved them. She took meals to town families when babies came or someone lay dying. She and Bud delivered food and clothes to mountain families who didn't attend services. God had called them to serve all the people—church attenders or not.

Ida Bealle's kitchen cranked out pies, cookies, and meals at a brisk rate. The town children knew that if Miss Ida Bealle stood on the porch after school, a snack of warm cookies waited. They swarmed the porch, devoured her cookies, and gave messy hugs. They waved as they skipped home, their smiles smeared with chocolate and crumbs.

Ida Bealle baked cookies on emotional days. Most Appalachian families crammed eight or more children into their tiny homes. Childless families were rare. Many people expressed sympathy for Ida Bealle and the preacher, but some whispered.

"Sin. It's sin in their life. God don't keep babies from people unless there's a reason."

The comments pierced Ida Bealle's heart, but instead of growing bitter, she baked. The little ones' sticky fingers and mischievous smiles were a balm for her broken heart.

She begged God year after year to bless them with a child, crying bitter tears every month. Her heart broke when friends and her sisters birthed baby after baby. She wrestled with joy for new life and sorrow for old barrenness. She loved her nieces and nephews and her friends' babies, but those babies didn't answer her prayers.

Why, God? Why don't you give Buddy and me a baby? I know we have enough love to provide a good home.

"Mmm . . . smells good in here." Bud sat down and grabbed several cookies, scattering crumbs over the table as he ate. "Hard day?"

She nodded. Bud wrapped his arms around her, pulling her close. She nestled her head into the spot on his shoulder where she fit perfectly.

"Why doesn't God answer our prayers?"

"He does, darlin'—his answer is no. God always hears and answers, sweetheart."

"This feels like a punishment, Buddy," she whispered.

Bud whispered into her ear, "It's all right. I know we want a baby, and I don't know why God doesn't allow it, but we must trust. We have to trust." He wiped her eyes and kissed her.

She smiled and tucked her pain away. There was work to do. Always work to do for the preacher's wife.

Dear Momma, September 7, 1961

Can you send me your spritz cookie recipe? I bake cookies for the school children, but they eat me out of house and home. I remember your recipe makes so many cookies. It will help me if I can stretch the ingredients.

Bud is well—keeping busy as usual. He's quite a sight perched behind the wheel in his old blue pickup, smiling ear to ear like a little boy.

We've seen three new families visit the church. They bring their sweet little ones to my classes.

Would you please tell the ladies thank you for the books and paper? We shared this box with the schoolteacher because she has thirty children in one room and no budget. If the ladies need an idea for the next box, please send pencils and art supplies for her.

We'd love for you and Daddy to visit soon. Bud and I are talking about a short trip back home this fall. He's working on arranging a speaker to cover services while we're gone. There's a fire-and-brimstone circuit-riding preacher he wants to contact. Our people don't love his sermons, but we all need a good shake-up now and then, plus Bud needs a break. He works so hard.

Love to you and Daddy and my sisters,

Ida Bealle Horne

Mom's Cookie Press Spritz Cookies

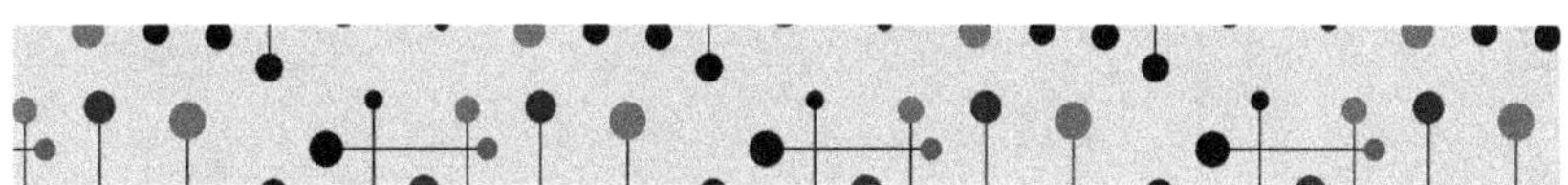

Time—10-12 minutes Temp—400°

1 c. Crisco

3/4 c. sugar

1 egg

1/2 tsp. baking powder

Dash of salt

2 1/4 c. sifted all-purpose flour

1/2 tsp. almond extract

1. Cream shortening; add sugar gradually

2. Add egg, unbeaten—beat well

3. Add sifted dry ingredients, and extract

4. Fill cookie press. Form cookies on ungreased cookie sheets. Bake.

 Yield: about 5 dozen

CHAPTER 24

After Cadence had unpacked, she hurried downstairs and found Fredonia and Miss Ollie working in the kitchen.

"So much to do!" Fredonia sighed.

Miss Ollie pushed tall glasses of iced tea across the table and bustled around the kitchen.

"Freddie, I came in once a week and kept an eye on things. Dusted and swept, fired up the stove when Ladies' Aid met. We used the front room—hope you don't mind."

"Of course not. It's not my house," Fredonia said. "What should we do, Miss Ollie? Start with the easy rooms?"

Miss Ollie nodded.

"Let's leave the outbuilding for last. The bedrooms should take a day."

"Who's moving in?" asked Cadence.

Miss Ollie turned and stared over her glasses. Cadence shivered..

"John Riley, I suppose," Fredonia said. "The church gave me time, but I've intruded on their hospitality far too long."

Miss Ollie stared at Cadence. Cadence stared at her tea and wiped condensation from her glass.

I wish we'd get on with the work. Anything is better than a stare-down by this "Miss Ollie" woman. Phew.

"All right, Cadence. We'll start upstairs. I'd like you to sort linens by type and stack them in the hallway. I'll do my room. You start on the others and check the closet in the hall; pull out all the sheets and towels."

"Got it." Cadence hopped up. "Thanks for the tea, Miss Ollie."

Miss Ollie's voice drifted up the stairs. "I don't know why you brought her. We don't need no strangers poking 'round here, Freddie."

"You hush, now," Fredonia said.

You have the best luck, Cadence. No one wants you here either.

"It shouldn't hurt anymore, but it does," she whispered.

Cadence laughed at the amount of linens she found in the small rooms. She examined the beautiful handmade quilts, and her antique-loving heart fluttered. She ran her hand along the crocheted edges of pillowcases and sheets, wishing for such talent.

She folded the linens and chose the quilt she would ask for if Fredonia let her keep one. She sorted alone and worked on her plans for Taylor.

Wonder where Fredonia is.

Cadence carried a stack of blankets to the hall and bumped into something. She peeked around the stack. Miss Ollie stood in her way. "Sorry, Miss Ollie. Didn't see you there." Cadence forced a cheerful smile.

"It's important to pay attention. Watch where you're going."

Cadence nodded.

"These aren't folded. Get it done before Fredonia sees that you can't follow instructions."

"Oh, I folded them, Miss Ollie . . ."

Miss Ollie turned and kicked a tall pile with her foot. Cadence stared at the woman's back and folded blankets again, double-checking each stack. Cadence wanted to please Fredonia, so she folded each item with crisp corners and piled them in neat piles.

Fredonia called from the bottom of the stairs, "How's it going up there?"

"Close to done. The closets have clothes and boxes. Do you want me to start on those?"

"No, leave it for tomorrow. I'll help in case there's anything important. I've checked out the projects and made a list. I'm afraid we'll be here for at least a week. Do you need to check in with your boss?"

"*You* aren't the boss?" Miss Ollie stepped behind Fredonia and stared at Cadence.

"I hired her to help for a few days, Ollie. She's not my employee." Fredonia smiled. "Come on down. Miss Ollie will have dinner ready soon, and we'll plan tomorrow's work. I don't want to wear you out on your first day."

Miss Ollie harrumphed and muttered her way back to the kitchen.

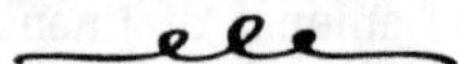

Miss Ollie served a dish called "hot brown" with a side of kilt lettuce. Cadence picked at the greens but forced herself to swallow when Miss Ollie stared.

Oh, what is this? Uggg.

Cadence grabbed her sweet tea and took several sips to clear the bitter green taste out of her mouth. The food settled in her stomach—a heavy lump.

If she keeps staring at me, I can't eat.

Miss Ollie jumped at a knock and hurried to the front door.

"Olivene, what are you doing here?"

Fredonia rolled her eyes and went to the door, and Cadence eavesdropped.

"Judge Crum, nice of you to stop by. What can I do for you?"

"Freddie," the man's voice boomed, "I heard you were back. Come to clean out yer momma's place, I imagine? I'm jest being neighborly. You know, I always stopped by and checked on yer momma, so when I saw that pretty pink car out there, I figured Freddie came back to the fold, so to speak. I says to myself, 'Wilbur Crum, you should stop by and see if Freddie needs any help.' So here I am."

"So nice of you, Judge, but we're finishing supper . . ." Fredonia trailed off as the man barged into the kitchen.

"Hey there, little lady. You come with Freddie?"

Cadence nodded.

"Judge Crum, won't anyone be expecting you tonight?" Fredonia asked.

"Nope. Thanks for the invite to dinner, ladies." He turned and smiled at Miss Ollie. She filled a plate and dropped it in front of him. "You know I love hot brown, Olivene."

"Freddie, I'm here to make you an offer." He shoveled food into his mouth, and it dripped down his chin. Lettuce tumbled down the front of his shirt.

Fredonia and Miss Ollie seemed uncomfortable, but the judge kept talking.

"This yer momma's hot brown recipe, Freddie?"

Freddie nodded.

"Mmmm. Miss Ida Bealle was quite the cook—that's for certain. You're jest as good, Olivene. Jest as good."

Pieces of the man's dinner tumbled down his shirt and across the table. Cadence pushed her plate away—appetite gone.

"Freddie, I stopped by to offer to buy the home place from you. Take it off your hands if you will. I know you don't want to worry about it when you're way up there doing whatever it is you do up north."

Fredonia broke in: "Judge, I don't own this property."

Judge Crum waved his hand, "Small details, Freddie. Small details."

He shoveled food and talked at the same time, and Cadence's stomach lurched. She laughed at his combed-over attempt; his thin hair did little to hide the bald spot. He grabbed Cadence's glass of tea and slurped it in one gulp.

"You're a judge?" Cadence asked. A sharp kick hurt her shin, and she glanced up, bewildered.

The man laughed as crumbs trailed down his cheeks. "Yep, little lady, I'm a judge. Not *a* judge—*the* judge."

"For the whole county. Right, judge?" Miss Ollie asked.

"Yes, ma'am. The whole county." He chuckled.

Cadence wrinkled her nose. He grated on her nerves. His voice. His laughter. His table manners.

I don't like him because he's a judge. I don't need to spend extra time around a judge if I'm plotting someone's demise.

How would this judge handle her case when she solved her Taylor problem?

When *I solve it—not* if.

This judge knew about life—he would side with her. She heard his booming voice in court, "Yes, little lady. Taylor Nash deserved it. You did us all a favor. Case dismissed."

Cadence shook her head and blushed.

"You look mighty happy there, little lady. You should stop over and see the courthouse sometime. I'd be happy to show you around."

"Sorry, Judge—she's busy here. We do need to get back to our work. Thanks for stopping." Fredonia stacked plates and set dirty dishes in the long white sink.

"I smelled chocolate when I came in. Miss Ollie, you bake dessert?"

Fredonia dropped into her chair and sighed.

Miss Ollie passed out giant slices of cake. "Judge Crum, you best be letting these ladies get back to their work."

"I know, I know, Olivene. I'm just trying to welcome Freddie home."

Cadence took a bite of the dark cake. "This is delicious, Miss Ollie."

"Miss Ida Bealle's recipe."

Fredonia stood. "Good evening, Judge. We have work we must finish before bed."

"I'm happy to help you ladies. What can I do? I always loved yer momma. She was good to me."

Fredonia walked behind the judge and nudged him to the front door. "Not a thing. We have it under control."

The judge stood at the door, staring around the room. "Well, good night then. Remember my offer, Freddie. I'll buy the property cash outright."

Fredonia shut the door and marched back to the kitchen.

"That man." Miss Ollie put her hands on her hips. "I declare—he could make the devil mad."

Fredonia chuckled. "You're saying a lot there, Ollie. Cadence, you didn't get a chance to finish your sweet tea before Judge Crum took it. Why don't you get a fresh glass and sit on the porch while Ollie and I clean up? I'll join you after a while."

Cadence made a beeline for the rocking chair and sank into the seat. She rested her back against the smooth wood. The creak of the chair and the groan of the porch boards made her sleepy.

She picked up her phone—three texts from Laura.

—Café busy today. How are u?

—Cadence, u ok

—Let me know when u want to come back to work. Hope u are fine.

Cadence wished she could tell Laura—

—I'm fine. Thanks for understanding. I went on a road trip with the lady I met. Having fun. Considering how to get rid of someone. Wish you were here.

She backspaced to delete before she bumped the send button.

—I'm ok. Will text you. Need at least a week. Hope to be back to work end of next week. Thanks for letting me rest.

Her conscience niggled at her lie but planning Taylor's demise didn't bother her one bit.

Okay. Maybe one bit.

Cadence leaned against the back of the rocker and listened to the rustling leaves in the oak tree. A bright red cardinal swooped past the porch and perched on a low branch. His loud whistle filled the air.

"I wish I could fly off like a bird," she whispered.

Fly off and ignore my problems or stick with my plan and remove the Taylor problem once and for all.

Ending the Taylor problem solved everything. No more blackmail. No new towns. No trying to fit in or hiding her past.

Yes, the Taylor problem needs a final solution.

Cadence smiled.

John Riley Blackburn prepared Sunday's sermon in the church office. He stood to stretch and peered through the windowpane.

Ah. The pink Cadillac. Freddie's back. I should stop tomorrow to check on her. I'll get Miss Ollie to feed me.

He glanced again; a young woman sat on Preacher Bud and Miss Ida Bealle's porch, her head on the back of Miss Ida Bealle's rocking chair, eyes closed. The old, warped church windows blurred his vision, but her smile hit like a lightning bolt. He jerked the window shade down and pushed his notes aside—his sermon focus gone.

Moments earlier he had struggled with Matthew 5, his passage for Sunday. *Blessed are they which do hunger and thirst after righteousness: for they shall be filled.*

Now he struggled keeping his mind off the mystery woman and her smile.

KILLED SALAD

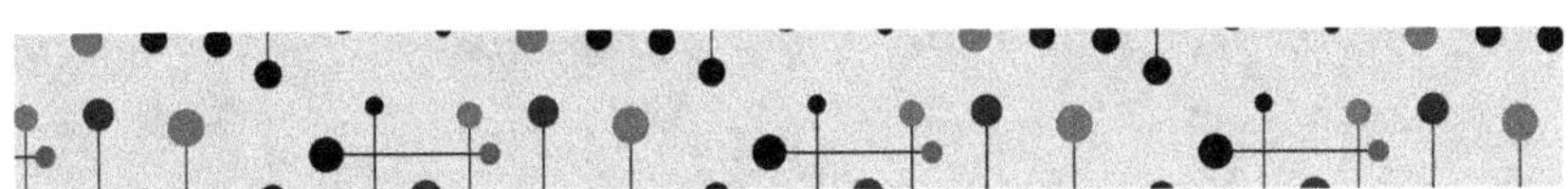

In the morning, pick a bowl of garden lettuce.

Wash it and make sure there are no slugs. Set it out to dry.

Rip lettuce into bite-size pieces and put into a big bowl.

Cook three or four slices of bacon. Cool bacon and crumble on top of the torn lettuce.

Cut the tops of several green onions and add to bowl.

Sprinkle with salt and pepper.

Heat bacon grease left in the skillet and pour it over the greens.

Optional: add 1 tablespoon of apple cider vinegar or lemon juice to the hot pan. Stir around and then pour over greens.

Toss the contents of the bowl to mix well and eat as soon as possible.

Garden lettuce is light and needs very little hot grease to kill (wilt) it.

Kentucky Hot Brown

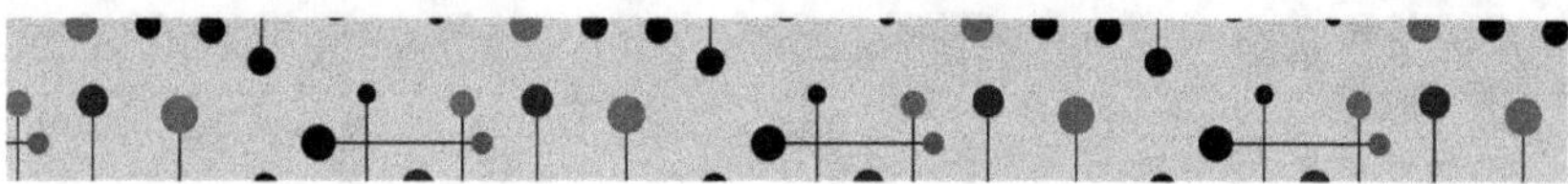

8 slices bread, toasted
leftover turkey
ham slices
1 ½ c. milk
3 tbsp. butter
1 tbsp. flour
pinch of salt and pepper to taste
2 c. Swiss cheese, shredded
1 c. sharp white cheddar, shredded
12 oz. bacon, cooked crisp
tomato slices

Grease a cast-iron skillet or a glass baking pan. Spread toasted bread in pan. Overlap if needed.

Layer with turkey and ham.

Make a white sauce with milk, flour, butter, and a pinch of salt and pepper. Stir over medium heat until thick. Stir in cheese and pour over bread and meat.

Top with crisp bacon slices and diced tomatoes.

Bake at 350 about twenty minutes or until bubbly. Broil for one to two minutes to make the cheese golden.

Serve hot.

CHAPTER 25

Cadence struggled with her Taylor problem while she rocked.
How?

The idea of running Taylor over with Cici seemed perfect—but murder? She imagined an unfortunate fire and insurance money—but no home. Telling the truth to Thatcher stopped the blackmail—but jail. She sighed.

The screen door creaked, and birds sang cheerful songs as the breeze blew through the leaves. Cadence closed her eyes and rocked, enjoying the peaceful surroundings.

"I brought a snack." Fredonia handed her a saucer with a wedge of chocolate cake.

"I hope it's a small piece—I can't manage another bite."

Fredonia shrugged. "Miss Ollie doesn't do small when it comes to cake." She settled onto the porch steps and sighed. "Phillips's mother found it appalling to have a daughter-in-law named Freddie." Fredonia laughed. "Phillip and I found a justice of the peace and married a few counties from home. We enjoyed a wonderful trip to Wisconsin and stopped at each of his accounts. He introduced me as his new wife every time, and I loved his pride in me. I believed nothing could go wrong. But then we pulled up to the Addison mansion." Fredonia sighed.

Deercrest, Wisconsin, 1981

"Phillip? Phillip Addison? Explain yourself, son." Abigail Addison stood with her hands on her hips, the color drained from her face. Phillip jumped out of the car and ran to open Freddie's door.

"Mother, meet my wife, Freddie." He wrapped his arm around Freddie's shoulders, but she shivered at her new mother-in-law's frown. She hadn't asked Phillip how his parents viewed his marriage. She imagined how her own parents viewed it, but they were far away in Kentucky. This woman stood in front of her—yelling.

"Your wife? Oh no, no, no, no, no, no, no." Abigail turned to the house and yelled, "Phillip Senior—come . . . here . . . at . . . once!" her screech escalating on each syllable.

She whirled to Fredonia. "What kind of ridiculous name is 'Freddie'? Are you pregnant? What do you want from us?"

Freddie's mind went blank, and her hands shook.

Phillip pulled Fredonia to his side. "Mother—stop."

"I will not stop, son. What have you done? Where did you find this charity case? Some diner in a little hick town?"

Phillip Sr. stepped behind Abigail, his hands on her shoulders. "Son, what have you done to upset your mother?"

"Father, meet my wife, Freddie." Phillip's smile reached ear to ear. His father stared, his Adam's apple moving up and down.

"Oh, son, you ought not to have done this. Come," he whispered. Phillip Sr. turned to the house. Abigail followed on his heels.

Phillip whispered, "It's okay. Come." He led Fredonia to a room off the marble hallway. "Wait here. I'll come back as soon as I can." The three Addisons stepped into the library and shut the door.

Fredonia waited and tried to slow her heartbeat. She took off her shoes and rubbed her feet in the plush carpet. Norris Creek didn't have carpet like this—houses like this either. Candles in wall sconces flickered, making her sleepy. She tried to remain optimistic, but every few minutes she heard muffled voices. The volume made it clear— someone was unhappy.

"Yes, I'm a hick, Mrs. Addison," she whispered. "I'm a hick, but at least I'm not a pregnant hick—not yet." Fredonia wouldn't speak of pregnancy to her mother-in-law. Whispering about it made her smile—and blush. Her momma would hush her if she heard Fredonia mention delicate matters. She would say, "Freddie Mae, ladies don't speak of this." She was correct. No lady Freddie knew used words like *pregnant* or talked about how it happened—always a big mystery to Freddie. She blushed again, remembering her husband's tender care.

"It's not a mystery anymore, Momma. I can't wait to be a mother. I hope I'll be half as good as you." She blushed.

The heavy library door opened, and she stuffed her feet into her shoes. She crossed her ankles and folded her hands in her lap to sit like a lady—not a hick. Phillip ran to her and rested his head on her lap.

"Freddie, I'm so sorry. I shouldn't have done this." His voice cracked.

"What do you mean, Phillip? You should not have done *what*?" Her heart beat fast while she absorbed the implications of his words.

Oh, God, please don't let him kick me out. I have nowhere to go. I have nothing.

Tears gathered, and her hands shook. "Will you send me away?" She ran her fingers through his thick hair and patted his back. "Phillip, look at me. What are you going to do?"

"Fredonia Mae Addison, I won't send you away. How could you believe that? I need you." He stood and held his hand out. "Come. We have to talk to them."

Fredonia smiled. "We talked—well, Mrs. Addison screamed, and Mr. Addison tried to calm her. Phillip pleaded. A day that lives in infamy." Fredonia chuckled.

"You see, I married the solitary heir to the Addison fortune. Their business structure gave the house and business to the oldest son when he married. The father moved into an advisory role, so our marriage changed Mrs. Addison's whole world. They moved to a smaller home, and Phillip and I moved into the mansion. And so began my war with his mother."

"Wow! You got the house and the money, and his parents were penniless? Why did his father do that?"

"I can't explain, but they weren't destitute. Phillip's grandfather structured the business a certain way, and Mr. Addison inherited it from his father—tradition. They didn't anticipate Phillip falling in love with a hick from Kentucky."

Fredonia smiled and shrugged.

"Did you and Phillip have lots of babies?"

Fredonia stood. "It's late. Enough rambling for one night, right?" She smiled and went inside. Cadence lingered on the steps in the twilight and imagined a wealthy, handsome stranger rescuing her and fixing the Taylor problem.

"No one ever rescued me, but anything's possible," she whispered.

Miss Ida Bealle's Chocolate Cake

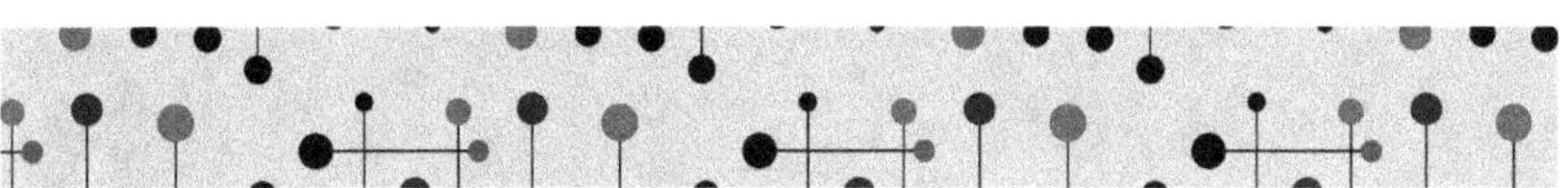

2 c. flour
1 tsp. salt
1 tsp. baking powder
2 tsp. baking soda
¾ c. cocoa
2 c. sugar
1 c. oil
1 c. milk
1 c. hot coffee
2 eggs
1 tsp. vanilla

1. Sift dry ingredients together. Stir in oil, milk, coffee, and stir for three hundred strokes.

2. Add eggs and vanilla and stir for three hundred more strokes. The batter will be thin.

3. Pour into two greased and floured nine-inch cake tins.

4. Bake at 325 for twenty-five to thirty minutes.

5. Cool for fifteen minutes before removing from pans. Cool completely on wire racks.

6. Frost with Poor Man's Milk Frosting.

Poor Man's Milk Frosting

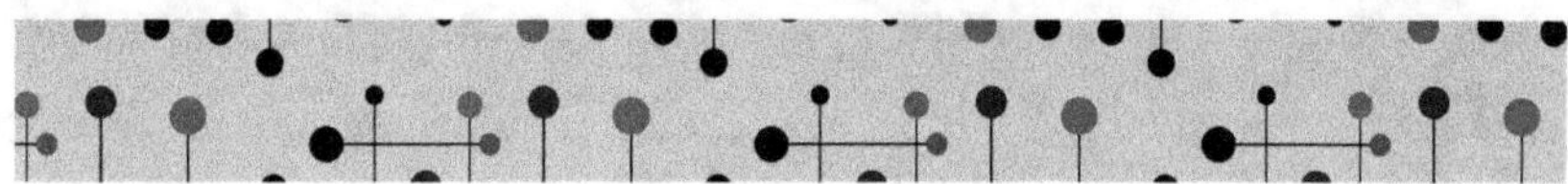

1 c. milk

5 tbsp. flour

½ c. shortening

½ c. butter, softened

1 c. sugar

1 tsp. vanilla

Put milk and flour into a saucepan and cook until thick, stirring so it does not burn. Put into the refrigerator.

In mixing bowl beat shortening, butter, sugar, and vanilla until creamy.

Add chilled milk and flour mixture and beat until thick and creamy, using lots of strokes or using your electric mixer.

Frost cooled cake.

Chapter 26

Norris Creek citizens and visitors are solemnly invited to attend the grand opening of Tansy's Donuts and Laundry on Rockhollow Road. Tansy Spurlock's new bakery sells fresh-baked donuts made from scratch every morning.

"Do your laundry and eat my donuts. I'll have coffee made fresh for you," Tansy says. She also says her shop has space to sit and rest and catch up with your neighbors.

Tansy hopes to have everything ready to open by Friday, June 15. Stop in and help her get her business running. Mention this article for a special discount.

—Norris Creek Gazette

"Who's Tansy Spurlock?" Cadence asked Ollie and set the newspaper onto the table.

"A young thing who's got no sense. That's what. I ain't buying donuts at a place people wash their dirty drawers, and I ain't washin' my drawers at a place selling donuts." She turned back to the old stove to flip pancakes.

The simple kitchen was a step back in time. Cadence loved the old stove—1940s from the style of lettering on the nameplate.

I'd love to have an old stove like this in my kitchen. I'll ask Fredonia if I can have it for my pay. Can she strap it on Cici?

She chuckled and imagined the beast of a stove strapped on the back of the pink Cadillac.

"What are you laughing about?" Miss Ollie leaned over the table. "We sure as the sun rises don't need a Yankee in here laughing at us."

Nice—I don't fit in here either. I've heard myself called every other name in the book, and now I'm a "Yankee."

"Morning, ladies. Ollie, the pancakes smell amazing. Thank you," Fredonia said. "Did I hear you talking about Tansy Spurlock? Lundy's daughter?"

"Yep. She's opening a donut and laundry shop." Miss Ollie's scowled and Cadence stifled a giggle. "Paper says yer solemnly invited. Who solemnly invites people to a grand opening?

"Tansy does—that's who. We should stop and grab a few donuts to support her." Fredonia winked at Cadence.

Miss Ollie scowled and shook her spatula. "I never heard of such foolishness."

"Cadence, I'll have you clean the root cellar today. Sort items by type, and haul broken things to the trash. Pile it behind the house, and I'll sort it. I'm afraid it's dusty, so grab a broom too."

"Which way?"

Fredonia pointed through the back door. "Take a left and open the doors in the ground. Reach above your head for the light."

Cadence stepped into a root cellar lined with shelves of Mason jars, garden pots, and cobwebs—lots of cobwebs.

She sorted jars into types and hauled boxes outside. After several trips up and down the stairs, her legs burned, and her dry throat hurt. She grabbed a framed embroidery she found stuffed behind a shelf. Pretty flowers surrounded words "The Truth Will Set You Free," and tiny stitches in the bottom corner said "Ida Bealle Horne."

I need water. I hope Miss Ollie isn't in the kitchen. I want a drink without her calling me a Yankee.

Cadence reached for the kitchen door handle and glimpsed her reflection in the window. She giggled at her disheveled hair, sweaty face, and a dark streak in the middle of her forehead.

Good thing I'm not trying to impress anyone.

She rummaged through cupboards for a glass. Voices drifted to the kitchen, but Cadence stayed hidden. Sweat dripped from her hair, and dirt stained her hands.

"Cadence? I need you for a moment!" Fredonia called.

Cadence guzzled the water and wiped the drips off her chin.

"Coming!" she called.

John Riley expected Miss Ida Bealle to come out of the kitchen. He missed her and Preacher Bud.

"John Riley, we'll have stuff you can share with your people. Can you grab it soon?" Fredonia asked.

"Absolutely. Tell me when."

When she heard a noise in the kitchen, Fredonia called, "Cadence? I need you for a moment."

A brown-haired woman peeked through the door, her face streaked with dirt.

Ah, the mystery woman.

John Riley held out his hand. "John Riley Blackburn. Pleased to meet you, Miss Cadence."

A rosy blush crept up her cheeks, and she reached to take his hand while she smoothed her hair with the other. She smiled, and John Riley's head swam.

What? Knock it off. You're the preacher.

"Cadence, this is Brother Blackburn. He's the preacher next door. I wanted to introduce you because he'll be around now and then while we empty the parsonage. Didn't want you scared with a strange man in the house." Fredonia winked at John Riley.

John Riley didn't know Miss Freddie well. Her rare visits to Norris Creek left him with a favorable impression. But he wished she had spent more time with her parents when they were alive.

"Miss Freddie, Preacher Bud, and Miss Ida Bealle were so good to me. Your daddy took care of me like a father when my daddy left. I'm a preacher because I loved him so much—wanted to be just like him. I'm happy to do whatever you and these ladies need. All you have to do is ask. Good day, Miss Freddie, Miss Cadence."

He wanted to skip across the lawn to church.

God, help me focus on you and not that brown-eyed beauty next door.

John Riley knew his sermon outline wouldn't get finished today.

Cadence's arms and neck ached from reaching above her head to sweep rafters. She emptied and cleaned the root cellar all afternoon.

At least it's cool down here. I wish I looked decent when Fredonia called me to meet the preacher.

The last time she talked to a preacher, the bottom dropped out of her world.

Grandmother Miggs's outdated house had become Audra's home. Grandmother loved her, but she was severe and strict. The kitchen smelled of cloves and cinnamon and gingerbread—Grandmother's favorite. The spicy cake wasn't Audra's favorite, but she enjoyed time with Grandmother. While they ate gingerbread, Grandmother asked about school and her friends.

If Audra was lucky, Grandmother told stories about her mother. She didn't remember much, but she remembered when Mom dropped her off. Grandmother hobbled outside and screamed, "You can't do this!" Her mother got into a car and sped away.

Why did Grandmother say I can't stay? Grandmother always lets me stay.

She dreamed her mother came back, but she never did. Audra was happy and safe with Grandmother, but Grandmother didn't want her.

They lived alone in the little white house. Audra worked hard in school and stayed out of trouble. Grandmother often rested, and many days when Audra got home from school, the neighbor lady waited.

"Your Grandmother's at an appointment and will come home tomorrow. You're to come with me for the night."

One afternoon Audra opened the door to a living room full of neighbors. She stood still.

What are they doing? Why are they sad?

Grandmother never invited visitors to their small house.

"Audra." The neighbor lady grabbed her and smashed Audra's face into her rough wool skirt. The lady squeezed her—hard. Audra heard murmurs and tried to keep the lady's skirt from poking her cheek. She didn't understand the words.

When the neighbor lady let go, Audra glanced around. "Where's Grandmother Miggs?"

The man from Grandmother's chapel bent down. Audra focused on the white square on his black collar and ignored his words.

"Your Grandmother went to the hospital today, and God took her home."

She frowned, "Well, if God brought her home, where is she?"

The neighbor lady squeezed her. "Heaven. Your grandmother is in heaven."

Audra turned and marched through the house, "Grandmother! Grandmother!" She peeked into the basement, the closets, and even the little cubby under the stairs. She ran up to the bedrooms and back to the living room.

"Where is she?" she yelled.

The neighbor lady repeated, "Your Grandmother Miggs went to heaven." The man cried. Audra March decided right then that if God took grandmothers from little girls, she didn't need him.

Cadence wiped her sweaty forehead with dirty hands and shook her head to clear the dark memory. She wasn't Audra anymore; she was Cadence, and chores waited. She grabbed bags of trash and lined the back of the house with boxes. She muttered to herself while wiping shelves. Meeting John Riley and remembering the chapel preacher left her unsettled and exhausted.

"God, you have never done a thing for me, not a rotten thing. If you think some handsome preacher in the middle of nowhere Kentucky will change my mind, you're wrong."

She wiped the shelf and gritted her teeth, "You ruined my life, and you need to fix it. If you help me get rid of Taylor, I'll try to believe you're worth something. Otherwise, you can back off." Something clattered at the top of the stairs, and she pressed her lips together.

"Who are you talking to down there?" Ollie peered into the cellar.

"Myself, Miss Ollie!" Cadence called. "You scared me!"

"Quit yer mutterin' and get cleaned up! Dinner soon!" Miss Ollie disappeared, and Cadence wiped the last shelf and checked the cellar. A shaft of light crossed a crevice near the ceiling—something glittered.

I should climb up and take a peek—but Miss Ollie. I'm afraid of her.

She hurried up the stairs and dropped the cellar doors closed. The smell of dinner drifted from the kitchen, and her stomach growled.

"Time to eat!" Ollie called.

CHAPTER 27

Christmas Eve, Turkey Creek Baptist Church, 1962

"When is cookie time?" A Preece boy tugged at Ida Bealle's skirt as she hurried around the church kitchen to find napkins and cups. "Soon. Now go back to your teacher." She shooed the little boy out of the kitchen and peeked out at the commotion. Children huddled in the corner, reciting their lines together, and Lolly Preece lined up shepherds. Another teacher straightened turbans.

Lolly rolled her eyes at Ida Bealle over the head of one of the Crum boys.

Ida Bealle flipped on the industrial-sized coffee brewer and added water. She listened to children running around the basement, costumes flapping behind them, squeals of excitement interrupted by Sunday School teachers calling, "Quiet!"

Christmas pageants stretched her patience, but she loved the familiar Bible passages and sweet children. The carols filled the decorated church, and gifts for all the children waited under a tree. She loved Bud's whisper in her ear when it ended, "Good job, Mrs. Horne." She might complain or roll her eyes and sigh with Lolly, but the Christmas pageant was the highlight of her year.

Organizing the pageant didn't bring her to tears these days. In past years the ache for a child hurt too much. She would come home after practice, crawl in bed, and cry a few—or a lot of— tears. Then she dried her eyes and went back to her busy life. Her wish for a child never lessened, but the reality of the situation settled in her heart. She and Bud loved the children in their community even though their own arms remained empty. Her pain was not as sharp now, but when she saw a mother caress her child or a baby melt into a mother's arms, the ache returned.

The notes of "Silent Night" drifted to the basement, and she heard Bud's deep baritone voice leading the congregation.

"Children, line up!" She smiled as children ran to line up behind her.

The noisy congregation milled around the basement munching on cookies. Bud drifted in and out of groups. He patted someone on the back, held a baby for a moment, spoke with several men. Children ran to him and pulled on his suit coat. He leaned down and smiled at a little boy; the smile on Bud's face made Ida Bealle's heart squeeze. He tousled the boy's hair and threw back his head to laugh when the boy whispered in Bud's ear.

She joined him, and he slipped his arm around her shoulders. "Good job, Mrs. Horne," he whispered. She smiled and followed him to the Christmas tree. The Ladies' Missionary Society had wrapped donated gifts and left them in a pile for the children.

Every child went home with a present. The news of Christmas gifts spread far and wide, and every year more children came. Most gifts were practical—mittens or hats. Many of the children who went to the program left without leaving a name. They stood in line, waited for their gifts, and disappeared into the shadows.

Bud and Ida Bealle talked to each child for a moment, then said a prayer, and sent the child off with a hug.

The gift pile dwindled, and a young girl stepped out from a dark corner. She held her hand out, and Ida Bealle reached behind the tree for a package labeled "older girl." The girl's dark eyes sparkled when she grabbed her box from Ida Bealle's hand. She hurried back to the corner. Her brown hair hung in a tight braid down her back, her dress faded and ill-fitting, her thin arms longer than the sleeves. The girl turned to the side, and Ida Bealle frowned.

The girl's thin body was obviously malnourished except for an unmistakably round abdomen. The girl slipped out the door. Ida Bealle shook her head. Surely she wasn't . . .

CHAPTER 28

Cadence sat at the table sipping coffee. Her arms ached from lifting heavy bins and boxes.

I won't survive if I have to lift this much tomorrow.

Fredonia sat next to Cadence with a glass of water. "Find any crazy cat ladies in the cellar today?"

Cadence giggled, "Thankfully, I did not."

Miss Ollie's frowned. "Prayer meetin' at seven. Eat quick and get cleaned up." She set dinner on the table and hung her apron on the wall. "I best be gettin' home myself, or I'll be late."

"Thank you, Ollie," Fredonia said. "You hurry on home. I'll see you later."

Fredonia glanced at Cadence, "Will you go tonight?"

"Where?"

"Prayer meeting."

"I guess I'll stay here if you don't mind."

I don't even know what "prayer meeting" is since I don't pray these days. Doubt I should admit that.

"Feel free to take it easy then, Cadence. I appreciate how hard you're working."

"Miss Ollie doesn't like me," Cadence blurted.

"Ollie was my mother's dear friend for many years. She's a good woman, Cadence, but she doesn't care for change, and she's protective of my parents' memory. Ollie watches out for me, the church, and the town. I hate to say it because I believe you're a good person, but Ollie doesn't look at you as one of her people. She'll keep her eyes on you." Fredonia shrugged. "I apologize if it bothers you. Don't let her upset you. Try to remember it comes from a helping place."

Being stared at and growled at is super-helpful.

"She called me a Yankee."

Fredonia laughed. She sat down her fork and wiped her eyes. "Oh . . . oh . . . that's funny. You—Yankee."

"I don't see why it's funny."

"'Yankee' is the ultimate insult around here, but Ollie forgets I'm a Yankee now. I'll ask her to go easy on you, okay?"

Cadence nodded. "I don't want her to think I tattled."

"Don't worry. I'm glad you're here." She cleared her plate and wiped the table. "I better scoot or I'll be late, and Miss Ollie will give me the side-eye."

Cadence sat at the table for several minutes and imagined living here. Church seemed to be a big part of their lives, but church and God made her uncomfortable.

I'll pretend to like church. I can fake.

She enjoyed the quiet pace in this small town and wanted to stay. She was jealous of Miss Ollie and "her people."

I wish I were someone's people.

Years of shuffling through foster homes had taught her how to keep the peace, keep opinions to herself, and be a chameleon. Audra became whatever the family wanted. She complied and went with the flow. Years of hiding from Taylor Nash had taught her to adapt. She pretended she didn't dream.

I can do this—march into that prayer meeting and pretend I know what's going on. Pretend I talk to God like they do.

She pushed back from the table. "I don't need anyone."

"What's that, Cadence?" Fredonia called down from the landing.

Cadence blushed. "Sorry, Fredonia. Thinking out loud."

Cadence wandered through the empty house, examining the pictures on the wall. Ida Bealle's face was proud in every photo. The love between Fredonia and her parents jolted Cadence, and she stepped away with a pang.

She read a verse with embroidered flowers and delicate stitches: *The Lord is gracious and full of compassion.* She turned away, her jaw clenched.

You've never been good to me. Where's all this compassion for little girls left without family?

She didn't believe the Lord was full of compassion. She couldn't. Her life proved he wasn't.

The comfortable living room made Cadence homesick, and she sat on the stiff sofa to rest. This room seemed opposite the plush living room in Fredonia's mansion, and she tried to imagine Fredonia growing up in this tiny house. Did Fredonia and Phillip Addison experience happiness? She needed to believe that some people got their fairy tales.

The fairy tale I want is getting Taylor out of my life.

She stepped onto the front porch and settled into the rocker. She rocked by pushing her toes on the porch and smiled at the creaky chair. A cardinal swooped by and dropped into the low branch across from the porch. Cadence smiled at the bird and his bright red feathers. The crest on his head stood straight up, but one feather flopped onto his forehead. She giggled at the feather bouncing as he whistled to the other birds.

Singing drifted through the open windows of the little white church. An instrument she had never heard added a gentle rhythm.

> *'Tis so sweet to trust in Jesus,*
> *Just to take Him at His word,*
> *Just to rest upon His promise,*
> *Just to know, "Thus saith the Lord."*
> *Jesus, Jesus, how I trust Him!*
> *How I've proved Him o'er and o'er!*
> *Jesus, Jesus, precious Jesus!*
> *O for grace to trust Him more!*

A sudden weariness overtook Cadence, and she closed her eyes.

I'm tired of running and hiding, and I'm tired of Taylor ruining my life, but I don't know what to do.

Her plans for Taylor energized her, but how would she accomplish it?

She glanced at the Cadillac, imagining a horrible accident. The image of Taylor under Cici's whitewall tires made her sick.

I can't keep running. Something has to change.

Cadence contemplated her choices: murder, move to another country, find a new name, start over in a new town.

See? No good choice.

In a few days, Taylor expected the money, and Cadence was broke. She hoped Fredonia's job lasted beyond Tuesday, but Taylor knew where she lived. She would force Cadence to pay somehow. Taylor always won.

What if I told Thatcher everything? I could ask for advice.

Cadence shook her head at the stupid idea. He would arrest her for admitting her part in the robbery or for plotting murder.

She sighed and walked to the end of the porch. Hopeless. Cadence knew this trip to Norris Creek prolonged the inevitable. When Taylor showed up to an empty house, she would rage. Her first mistake in a lifetime of errors—believing Taylor was her friend.

Why was I so stupid? Why would a rich girl want to be the friend of a sad, lonely kid? Now I'm an unhappy, lonely adult, and she's still using me. When do I get what I want?

While Cadence stewed over her miserable existence, the church doors opened. She backed into the corner, hoping the people on the lawn didn't see her.

They chattered and laughed, and the children played hide and seek. Ladies surrounded Miss Ollie, laughing at something she had said. A beautiful smile spread across Ollie's face, and she completely changed.

She can smile.

Men congregated under a tree—deep voices filled the air. Light shone through church windows and cast a halo over the crowded lawn. Laughter rang out, and children giggled, calling to each other in their game. Men slapped each other on the back, and the women laughed.

They all belonged—even Fredonia. Cadence found her in the middle of a circle. The women hugged her and smiled.

Cadence stood in the shadows. Tears pooled in her eyes and spilled down her cheeks. She ran inside, letting the screen door slam.

Cadence hurried to bed, hoping to fake sleep before Fredonia returned. She wasn't in the mood to chat—no way to explain her tears.

They had emptied her room this afternoon; only the bed remained and the discolored spots on the walls where pictures had hung. Cadence crawled into bed, pulling the coverlet over her. The open window overlooked a tree, and voices and laughter from the churchyard drifted into the room—too much tonight. She hopped out of bed and stared at the people gathered below.

A dark-haired man moved from group to group: the pastor. He talked to people and laughed, then chased a group of children playing tag. The children shrieked when he tagged one. The pastor ruffled the heads of a few boys and spoke to children jumping up and down for attention. She narrowed her eyes and folded her arms across her chest. The easy interactions reminded her that she didn't belong.

Go home. Don't you people have better things to do?

Something crinkled under her foot, and she tried to lift the end of the iron bed frame to grab it.

"Oooff! It's heavy," she grunted. She climbed back into bed and sunk her head onto the pillow. The soft bed and crisp sheets lifted her spirits until she turned the paper over: "5 Ways the Truth Sets You Free." She snorted and flung it across the room.

Are you even kidding me right now? My truth is that I don't belong anywhere. No one loves me, and I'm a criminal. So there you have it.

She rolled over and stared at the wall, her mind racing, keeping her awake.

Cadence woke long before the sun rose and stared at the ceiling, unable to forget the title of the paper she found last night.

Telling the truth isn't my goal—no more Taylor is the goal. I don't need to tell the truth. God needs to tell the truth. Why did he take my grandmother and leave me alone?

She rolled over and punched the pillow, trying to get comfortable. Her grievances kept her awake—God, Taylor, and the foster care system. Now Miss Ollie and her unfair treatment went on the list. She flopped over.

I have to figure this out. I can't go home without the money, and I can't stay here, where I stick out like a sore thumb. I can't tell Laura. I can't talk to Thatcher—ha. Big no. Thatcher does not need to know what I've done. I can't tell Fredonia, or she'll make me find my own way back to Wisconsin. Miss Ollie will call that "Judge" and have him over here in a flash to arrest me. What if I stay here and work at Tansy's donut and laundry?

She laughed at Miss Ollie's proclamation: *"I ain't buying donuts at a place where people wash their drawers."*

Cadence tiptoed downstairs to prepare for another day of work. One of the steps creaked—the sound loud in the quiet house. She stood still for a moment, frowning at the offending step, but no one stirred.

She had dressed in her favorite blue shirt and comfy jeans and had wrapped her hair in a red gingham scarf. She was ready to tackle the day.

"You're Rosie the Riveter," Fredonia said.

"Oh, Fredonia! You scared me—I didn't hear you."

"It's a wonder with that creaky step. I better get it fixed."

"It's softer than the others. Hope I didn't wake you when I came down."

"No. I tossed and turned. You sleep well?"

"Like a baby. Where's the coffee?"

Fredonia pointed to the vintage percolator on the stove. "Mmm . . . it's good stuff."

Cadence filled a large mug with steaming coffee and wrapped her fingers around the warm cup.

"You should sell it at your fancy coffee shop in Deercrest." Fredonia laughed.

Cadence giggled. "Good idea. It would sell. Tell me the rest of your story, Fredonia. Did you get a happy ending?"

Fredonia stared into her mug; tears pooled in her eyes.

"There's not much more to say, and it's not my favorite part of the story."

CHAPTER 29

C adence waited, hoping Fredonia's story wrapped up in a happy ending.

Fredonia cleared her throat and took another long sip of coffee. "Phillip and I enjoyed four beautiful years of marriage. We enjoyed each other, and our new life was a dream, perfect—other than his mother. She never got over her hick daughter-in-law, Freddie. She hates me to this day, by the way."

Fredonia grinned. "We set up housekeeping, but in a mansion the size of the Addisons', there wasn't much for me to do. The staff did the work, so we spent our time getting to know each other and creating traditions. I decorated our main rooms more to my liking—much to the horror of Phillip's mother. Phillip supported me and tried to keep her from making me miserable. She tried to ruin my life. Oh, how she tried! She showed up unannounced when Phillip was away on sales trips. She walked through the house, berating changes I'd made. I never wondered where I stood with Mother Addison. She hated me, and everyone knew it."

Fredonia sipped her coffee, a smile pulling at the corners of her mouth.

"I don't know why I laugh. I'm used to it after forty years. She still shows up unannounced."

"She's alive?" Cadence asked.

"Yes. Alive and well and hating her child's widow."

Widow? No. Cadence swallowed hard over the lump in her throat.

"Phillip and I traveled together on occasion. I enjoyed the extra time with him and loved seeing him in action. He was an excellent representative for his father's business and a good salesman. We stopped to see Mother and Daddy a couple of times, and they tried to accept him. Phillip asked me to go on the trip that last time, but I wanted to attend a ladies' tea at the country club. If I went, his mother might see that I tried to conform to her ideal. I kissed Phillip goodbye and promised I'd go next time."

She held her coffee cup; emotions flooded her face. "There was an accident. We don't know what happened, but Phillip died on impact." Her voice cracked, and her lips trembled. A tear rolled down her cheek.

Cadence sat stunned. *So much for happy endings. See, God, why I don't believe anymore? You took Grandmother from me. You took Phillip from Fredonia. Who are you good to? Not anyone I know.*

Fredonia cleared her throat and sighed. "He died thirty-six years ago, but sometimes the emotions ambush me." She refilled her coffee, holding the percolator above the stove. "Refill?"

Cadence nodded and held out her mug. "I'm sorry, Fredonia."

"Well, 'sorry' doesn't change anything. Phillip was a good man, and we lived a happy life. I have no regrets."

"You stayed up north?"

"Ah . . . well, it's one reason my mother-in-law hates me. If I left, the house and business income revert to the Addisons. In the beginning I was too grief stricken to decide, and I refused to leave the home where Phillip and I created our memories. I felt his presence there. I also didn't want to face my parents because I had hurt them when I ran off. I don't regret marrying Phillip, not even *how* I married him, but I was still young—twenty-two when Phillip died." Fredonia shrugged.

"So I stayed in Deercrest and held on to my rightful position as the widow of Phillip Addison. Phillip's father was kind to me and tried to keep Mother Addison from causing trouble. But she was—*is*—a sneaky one. I imagine she's at the house right now redoing a room or bossing my staff around."

Fredonia smiled at Cadence and stirred her coffee long after the cream had mixed in.

"I came back for visits because I do love Norris Creek. But I was too stubborn to let Mrs. Addison win, and in time Deercrest became home. I'm busy there and have friends."

"Did your parents ever visit you in Deercrest?"

"Once. They were amazed. Daddy said, 'Freddie, I got lost in here last night!' Momma worried about how I kept such a large home clean. She loved cooking in my kitchen and made her famous recipes. She fed them to my staff, who adored my parents, by the way. But the trip was too much for them. Daddy refused to get onto an airplane, and Momma refused to come without him. I made my way back to Kentucky now and then, and we made peace. They accepted it." She shrugged.

"Why did you wait so long to clean out their house?"

Fredonia stared into her mug for several seconds. "It's hard to admit they're gone. So I delayed, knowing that the church was patient. But a couple of weeks ago I got a letter from the deacons asking me to consider removing my parent's items. The church needs the space, and it's time. It's been time for a long while, but I pretended I hadn't lost everyone important in my life."

Cadence nodded; she understood loss. She sipped her coffee and let Fredonia reminisce.

Fredonia tapped the table and stood up. "John Riley's coming over today to help me haul stuff out of here. Did you find anything to keep?"

"I love the red-and-white quilt and the pretty pillowcases."

"Perfect. Set those in your room. We better get busy. I want to empty the closet under the stairs today. We're making good progress, and I hope to wrap up by Monday or Tuesday and get home."

Take as long as you like, Fredonia. I'm in no hurry. No hurry at all.

Emptying the closet under the stairs took hours. Cadence pulled out boxes and carried each one to the living room, where Fredonia sorted.

"Fredonia, this closet is huge; it goes on for miles." Cadence wiped her brow and retied her headscarf.

"It was my favorite when I was little. I'd crawl in there with my blankets and dolls and have tea parties. One time I fell asleep and worried mom sick. When I woke up and crawled out, she was at the table crying. She grabbed me and hollered, 'Where did you come from?' I showed her, and she never let me shut the closet door again." Fredonia chuckled.

Cadence returned to hauling boxes and wished for memories of her own mother. Sweat and dust mixed on her forehead and cheeks. She wiped her face with a grimy hand and left trails of dirt behind.

Pictures, papers, and craft supplies spilled out of the boxes in the living room. Fredonia lifted an unfinished knitting project. "Mom always worked on a project or twelve. 'Idle hands are the devil's workshop,' she said. Her hands always moved—that's for certain."

"I tried to teach myself to knit," Cadence said, eyeing the delicate work in progress. "I'm not doing well."

"Ollie knits. I'll ask her to teach you." Fredonia winked.

"What?" Miss Ollie stepped into the room, wiping her hands on an apron. "What did you say about me?"

"I said you knit. Cadence is trying to learn and needs a teacher."

Ollie harrumphed. "I'm busy, Freddie. Don't you go thinkin' I'm sitting around waiting for chores to do." She marched back to the kitchen, muttering.

Fredonia shrugged and rolled her eyes. "I'll set aside mom's needles for you to take home. We'll find someone in Deercrest to teach you."

"Sounds perfect," Cadence said. She hurried into the closet to grab another box. "Fredonia, can you grab this box for me?"

She turned and bumped into the minister. "Ope, sorry."

"Not a problem, Miss Cadence. Let me grab it. Miss Freddie wants to speak with you."

Cadence wiped her hands on her pant leg and crouched to get through the closet door.

John Riley set the box onto a pile. "Miss Freddie, you have your work cut out for you today. Who knew Miss Ida Bealle kept so much stuff?"

"They lived here a very long time, and Momma was a bit of a saver. What's your plan today, John Riley?"

"Well, the first thing I need to know is what is *ope*?"

Fredonia laughed. "Oh, my dear boy, this is what we call a 'Wisconsin word.' It's a cross between *oops* and *sorry*."

His eyes twinkled. "Gotcha, Miss Freddie. You don't say those words, do ya?"

She shook her head, "No, sir, and I don't say *bubbler* either."

"What's wrong with *bubbler*?" Cadence asked.

"Another Wisconsin word, my dear. No one else says it." She turned to John Riley. "Drinking fountain."

He rubbed his chin and shrugged. *"Bubbler,* huh? Never heard it, but I like it."

"Where will you take all this?" Freddie asked.

"I have a few mountain families in mind. Some families in Little Ivy can use the help."

"Perfect. I haven't heard about Little Ivy in years. Has it changed much?"

He sighed. "It's a rough area, and I don't go out there at night. But some of the people are trying hard. I want to help. They need to know of Jesus's love same as us."

Fredonia smiled. "You're a good man, John Riley. You remind me of Daddy. Cadence, you go along today. You'll get to see our beautiful scenery. John Riley, come home the back way—show her the valley."

John Riley's dilapidated blue pickup sat under the tree near the pink Cadillac. The scraped paint and missing fender gave it a mournful appearance. He closed the tailgate and patted the side of the truck. "Come on, Old Blue. We have work to do."

Cadence laughed.

"What? Old Blue needs a bit of encouragement when we head up the mountain. She's an old girl, but I love her." He grinned and ran around to help Cadence climb into the cab.

When the truck turned onto Main Street, Cadence scanned the buildings, hoping to find an antique store.

"Looking for something?" John Riley asked.

"An antique store and the donut and laundry store."

John Riley threw his head back and roared. "Tansy's place? Oh, man! I bet Miss Ollie made comments. Donuts and laundry." He shook his head. "It's on Rockhollow Road back a block or two. I can show you on the way home, but if you buy donuts, you better eat them before Miss Ollie catches you." He laughed again.

Cadence noticed children waving at the truck, adults too. "You're popular."

"Not always popular. Sometimes everyone's angry with me but today's a good day." He waved at a boy running alongside the truck, and the little boy's face lit up.

"Why?"

"Well, for starters, I'm the new preacher. Miss Freddie's daddy held the job for fifty years, and they still see me as the Blackburn kid from Little Ivy. Unpopular decisions, or a sermon hits too close to home. People don't like it when I preach on their sin."

"Why?"

"Why what? Why don't they like when I preach on their issues?" He smiled. "Hasn't a preacher ever stepped on your toes in a sermon?"

"Church isn't my thing." She stared out the window.

"It's okay, Miss Cadence. God loves you."

Her stomach churned. *Why all the God stuff? God doesn't love me, Mr. Preacher. You want him to exist, but he doesn't. If he were real, he'd get me out of this mess and bring my grandmother back.*

"What's your story, Cadence?" John Riley broke the silence.

"My story?"

What does he know? She took a deep breath—her heartbeat raced and she wiped clammy hands onto her jeans. *How did he figure me out? What did I say?*

"You know—your story. What do you do up there in Wesconsin?"

"Wis . . . *Wisconsin*." She smiled, and he grinned.

"Yes, my accent. Apologies to you, Miss Cadence. *WISconsin*."

"I'm a barista at a coffee shop, and I help the owner with the baking."

"Aha. Explains why you want to check out Tansy's Donuts and Laundry." His warm laughter filled the cab. "What else do you do up there? Any family?"

"My life is rather dull. I work, and I shop at antique stores on the weekend." She shrugged, sidestepping the question about her family.

"Well, boring is good sometimes, right?"

"What about *you*? What do *you* do?"

"Me? I'm the preacher around here."

"But you only work Sundays and the hour meeting the other night? What else do you do?"

He shook his head and laughed. "Oh, Miss Cadence, if I only worked on Sunday and Wednesday night, I'd be a fat, lazy man."

They turned onto a small winding road. It narrowed, and trees brushed the sides of the truck. They bumped along until John Riley pulled to a stop behind a rusty truck held together by zip ties and duct tape. A big hairy dog ran around the truck, barking. Cadence pushed the lock on her door, her eyes wide.

"Oh, don't you worry about Calhoun. He's a good dog. It's his owner we have to worry about." He winked at Cadence and nodded to the porch.

A barefoot woman stood on the porch, a shotgun leveled at the windshield.

CHAPTER 30

*N*orris *Creek, Kentucky, Christmas 1962*

Ida Bealle leveled an angry gaze at her husband. "Bud, I saw it with my own eyes. She's a little girl, and that was a baby." Ida Bealle slammed mugs on the table, spilling coffee. "Why? Why, Bud? We don't get a baby, but young girls from Little Ivy do?" Her voice shook, and she pressed her lips together. She sighed and plopped into a chair.

Bud held his mug in his hands.

"Well?"

"Ida Bealle, you don't understand."

"Understand what, Bud? God blesses teenagers, but he won't bless *me*? He blesses *sin*, but he won't bless *me*?" The tears she held back spilled down her cheeks. She pushed her chair back, tipping it over, and pointed to her husband. "It's not right, and you know it."

"Someone did it to her, Ida Bealle."

Her cheeks blushed. She covered her face with her hands, willing herself calm. Her voice trembled. "Bud, you mean to tell me . . ."

"Yes. So many hard situations, Ida Bealle. I try to shield you, but—"

"Who?"

He shrugged. "A dad? An uncle? A brother? A neighbor?"

"Bud. Fix it."

"I can't, Ida Bealle. I've tried."

"Call the police. Call someone."

He pulled her into his arms, and she rested on his shoulder, but she wanted to pound someone.

"I've tried. Don't you know I've tried? No one listens."

His arms tightened around her, and his voice caught. She knew he held back tears.

"If she won't say who, Ida Bealle, there's nothing to do, but if she does say who, she has nowhere to go."

"It's hopeless." His wool suit coat scratched her cheek. She nestled in closer. The ugly truth made her hurt, but the loathsome truth of her judgmental heart hurt more.

"It's never hopeless, darling. But God . . ." He lifted her chin and kissed the tip of her nose.

Bud whispered their favorite Bible passage, and Ida Bealle joined him, her voice shaky. "But God, who is rich in mercy, for his great love wherewith he loved us . . . that . . . he might shew the exceeding riches of his grace in his kindness toward us through Christ Jesus."

"Always remember—'but God,'" Bud said.

Ida Bealle nodded, "How do you do it, Bud? How do you see all this and stay sane?"

He smiled his heart-melting, lopsided grin and shrugged. "I serve an amazing God, and I happen to have the most beautiful wife in the world." He pulled her close and rested his chin on top of her head.

She laughed, unable to resist a tease. "Indeed you do, Bud Horne."

CHAPTER 31

Cadence's eyes widened. "What are we going to do?" She blew out short breaths.

"Run? Scream?"

"Which one?" she asked.

"Nah, we're okay. I was teasin' ya." He rolled the window down and leaned out. "Missus Preece, it's me! John Riley!"

The woman on the porch stared a moment, then leaned the shotgun against the house. She hurried down the steps, hollering at the dog.

"Calhoun, you come back here now! Don't you be slobbering on Brother Blackburn!" She reached for the dog's collar. "Sorry, Preacher. Weren't expectin' ya today."

John Riley hopped out of the truck. "I know. I'm early. But I have some stuff back here you can use."

Mrs. Preece nodded to Cadence when she got out of the truck. "This yer girl, Brother Blackburn?"

Cadence blushed.

John Riley smiled and winked. "Nah, Missus Preece—this is Cadence. She came down from Wesconsin to help Miss Freddie clean out Preacher Bud and Miss Ida Bealle's place."

Mrs. Preece eyed Cadence and smiled. "I ain't never met no Yankee, but you look nice."

John Riley threw back his head and laughed. "Now, Missus Preece, you be sweet to Miss Freddie's friend."

Mrs. Preece nodded. "I guess she cain't help where she's from now, can she, Brother Blackburn?"

Cadence waved at three little girls in the doorway. A chubby toddler with a mop of curly ringlets waved. Cadence smiled and waved back. The other two stepped inside the house, but the chubby baby took her thumb out of her mouth and smiled.

Mrs. Preece turned and held out her hand to the little one. "This here's my Lolly. She likes meetin' people jest like her Great-Grandma Lolly. The other two are shy." Lolly ran to her mother and pulled on her skirt. Mrs. Preece leaned over and scooped her up, settling the little girl onto a hip. "You say hi to Preacher, Lolly."

The chubby baby laid her head on her mother's shoulder and hid her eyes. John Riley reached out and tousled her hair.

"Good afternoon, Miss Lolly." The toddler smiled around the thumb in her mouth and snuggled close to her mom.

John Riley turned to the back of the truck. "Missus Preece, Freddie said you should take whatever you can use. We're going on up the mountain 'til everything's gone, but you're our first stop." He opened the tailgate and pulled boxes close to the edge.

She flipped through the boxes and made a small pile. The lady's eyes brightened when she found the books. She selected a few and stepped away from the pickup.

"That'll be good, Preacher. Thank you for thinkin' of us. Come on in and have a bite before you leave."

"We have a few more stops. We better get on." John Riley said.

"I cain't have the preacher go on past my place without offering a bit of something. Come on in for tea. Orv won't forgive me if I let you leave hungry. Come on now," she said and hurried up the path to the cabin.

John Riley shrugged his shoulders and motioned for Cadence to follow.

The kitchen used most of the space in the tiny home, and a blanket hung between the rooms to add privacy. Cadence wondered how they crammed everyone into this space.

John Riley patted the bench beside him, and one of the little girls crawled up next to him. "What did you do today, Miss Grace?" he asked.

"We chased the kitties and got dirty, and Momma made us come inside and take a bath," she said, frowning.

"Good thing I did, little girl. You three were a muddy mess. What if Preacher saw you all dirty? Pffft!" She sighed, but a smile tugged at the corner of her lips.

Mrs. Preece set a pitcher of iced tea onto the table. She added a plate of cookies, a bowl of apples, and slices of banana bread.

John Riley poured tea and set food onto the plate in front of Cadence. Her eyes bugged out, but John Riley put his finger on his lips and shook his head.

"Will you join us, Missus Preece?"

"No, sir. You eat up. I gotta get the beans cooking." She smiled at John Riley and admonished the girls, "Don't get crumbs on Preacher's nice shirt."

"They're okay. What're a few crumbs between friends?" He turned to the little girls, and in a playful, loud voice, said, "I'll tell you what bothers me. Laughing and fun. No laughing and no fun when I'm here." He bugged his eyes at the girls, and they shrieked.

His eyes lit up when the little girls laughed.

What's your story, John Riley?

He drained his tea and popped the banana bread into his mouth. "Lots of stops ahead. We better scoot."

The girls waved at Cadence and yelled, "Bye, Preacher!"

"See you Sunday?"

"I hope so, Preacher. We'll see what Orv is up to. I'll try to talk him into it. He took my dulcimer to town to get it fixed. If it works out, I'll come play it for prayer meetin'."

John Riley nodded. "I'd love to have you play your dulcimer for prayer meeting. You know you're always welcome. If you need a ride, call me. Thank you for the tea—delicious."

Mrs. Preece pushed a wrapped loaf of bread into John Riley's hands.

"Can we pray before we leave?" John Riley asked.

The lady nodded and gathered the girls around her. John Riley stepped toward them and took Mrs. Preece's hand. One of the girls reached out her pudgy hand, and John Riley took it into his and prayed.

Cadence stood at the door listening.

"Father, we bring this beautiful family before you, asking you to provide for them and pour your blessings on them. Bless Orv and keep him safe in the mine. Keep these precious girls safe as they explore your creation and help them obey their Momma and you. Dear Lord, bless Missus Preece for her hospitality. Give her a special blessing today and help her to know she's precious in your sight and dearly loved. In Jesus's name we pray."

"Amen!" the girls called in unison.

John Riley tousled each blond head and laughed. "Amen indeed, ladies."

"That was right nice, Preacher." Mrs. Preece said. "Thank you."

Cadence's phone rang—Laura.

"Cadence, I'm glad you picked up because I was going to stop over yesterday, but the café got busy. Are you resting?"

John Riley waited inside the door. *Does she know it's on speakerphone? Should I barge out now and interrupt or stay here and pretend I can't hear?*

"When will you come back to work?"

John Riley didn't hear Cadence, but he heard the woman and pieced most of the conversation together.

Interesting indeed, Miss Cadence. You are not resting. Why does your boss believe you're sick?

"Oh, I meant to tell you your friend stopped in yesterday looking for you. You know your friend Taylor. Nash?—yes, Nash. It was nice of her to stop in and check on you. I told her you came down with a touch of something. She said she can't wait to catch up with you, so I gave her your phone number. I don't remember you mentioning her before."

John Riley opened the screen door to hurry past Cadence, hoping she didn't realize he had heard.

Cadence stood at the end of the porch overlooking the Preeces' yard, her back turned to him. He tiptoed across the porch and heard Cadence loud and clear.

"What? You gave her my number, Laura? Taylor Nash is a horrible person—a waste of human flesh. Please don't speak to her about me again. Ever."

John Riley hurried to the truck, wishing to hear the end of the conversation. He wanted to correct her—no person was a waste of human flesh. God can redeem any situation.

Was she teasing?

John Riley fiddled with the radio and fought against his desire to pull her in his arms and kiss her worries away. He ran his fingers through his hair and blew out a breath.

John Riley Blackburn, you are in trouble.

Cadence rode facing the truck window, but all she saw was Taylor Nash worming her way into Laura's good graces.

"She seemed nice." Cadence replayed Laura's words.

No, Laura—she's not nice. She's evil. She looks beautiful, but inside she's rotting and can't wait to ooze her rotten slime all over you.

She held her phone, waiting for Taylor to call and taunt her. Taylor enjoyed backing Cadence into corners, making her shake with fear. When it came to Taylor Nash, Cadence quivered like a blob of jelly.

Her phone buzzed.

Hi Cadence so sorry didn't think before sharing your number.

....**It's ok.**

We ok?

....**yeah fine**

Ok take it easy see you soon

She slipped the phone into her pocket and stared out the window.

This town is beautiful. What if I stay? I'm not an obvious Yankee or anything. I can blend in with no problem.

She rolled her eyes. *I have nowhere to go. Nowhere to hide, and Taylor has my phone number. What else can go wrong? I'm one disaster after another.*

She sighed.

"You okay?"

She smiled a weak smile, "Those little girls are sweet. They sure liked you."

"They *are* sweet. Little spitfires too." He chuckled.

"Do they go to your church?"

"They'd like to, but her husband, Orv, works in the mine. He's tired on Sunday, or he's drunk, so they don't come in for church. Most of these people we'll see today don't come to church."

"Why do you help them?" Cadence didn't understand John Riley. He ran all over the mountain to give things to people who never came to his church.

What a waste of time!

"I help because I love them, Cadence. God brought me here to serve this community—it's what I do. People don't have to attend my church for me to care about their lives."

Cadence nodded. She didn't understand, but she doubted she would ever understand his God thing.

"What's your story?" she asked.

"Mine?" John Riley asked. "What do you want to know?"

"You said God brought you here. How do you know?"

"I grew up here."

"Here? In Norris Creek?"

"No. Here in Little Ivy. I wasn't a townie. We lived way back in the worst part in a small cabin, and we were dirt poor. No neighbors nearby, so life was Momma and me. Daddy worked in the mines and drank all weekend. I went to school in town when the weather wasn't bad, but we rarely went to church. Daddy didn't allow it."

"You were nice to the lady because of your childhood?"

"Yes. I understand her situation. It feels close to home. Mrs. Preece is a good woman who loves her babies, and she loves Jesus. She loves her husband too, even though he doesn't make life easy for her."

"No brothers or sisters?"

"Nope, just good old me." He grinned. His grin made him look like a little boy, and her heart did strange flops.

"You?"

"Siblings? No."

He nodded. "Then we understand each other too."

"How did you become the preacher if you never went to church?"

"I didn't say we *never* went to church. We went every Sunday after Daddy disappeared. Momma learned to drive the car and riding down this mountain with her on Sunday morning was an experience and a half." He laughed. "She raced down these roads, and I held on for dear life. Preacher Bud watched out for us like he watched out for all the mountain families. He brought food and clothes and Christmas gifts. I loved when he brought books. I never got enough books. I'd read them over and over 'til he came back, and I swapped him for new books. He was my library.

"I asked lots of questions about God, and he brought me his church books. I was so proud to read Preacher's books. I guess you'd say I was an odd kid, but my favorite was his dictionary of theology."

Cadence nodded. She didn't know what *theology* meant, but yes, she thought he was odd.

CHAPTER 32

Cadence hopped out of the pickup at every stop, and John Riley introduced her as "Miss Freddie's helper from Wesconsin." The people nodded in her direction, but John Riley got all the attention.

Every homemaker insisted they eat—cakes, cookies, pies, and cornbread. Every house offered a glass of sweet tea. Cadence's teeth hurt as she sipped yet another glass of sugary tea.

John Riley laughed with the children and teased the older kids. He chatted with the adults and wove questions throughout the conversation, drawing out information.

Slick if you ask me. Wonder if they realize what he's doing? They tell him all this personal stuff, and he still gets more out of them. What's your game, John Riley?

Cadence predicted his questions and played a secret game.

Oh, there's the health question. Next, ask about jobs—bingo. Then the prayer at the end, where he gathers the family, touches a shoulder, and prays out loud.

His long prayers made Cadence uncomfortable. John Riley prayed as if he and God knew each other.

They don't even know he's playing them. He's good.

By late afternoon they had emptied the pickup bed, but the backseat overflowed. Cadence counted one loaf of banana bread and two white breads, two chocolate cakes, a case of Cheerwine soda, a pound of bacon, and six dozen cookies.

Cadence shook her head in disbelief. "This is a lot of food."

John Riley laughed. "Life as the preacher has some benefits. They take good care of me around here. Miss Freddie said to take you home the back way so you can enjoy the scenery."

Cadence turned from the window. "You're good, you know."

"In what way?"

"You get those people to tell you all their problems, then you pray with them, and boom—everyone feels better. Do they know it's all a game?"

It's not right, John Riley—playing games and offering hope.

"What I do is not a game, Cadence. I *care* about these people. I'm not playing with their lives. Ministering here is my calling—my life."

Cadence shrugged.

"Preacher Bud's interest in me wasn't a game. He didn't give me false hope. He met our needs and cared for us. He helped me become who I am today."

"So you recruit preachers?"

He smiled. "You misunderstand, Cadence. Yes, I became a preacher because of Bud. He and Miss Ida Bealle paid for my seminary training because he saw God's call on my life, not because he recruited preacher boys. They did so much to lighten my load. Life's not easy."

"That's the first thing you've said all day that I can agree with." She turned to the window again and gazed at the valley. A small cabin sat below in a V where two mountains met. Clothes hung on a line behind the house, and a dog ran around the yard. Cadence's heart ached. She wanted home—somewhere to belong.

Is a little bit of peace too much to want? Am I unrealistic?

"What's been hard for *you*, Cadence?" John Riley asked in a low voice.

She turned, her eyes wide as a wave of anger crashed over her.

"How dare you ask me your questions? I'm not one of your mountain people, John Riley. What's been hard for me?" she turned to the window, tears pressed the back of her eyes. A lump formed in her throat, and she clenched her fists and bit her lip.

What hasn't *been hard, Cadence? That's the question Pastor Blackburn should ask.*

John Riley gripped the steering wheel and tried to form a reply.

Hit the sore spot. I didn't aim for it but seems like she needed to get that out. A little help here, Lord?

He resisted the urge to fill the silence with chatter and considered pointing out the scenery. He knew stories about each homestead—history from decades past and current lore. He considered pressing Cadence on the question left in the air. Then he decided a conversation about the weather a better option.

Her anger didn't surprise him. He saw every emotion and reaction by now. He knew people hid hurt and anger for a short time before feelings boiled over. What surprised him was his level of concern. He cared for her as a pastor—sure. God had allowed their paths to cross for a reason, but his concern and curiosity for the brown-haired beauty in his passenger seat involved much more than his pastor heart. A warning thumped in his chest.

Watch yourself, John Riley. You tread on dangerous ground.

He adjusted the volume on the radio and turned. "How about the weather?"

Cadence breathed a sigh of relief when John Riley quit asking questions. She gained control of her swirling emotions and pasted on her "life is fine" face as they entered Norris Creek.

"Streets are quiet at suppertime," John Riley said.

"Do I see a bookstore?" Cadence pointed to a small gray shop set back from the street.

"Yep. Miss Lou's. Never know what you'll find in there. She sells bait, too, if you fish."

"Books and bait? Donuts and laundry? Why so many double businesses?"

John Riley shrugged and grinned. "Limited space, I guess."

"Judge Crum is here, looks like," he said when they pulled into the parsonage. "Wonder what he's after?"

"He stopped the other day and told Fredonia he wanted to buy the house."

John Riley wrinkled his brow, his jaw clenched. He ran around to open the door for Cadence. "I'll pretend you didn't tell me, and I'll let him talk a bit. See if I can figure him out."

The screen door opened, and Miss Ollie stepped out. "Supper's ready. Get a move on."

"Yes, ma'am." John Riley grinned.

Cadence noticed empty boxes and stacks of papers and photos—making progress.

"You're back. Judge Crum will join us for supper again." Fredonia's voice was pleasant, but she rolled her eyes at John Riley.

"Judge." John Riley nodded in Judge Crum's direction.

"Preacher."

"You say the prayer, Preacher," Miss Ollie directed from the stove.

"Let's pray. Father, we thank you for this warm home and the people gathered around. Thank you for providing food and company. I give thanks for Miss Ollie and her fine cooking and willingness to serve. Thank you, Lord, for Miss Freddie's strength to sort through all her momma's stuff. Give her fond memories and fill her heart with joy as she works. Thank you for the gifts she shared with our mountain families today. Bless her for her generosity. Thank you, Lord, for Judge Crum and his good service in this community. And, Lord, we thank you for our new friend, Miss Cadence. Bless her for the help she gives Miss Freddie and for her kind help to me this afternoon. Amen."

Heat rose in Cadence's cheeks. She didn't remember anyone thanking God for her presence before. She glanced up to see Fredonia staring at her with an odd smile.

"What did you two do all afternoon?" Judge Crum bellowed from the far end of the table.

John Riley recounted their stops and the items they left at each home.

"Did Mrs. Preece say Orv's behaving? I ain't seen him in court for a while," Judge Crum asked between bites.

"Judge Crum, discussing Orv's court cases isn't proper for a man of your position, is it?" Fredonia asked.

Judge Crum ate like a child, and crumbs fell down his shirt like Cookie Monster. Cadence stifled a giggle and bit her lip.

"Come on now, Freddie. We're all friends here. I ain't sayin' nothing we all don't know," Judge Crum said in complaint.

"Well, my friend Cadence here doesn't know. And I prefer pleasantries at my table, sir." She fixed her gaze on the judge. "Please."

"All right, Freddie. I'll behave myself."

John Riley laughed. "Judge Crum, when did you ever behave yourself?" The judge burst out in a loud guffaw and slapped his knee.

"You preaching to me, John Riley? It ain't Sunday."

Cadence heard the light banter, but the tension buzzed under the surface. Miss Ollie didn't like the judge, and Fredonia tolerated him from what she gathered. John Riley's voice sounded pleasant, but Cadence remembered his clenched jaw in the pickup.

"You know me—I preach everywhere I go." He winked at Judge Crum.

Miss Ollie served Cadence a generous plate, but her stomach groaned from the treats she had eaten all afternoon. She took several small bites of the breaded fried meat and tasted onion and a hint of garlic. "This meat is delicious, Miss Ollie. What kind?" Cadence asked.

"Whistle pig."

Cadence set her fork on the table, and food rolled in her stomach. She struggled with a gracious reply or at least a non-Yankee comment. "Uh—'whistle pig'?"

John Riley nudged her knee under the table. His eyes twinkled, and he grinned. "Miss Ollie's messin' with ya. Aren't you, Miss Ollie? You wouldn't serve groundhog to a first-time visitor?"

Ollie laughed. "Okay, okay—country fried steak."

Miss Ollie's joke hurt Cadence's feelings, but her stomach quit rolling, and she breathed a sigh of relief.

"I like whistle pig," Judge Crum hollered from his end of the table.

"Judge, did you stop by for a particular reason?" John Riley asked.

"Gotta check on the ladies. Plus, I hankered for some of Miss Ollie's cooking." He winked at Ollie, and she scowled at him. "Don't you scowl at me, Miss Ollie. You know you're gonna marry me yet."

Ollie threw her napkin onto the table and pushed back. "Judge Crum, wash your mouth out with soap!"

The judge roared with laughter, and Cadence grinned, pleased with Miss Ollie's discomfort.

"Miss Freddie," John Riley said, "I'm thinkin' my pickup is about to give out on me. Sell me your fancy pink car out there. How much?"

Freddie laughed so hard she wiped her eyes. "Can you imagine the talk if the preacher started driving a pink car? But for you, John Riley, I'll sell Cici for fifteen thousand. "

"Hey, you told *me* thirty," Cadence protested.

"Well, you're a big-city girl, Cadence. But Brother Blackburn is a poor country preacher. He needs a deal." She winked at John Riley, and John Riley winked at Cadence.

Fredonia reached over and patted Cadence's arm. "Don't you worry —Cici's not for sale. I'm teasing both of you, but enough foolishness. Thank you for coming by, Judge, but I have lots to finish tonight. I'm sure I'll see you before I leave." She stood and walked to the front door.

"You're gettin' above yer raisin' now, Freddie. Don't get high and mighty on me. I need to talk to the preacher here about buying this place."

John Riley sat his mug on the table and wiped his mouth with a napkin. "Judge Crum, this home isn't for sale. You know the parsonage belongs to the church."

The pastor's voice sounded calm, but his face was hard to interpret —not the kind, pastoral man she had observed all day.

The judge cleared his throat and set his napkin down. He stared at John Riley. "Well, preacher boy, you misunderstood me. I'm not asking —I'm buying."

John Riley stood up, "Judge Crum, let's not ruin the ladies' supper. You're welcome to attend our next board meeting and discuss ownership of this property. But how about you and I take our leave and let these ladies get back to their projects?"

Judge Crum eyed John Riley for a moment and blew out his breath. "Sure, Preacher. We'll talk about this in front of the board. Lookin' forward to that meeting. Night, ladies." The door slammed.

"Thank you for dinner, Miss Ollie. Miss Freddie, I'll stop by tomorrow for the next load," John Riley said.

He smiled at Cadence and winked. "I hope you'll help me tomorrow, Miss Cadence."

Cadence nodded and looked away. Her heart skipped a beat.

"I plan to stop for a dozen of Tansy's donuts," he said.

"Don't you dare, John Riley Blackburn!" Miss Ollie grabbed a broom and chased the preacher out the door. John Riley chuckled and howled as he ran to his truck.

CHAPTER 33

After supper Cadence joined Fredonia and Ollie and listened to their stories. Fredonia's baby pictures made Cadence smile, but a stab of jealousy twisted her heart. Fredonia belonged in Norris Creek—her parents wanted her.

Cadence wished for piles of memorabilia and pictures of herself as a child. She wanted stacks of papers about her family stories and wanted what she didn't have—somewhere to belong.

She examined pictures and half-listened to stories; her mind wandered to Taylor. Her stomach lurched.

I have options. One—figure out how to pay her, knowing she'll blackmail me again. Two—run her over with Cici. Three—three what? I have no idea.

"Cadence?"

"Sorry." She handed a pile of photos to Fredonia.

"I said Ollie and I are going to listen to our favorite radio preacher. Care to join us?"

Cadence stood and stretched—her stomach churned. "I'm exhausted. I'll turn in if you don't mind."

Fredonia nodded, adjusting the radio dial. Peaceful piano music floated through the room, and Cadence considered staying—anything for peace, even a radio preacher.

"Join us this evening as our pastor shares God's desire for truth." The announcer's voice boomed over the piano music.

Cadence escaped to the bathroom, not interested in truth—too much deception in her story. She brushed her teeth and scrubbed her face— the voice from the radio drifting through the house.

"God's Word teaches truth. What lies have you told? Who have you harmed with your lies? God knows who you are inside, no matter what story you tell the world. Ask God to give you strength. Obey. Tell the truth and ask forgiveness for the wrong you've done."

Cadence rushed up the stairs, the radio preacher's annoying voice following her.

"Living a lie keeps you in a cycle of anger, pain, and bitterness. Acknowledge what you've done and pray to God for mercy. But don't stop there—talk to those you deceived. Ask for forgiveness. Tell the truth."

She dove into bed, squeezing her eyes shut. The words mocked her.

"Ask them to forgive you. Tell the truth." Cadence sighed and pulled the covers over her ears, trying to stop the words from settling in her mind.

"I'm not lying," she said. "I'm keeping myself safe. There's a difference."

She sank into the pillow, closed her eyes, and tried to forget.

John Riley worked at his desk in the church office, his head in his hands. He tried to pray, but words failed—Judge Crum, Cadence, the pain he had seen in his people. He tried to sort his jumbled thoughts. He smiled, remembering the afternoon spent with Cadence. Her brown hair blew around her face as they drove. His heart pounded at her smile when she met the Preece girls. Her laugh. Her eyes.

"God, I need help," he prayed. "I need to work on this sermon—not dream about a brown-eyed beauty who's running from you.

He paced the office quoting the scripture he chose for Sunday, "And your ears shall hear a word behind you, saying, 'This is the way, walk in it,' when you turn to the right or when you turn to the left."

He continued pacing. The sermon taught his people to follow God and tune hearts to his leadership. Not complex, but he sat with a blank screen and one verse.

He plopped into the swivel chair and picked up a pen.

Will handwriting kick my brain into gear? Nope. Nothing.

John Riley had lived focused on ministry for several years—no girls to distract him. He dated a girlfriend or two in high school. Preacher Bud encouraged him to wait for God to bring a special lady to him like his Miss Ida Bealle. He had ignored Preacher Bud's warning when he was young. He cared about girls and fun, and while John Riley loved Miss Ida Bealle, she wasn't his type of girl.

In seminary he spent time with several young women. Where better for a preacher to meet a wife? A woman ready to serve God—perfect choice for a young minister. He fell head over heels for a beautiful girl with rosy cheeks, sparkling eyes, and curly blonde hair. He spent every moment juggling classes and making excuses to spend time with her.

The engagement lasted six months. John Riley counted his blessings. They were the perfect couple. She was petite and blonde while he was tall and dark. Her humor and impulsiveness countered his seriousness. Holly made him laugh, and John Riley made her study. After graduation John Riley moved home and helped Preacher Bud. He and Holly dreamed about their home and ministry and planned their happily ever after.

On spring break he brought her to meet his mom and show her Norris Creek. He pointed out the house he hoped to buy with space for a garden. In his excitement, he didn't ask why her lip curled when he talked about their children playing in the creek. He tried to explain away the shock in her eyes when they drove around town. He ignored the tone behind her comments, the faces she made behind his mother's back. He pretended he didn't hear sarcasm when she talked to Miss Ida Bealle.

One thing he didn't miss was the ring she dropped into his hand a few days after they returned to seminary. "You're a nice guy, John Riley, but this will not work. I wish you well," she said.

John Riley stared at her blonde curls bouncing as she walked out of his life. The ring sat in his hand as a cold, hard lump.

He heard about Holly on the alumni page. She had married one of his friends—a good friend. No kids. They ministered at a megachurch in Los Angeles. From the pictures they shared, she seemed happy. He hoped so. She had broken his heart, but John Riley wasn't the type of guy to wish ill on anyone—not even pretty girls who crushed his dreams.

He shook his head and grinned. "I wish you well too, Holly."

No one had sparked his interest since. There were women—oh, there were women. Every mother within a hundred miles made sure John Riley knew her single daughter. Casseroles showed up on his steps with perfume-scented notes, cookies on his desk after services, shy smiles and invitations to dinner.

John Riley wanted a wife and family but chose to honor God with his singleness. If God wanted him to marry, he needed to hit John Riley over the head and tell him. He wanted a wife who stole his heart and captivated him. No one came close—not until Cadence Audley came to town.

God, what are you doing?

He swiveled back to the computer, intent on writing his outline before he went home. He reached for the mouse and remembered Cadence's phone conversation on Preece's porch.

Let's see who you are, Cadence Audley, and let's check out Taylor Nash too.

Cadence tossed and turned, the words of the radio preacher churning in her mind. She dreamed she was a judge in the courtroom pointing at those who had hurt her—Mother for abandoning her, Grandmother for dying, foster families for treating her like a chore, friends who used her, men who preyed on her.

Taylor stood in front of the bench, and Cadence jumped down, her judge's robes fluttering. She sat behind the wheel of Cici, backed over Taylor, and pumped her fist. Victory. Cadence settled behind the judge's desk, gathering her composure. The bailiff opened the door for the next hearing—the Boyds family. She turned away from their gaze, tapping her gavel on the bench.

"Case dismissed. I've done nothing wrong." She stood to enter chambers and ignored their stares. "I didn't betray you. I've done nothing wrong."

Cadence stared into the dark bedroom.

"I've done nothing wrong," she whispered. She shifted from side to side, trying to get comfortable. The ache in her heart kept her awake. She replayed the trip to the mountain with John Riley. The people demonstrated happiness despite poverty and miserable conditions, and John Riley showed love to every person. She smiled, thinking of his blue eyes and how the corner of his eyes crinkled when he smiled.

She threw off the blanket. "Enough foolish dreams, Audra. A preacher is the last mess you need in your life. John Riley is a preacher, and Thatcher Stevens is a police officer," she said. "Why can't I find a guy with a regular job? A normal guy is all I want."

She dug out work clothes and tiptoed to the kitchen. Coffee and a sunrise sounded perfect.

In the dark kitchen Cadence switched on her phone light in search of the coffee pot. She found coffee grounds, but the coffee pot was nowhere in sight. She searched through cupboards and found the old aluminum percolator, then smiled at the click-click-click when the gas flame ignited. The vintage stove was a beauty—a Hardwick with a back vent similar to the grill on an old car. A timer shone a pale light. This kitchen reminded her of Grandmother's kitchen—hers too.

She sat at the red Formica table waiting for coffee. The clock ticked, the percolator bubbled, and Cadence wondered what project to work on today. They had made progress, but the living room needed sorting. John Riley planned to clear furniture and small things when she and Fredonia left for Wisconsin.

She finished the root cellar the other day, but Fredonia wanted her to sort the shed out back.

The root cellar.

Cadence turned off the flame and grabbed her phone, racing to the cellar. She struggled with the latch for several moments but finally tugged the doors open and walked into the dark cellar. Her gaze swept the clean shelves. With the floor swept and the cobwebs knocked down, the cellar was a new space. She hunted for a chair or sturdy table to climb onto. The shelves were too heavy to drag, so she tugged a small table under the spot. She grimaced, waiting to crash to the floor, but the table held. She reached into the crevice and patted around.

Did I imagine seeing something?

Straining on her tiptoes, she willed the rickety table to hold her and reached again, flattening herself to the wall. Her tongue hung out as she reached and patted around the crevice.

"Nothing—boo," she complained to the empty cellar. She got down and then stood on the stairs, pointing her phone light across the cellar. The light was dim, but she knew something hid up there.

She pushed the table under the shelf for later, but now she needed coffee. She stepped out of the cellar—and bumped into Miss Ollie. "Oh, Miss Ollie! You scared me!"

Ollie stared at her, her eyes hard. "What are you doing down here this early?"

"How did you know where I was?"

"I came in to put on coffee and start breakfast and found the coffee pot on the stove. The back door was open. It weren't hard to guess someone was out here."

"I couldn't sleep," Cadence shrugged. "I wanted to finish down there."

Ollie stared at her for a moment, then nodded toward the kitchen. "Coffee's ready."

Cadence decided to search later—when grumpy Miss Ollie didn't hover.

CHAPTER 34

May 1963, Norris Creek, Kentucky

Storm clouds hovered over the valley. Thunder and lightning rumbled outside, and rain streamed down the windowpanes. Ida Bealle curled next to Bud, tucked under the red-and-white quilt to keep out the damp air. Bud slept sound. She smiled at his whistling snore and dozed until lightning cracked. She whispered a prayer of thanks for their snug home. A clap of thunder woke both of them, and Bud pulled her close. "Wow—a loud one!" he whispered against her hair. She nodded; her eyes closed.

The rumble continued, and Ida Bealle drifted in and out of sleep, confused. She sat up in bed and listened.

"Bud, that's not thunder." She shook him. "Bud, wake up! Someone's at the door!"

Bud sat up and rubbed his eyes. When the banging grew louder, he walked to the window and peered out. Lightning crackled through the sky and illuminated the mountain in the distance.

He crawled into bed and snuggled beside her. "Nothing's out there—just the storm," he murmured and drifted back to sleep.

She nodded, closing her eyes—so tired—then another bang.

Bud jumped up and slipped his arms into his robe, tying the belt as he hurried downstairs. She grabbed her dressing gown and followed through the dark house. The bang grew more insistent.

Ida Bealle glanced at the clock. Two o'clock. Bud motioned for her to stay back.

A woman stood at the door; her scarf dripped rain onto the blankets she held out. Her wrinkled hands gripped the blankets. "Take her. She's your'n." Her voice cracked as she shoved the bundle into Bud's hands. She disappeared into the night before they could say anything.

Bud set the bundle onto the table, and Ida Bealle grabbed at the blankets, pulling them open. When she pulled back the last layer, they both gasped.

A very tiny, very new baby with downy blonde hair and pink skin lay on their table, sound asleep. A worn cotton diaper on her bottom was all the baby wore.

"Oh, Bud." Ida scooped up the baby and clutched the bundle to her chest. The pieces of her empty heart overflowed.

Bud grabbed his coat and hat and ran after the woman, the door slamming behind him.

Ida Bealle wrapped the blanket around the baby while tears flowed. The tiny baby nestled her head under Ida Bealle's chin. Sweet puffs of warm baby breath fluttered on her neck. She smiled and rubbed the baby's back, a soft circular motion over and over until she fell asleep with the baby tucked in her arms.

The storm stilled, and the morning sun was peeking through the clouds when Bud came home. Ida Bealle snuggled the baby on the sofa, too afraid to get up. The dream might disappear if she moved.

Ida Bealle's eye sparked, and she stared at her husband with a hint of defiance. "We're keeping her, Bud. She's ours. You heard her."

Bud nodded and went up the stairs to bed.

CHAPTER 35

C adence poured coffee from the percolator and thick swirls of cream into the heavy mug. "Mmmmm—smells like home."

Miss Ollie stared, and Cadence turned away, stirring her coffee with a thin teaspoon. "What will we do today, Fredonia?"

"I haven't decided. The back shed, boxes in the living room, my father's study. We're making progress, but there's still so much to do. I'm exhausted already."

"Don't you worry, Freddie. We'll get done." Ollie set toast onto the table and slid jars of jam and a butter dish across the table. "Get eatin'. Bacon's ready in a jiffy."

If Miss Ollie tattled on her and forced her to explain why she had gone to the cellar this morning, she didn't know what to say. She needed to figure out what was in that cubby before she said a word.

"Miss Ollie, how'd you get this bacon so straight?" she asked. "Mine always shrivels up in a twisted mess."

Ollie stood a little taller at the stove and smiled. "My momma taught me—have to use a press."

Cadence didn't know what Ollie meant, but the smile transformed her.

I can win her over yet. Keep the compliments coming. She likes them.

"Coffee's delicious too. How many scoops do you add to the percolator?"

"Four." Ollie turned back to the stove to spoon bacon grease into the little jar on the back of the stove.

"I have one of those." Cadence pointed to the jar. "I didn't know what it was."

"You didn't know what was?"

"The little round jar."

"You can't read 'grease jar'?" She slid her finger under the letters as if teaching Cadence to read. "'Grease jar,'" she said, a hint of sarcasm in her voice.

Cadence shrugged and smiled at Ollie. "Cut me some slack, Miss Ollie. Mine doesn't have letters on the front."

Ollie rolled her eyes and went back to scrubbing the stovetop.

"One more cup of coffee and then back to work, ladies," Fredonia said. "Cadence is right, Ollie. This is good joe."

Ollie smiled at the compliment. The smile made her face friendly instead of severe—a rugged beauty.

"You should smile more, Miss Ollie," Cadence said.

Ollie turned from the stove. "What did you say?"

"To work, ladies." Fredonia stood and patted Ollie's shoulder. "Thanks for breakfast. What would I do without you?"

Ollie smiled again and turned back to the stove. "You'd starve."

Fredonia laughed.

Cadence followed Fredonia's directions, running back and forth for several hours. "Fredonia, I need a break." she gasped after lugging a heavy box to the hall.

Fredonia waved her hand across the piles. "Sorry. I'm reminiscing and reading, and you're doing all the dirty work. Grab a drink and sit on the porch for a bit. I'll work 'til you get back."

Cadence found tea in the refrigerator, gulped a glass, refilled it, and sat in the rocker, thankful for rest.

In the churchyard children chased each other, screeching when tagged. Their laughter filled the yard between the church and the house. Little ones dug in a sandbox, and a red-haired girl swung on a swing hanging from a tree branch.

Oh, to be a kid again! Have fun and let everyone take care of you.

She frowned. *Her* childhood wasn't carefree and fun.

I'd rather be a grown-up in charge of my own life, no one telling me what to do.

She laughed. She was *not* in charge of her life. She sat on a porch in Kentucky, hot and sweaty, clinging to a dripping glass of iced tea because a certain someone dictated her life—controlled her.

Four days till D-Day. Hey, Taylor, newsflash: I don't have the money.

She sighed. *What do I have to do to get free of Taylor? I can't get free. She'll come back.*

Cadence checked her phone several times, shocked. No texts—nothing.

The lack of contact from Taylor unnerved her, and her conscience was pinched for lying to Laura. Cadence liked her boss—a lot. Laura treated her well and was honest and fair, and she mothered her employees too. She didn't expect to find friendship at the Muddy Cup Café, but she appreciated Laura and worked hard. Cadence was a good employee and a respectable citizen.

See, Laura, I know you hate liars, and I didn't mean to lie to you. No. I meant to say that I'm skipping town for a few days to lay low because I don't have ten thousand dollars. But, hey, don't worry about me. As soon as I get Taylor out of my life, I'll go back to work, and we'll pretend nothing happened.

She glanced under the oak tree at Cici's whitewall tires and shook her head.

No. I have to think of another way to fix this. All my troubles are gone if you're gone, Taylor—all of them.

"Cadence?" Fredonia's voice interrupted her swirling thoughts.

"Coming."

"Old church pictures." Fredonia sat in the middle of boxes. She held up a fist full of black-and-white photos and handed one to Cadence.

"I love the '50s. The ladies are beautiful," Cadence said.

Fredonia smiled and handed her another photo. "My mom."

"She's pretty." Cadence examined Ida Bealle, who wore a polka dot dress, white heels, and a chiffon scarf wrapped around her hair. "Is this why you wear scarves when you drive Cici?"

Fredonia laughed. "Well, yes, but I don't want my hair in my eyes. Help an old lady up, please." She reached for Cadence and groaned as she stood. "Take this box over to the church, okay? I saw John Riley's truck earlier."

"How will I find him?"

"The open door behind the altar." She handed the box to Cadence with a grunt. "Careful—I'm not sure how secure the bottom is."

The hinges creaked when Cadence tugged the church door open. She smelled her favorite scent—old library. She paused to examine the entryway's stunning woodwork. A rope hung in the corner, and she craned her neck up to find a brass bell high above. Rows of shining wooden benches lined both sides of the church, and a heavy wooden cross hung on the wall. A piano sat to the side—piles of red books on top. Cadence noticed the same books on the back of the benches. She tried to remember the last time she had gone to a church—not since Grandmother died.

She headed to an open door behind the piano.

"Cadence, let me grab this," John Riley said. "I heard a noise out here, but I expected someone else."

"Fredonia sent me with these church pictures." She held out the box and John Riley's fingers brushed hers. She pulled her hand away and her eyes widened at the zap she felt when he touched her.

John Riley grabbed the box. "Follow me. Let's check them out."

The plain office held a desk and shelves full of books. *Practical Theology, Counseling for Christian Couples, Essays on the Book of Job, Christology, Pilgrims on the Way, Ecclesiology.*

Her eyes glazed over, and she stepped to the window—a game of tag in full swing in the churchyard.

"You have a playground?"

John Riley shrugged. "The playground at school isn't safe, so I managed to get this one approved last year."

"Doesn't the noise interrupt you?"

"Never," he replied, smiling. "Their noise helps me write my sermons. Happy children boost my mood."

"What else do you do for them?"

"The children?" he asked, moving back behind his desk while shuffling photos.

"The people."

John Riley pointed to a chair across from him. He leaned forward and smiled. "Well, Miss Audley, I'm glad you asked."

She heard most of what he said, but his smile distracted her. His blue eyes shone while he talked about the library he had established up the mountain for the people in Little Ivy, a food pantry, and literacy clubs. For a brief moment she imagined she helped him. Here. In Kentucky— so many worthy projects. For a split second, she wished she was the kind of girl he would choose for a wife. She wanted to work alongside someone so energetic—so giving. Norris Creek was a town she might call home—a place of peace and rest. She wanted to stay.

Oh, Cadence. Don't fool yourself. You're not the kind of girl a decent man wants. You're the kind of girl who's left for last—when there isn't anyone else. You're not preacher's wife material.

"And I plan to set up a parent mentor program soon. I'll have to work with people who are parents, though." He shrugged and leaned across the desk. "What do you think?"

She tucked away her longing for a carefree life and tried to answer his question without admitting she daydreamed about him while he talked.

"Wonderful, but how do you have so much energy?"

"God." He nodded toward the window. "Of course, those kids motivate me. I want them to have their needs met so they can grow into the life God intends for them."

She turned away—God again. The sliver of hope floated off, carrying her dreams away—like a balloon.

You aren't the type of girl he wants, Cadence. Get your head out of the clouds.

"Fredonia said she has another load ready for you."

"Perfect. I'll come over around one. You'll go with me?"

Cadence nodded. John Riley's smile shattered her resolve. She was helpless to say no.

CHAPTER 36

A note hung on the screen door.

Ollie and I ran to the hardware store—needed exercise. Back around 1.

F

"My chance," Cadence whispered and hurried to the backyard in search of a ladder and found one hiding in weeds. She ran to the cellar, stopping to catch her breath and wipe sweat from her eyes. She breathed a sigh of relief when she tugged the cellar doors open.

"Good grief—after all this work, there better be a treasure up there." She leaned the ladder against the wall and tested each rung before attempting to climb.

"Here goes nothing." When she got to the top, she pointed a flashlight into the deep hole and squinted. "There's something," she whispered. "Ugggh—my arms are too short."

Call John Riley. No, if it's empty, I'll look foolish.

She spied a broom and poked it into the space until something clanked. "Yes." Cadence pushed and maneuvered until she reached a heavy tin.

Did the news anchor who opened Al Capone's vault feel this nervous?

The anticipation made her heart pound, she tried to open the lid with shaky hands, but the rusty lid didn't move.

Investigate later. If Miss Ollie finds me down here again, I'll have to explain. What if there's nothing to explain?

She dragged the ladder behind the shed and pushed it far into the weeds. She didn't need Miss Ollie noticing the disturbed weeds and asking questions. She hurried to her room to hide the tin before anyone found her snooping.

"Nothing but junk, I bet," Cadence whispered, tugging on the lid. She grabbed an ink pen and pushed it between the cover and tin to pry it open.

She listened for a moment. Quiet. She checked the time. Twelve fifty —hurry. If they came home before she finished, she would hide the tin and freshen up—her excuse for hanging out upstairs. She pulled the lid open and stared, then pushed the top back on and stuffed it under her pillows.

Breathe, Cadence, breathe. Oh, my word.

She sat on the bed, her mind racing. She pulled the tin out and held it on her lap.

I can't keep this.

She opened the tin and rifled through the contents. A stack of papers and envelopes seemed interesting, but the roll of hundred-dollar bills made her gasp. She counted—one hundred fifty hundred-dollar bills.

This money solved her problems—no need to commit murder or create a dreadful accident for Taylor.

She held the tin on her lap and wrestled with her conscience. If she hid the money and reported the envelopes, she might get away with the plan.

What if the envelopes mention the money?

"I have to open the envelopes. Fredonia's rich. She doesn't need this," Cadence whispered. She held the money and closed her eyes, and a weight rolled off her shoulders. With this much money, her identity in Deercrest stayed safe. She would stay in her little white cottage with her treasures and work for Laura, pretending she was a decent, upstanding citizen.

Voices flashed in her conscience.

Grandmother: "Honesty is the best policy."

Laura: "I hate it when people lie to me."
Fredonia: "I'm so glad you came to help me.
The radio preacher: "The truth will set you free."
The memory of John Riley's smiling eyes flashed and she took a deep breath.

What do John Riley's eyes have to do with this? I won't see him after I leave. She shook her head to banish the image of those twinkling blue eyes.

She pushed the tin under the pillows and checked her hair and face for dirty spots or clinging weeds. Her phone beeped.

—Hey Audra, good to see you.

—Can't wait for Tuesday.

—Met Officer Thatcher. He's nice. Stays busy looking for crooks.

—T

Cadence deleted the messages and dropped on the bed; bile rose in her throat. She glanced at the pillows and took a deep breath.

"'*Take the money*' it is," she said, feeling both relieved and disgusted.

The screen door slammed. "Cadence? You here?"

Cadence peeked in the mirror, her cheeks bright red—guilty.

"Up here!" she called.

Three more days, Cadence. Keep it together three more days. No one will ever know.

She joined Fredonia and Miss Ollie in the living room.

"We're almost finished with this room but ran for tape and twine. I tried to talk Ollie into a stop at Tansy's, but she wouldn't let me." Fredonia winked.

Ollie waved her hand in the air and marched to the kitchen. "I already said my piece about eating donuts where people wash their drawers."

Fredonia giggled and shrugged. "I tried."

Cadence noticed Fredonia teased Miss Ollie often, but their care for each other peeked through the banter.

"What were you busy with while we were gone?"

"I ran those pictures over to the church, and John Riley showed me around. I watched the kids on the playground behind the church. Looks like they enjoy playing over there."

Fredonia nodded. "He does a lot for the community—like my daddy. It's good to see."

Cadence nodded and turned away from Fredonia—too much guilt.

"I don't know how he has the energy for half the things he does," Fredonia went on. "He's always working on projects."

Cadence nodded, worried her face might give her away. Did her forehead flash a neon sign, "Guilty"?

"Why don't you run over and tell him to come for lunch—then he can load up again." She waved her hand over a pile near the door. "This stack is ready to go, and if I hurry, I can add a little more before you leave."

Cadence hurried to the church, relieved to step away from Fredonia's gaze.

How will I keep this up for three more days? Keep my head down. That's how.

When she crossed the lawn, she heard heated voices, but the wind garbled the sound.

Why would anyone argue in church?

Cadence opened the heavy doors and stepped into the cool church— the voices clear.

"No. I told you it's not possible." John Riley's voice drifted across the sanctuary.

"It *is* possible, and I told you I'm buying it."

Oh, great—Judge Crum. He'll notice my guilty face and know.

"We'll settle this at the meeting tomorrow night. There's no reason to discuss this without the board present."

"Wait a minute, son. This is between you and me. I'll give you whatever money you need for your community projects if you side with me at the meeting. Our secret—a gentleman's deal."

Cadence waited to hear John Riley take the bribe.

"No, Judge. It's not how we operate."

"Oh, JR," the judge chuckled. "Would be a shame if the town heard what your momma did to your daddy. Wouldn't want the news gettin' out now, would ya, Preacher?"

"Is this a threat, Judge Crum?" John Riley's voice rose.

"Settle down, boy. I'm an officer of the court; of course, I'm not blackmailing you," he said with a laugh. "No one would believe you if you told them, but if I talked about the questions surrounding your daddy's disappearance . . ." he trailed off.

"Judge Crum, you need to leave. We'll discuss this with the board."

Cadence moved to the door and stepped out. She came back in and slammed the door, "Hello?"

The judge walked down the center aisle with a smirk on his face. John Riley followed, his jaw clenched, and his eyes flashed.

"Fredonia said to come for lunch."

"Not today, little lady." Judge Crum tipped his hat. "Got court in twenty minutes." He hurried past her. "Good day, Preacher."

John Riley nodded. "I'll head over in a few minutes." He turned back to his office. The door clicked shut.

Miss Ollie hollered when Cadence came in, "Cadence, I need a hand getting lunch on the table! Set out dishes. Is John Riley coming? I saw the judge over there. Don't tell me he wormed his way into another meal."

"No, he has court."

"Good. Four settings then." She pointed to the cupboard. "Dishes in there. Napkins in the drawer. Can you find the salt and pepper? Butter. Oh, and slice the bread."

Cadence moved fast, too afraid of Ollie to linger.

The screen door creaked, and John Riley's voice floated to the kitchen. Butterflies tickled her stomach.

Oh, girl, stop. You don't deserve a man as decent as John Riley, and he doesn't deserve someone like you. Quit acting like a schoolgirl and set the table. Focus on what's important—getting rid of Taylor.

"John Riley, was Judge Crum over there? What's he want?" Ollie called out.

"He wants to buy the parsonage." John Riley and Fredonia stepped into the kitchen.

Fredonia shook her head. "I don't understand him. Why does he want the parsonage?"

"I'll tell you why." Ollie pointed the wooden spoon at Fredonia. "In his mind, he owns this town and gets what he wants. He throws his money around, scaring people. He's ruined the downtown. Did you see that monstrosity of a courthouse when you came into town?"

Ollie shook her spoon again. "He insisted we build a second courthouse. What town the size of ours needs two courthouses? Nothing wrong with the old one, but Judge Crum wanted a new one. We're still paying taxes for the ugly thing, and the old one sits empty. Man has no sense."

"Miss Ollie," John Riley said, cutting into her tirade. "The Bible says to love everyone. No need to tear down the judge."

"No need 'cause everyone knows it!" Ollie huffed. "Now sit yerself down and eat. Food's gettin' cold while you're jawing."

John Riley grinned. "Yes, ma'am. Ladies, after you."

Listening to John Riley's prayer, Cadence wished she believed God existed as she did when she was little. John Riley talked to God as if He existed, but Cadence knew better. If God was real, people like Judge Crum and Taylor wouldn't have power. The judge was out of her hands, but Taylor wasn't.

Yes indeed, Taylor Nash. I don't know what I'll do, but your days of pushing me around are over.

CHAPTER 37

After lunch Cadence helped John Riley pack his pickup with Fredonia's cast-offs. He helped Cadence into the truck and ran to the other side. When he slid behind the steering wheel, he turned to her and grinned. "We're off."

His blue eyes and dazzling smile took her breath away.

Why is he so good looking?

He parked in front of a small store.

"You're stopping at Tansy's? I'll tell Miss Ollie."

John Riley tapped his finger on his lips. "Shh. Don't you get me in trouble with Ollie, Miss Cadence. I have to support Tansy 'cause she goes to my church."

The shop smelled of yeast and sugar with a hint of cinnamon and chocolate. Tables covered in red-checked cloths and vases of dainty white daisies filled the cheerful space. A woman and small children sat near the window. The little boy licked the top of his donut, his face smeared with chocolate.

"Preacher Blackburn!" called a smiling woman behind the register.

"Afternoon, Tansy. Meet Miss Cadence. She came to help Miss Freddie clear out the parsonage."

The woman frowned at Cadence and turned back to John Riley with a big smile.

"How did opening day go for you?" he asked.

"I sold out of long johns the first hour. Pick a donut—on the house."

John Riley exclaimed over the options, "Mmm mmmm, Miss Tansy. You're gonna make me take up jogging again so I can eat here more often. How about a chocolate donut with sprinkles—to go, please?"

She laughed. "No worries, Preacher. You look fine. Jest let me put it in a poke for you to carry."

Cadence watched a rosy-red blush creep up the woman's cheeks.

Hmmm. Miss Tansy has a crush on the preacher.

"What about you, Cadence?" John Riley asked.

"Nothing for me. I'm full from lunch."

Tansy stared at Cadence a moment before bagging John Riley's donut. When a woman came through one of the back doors carrying a basket of laundry, Cadence stifled a giggle. The laundromat wasn't a joke. She turned into Tansy's stare—her look reminded Cadence of Taylor.

On the way up the mountain, John Riley turned to Cadence. "How rich is Miss Freddie?"

"What?"

"How much money does Miss Freddie have?"

"I don't know. Why?"

"It's a topic of conversation around here. I know she's well off, but how well off?"

Why did he want to know? Why did Fredonia keep it secret?

"Did she ask you not to say?" John Riley asked.

Cadence didn't know how to answer. She had decided to keep the money she found because of Fredonia's wealth. But did everyone need to know her net worth? She kept it from them for some reason.

"I don't know how much she has, but when I went to her house, I thought I read the address wrong and was worried security would ask me to leave."

"Why?"

"She's rich."

"Rich? Or *rich*?" He grinned.

"Rich," Cadence said. "And add a couple more."

John Riley let out a low whistle.

"You won't tell her I blabbed?"

"No. I've wondered why Miss Freddie stayed up there, but I guess there's nothing for her here. We can use her help. Her money, I mean." He shrugged. "It's not my place to say. Please don't repeat me."

Cadence nodded. "What do you need help with?"

"So much—a youth center for starters." He shared his ideas for the community, and Cadence watched, fascinated by his excitement. He told her about his dreams for the people and how he wished to alleviate the pain their poverty caused.

"I'm good at planning and have ideas—we need so much. But it comes down to finances, and I don't have them. Others see the need, but we don't have money." He smiled and shrugged. "So I pray. God will care for us in his time. I don't want to push, but if Miss Freddie realized our needs and helped, lives would change."

Cadence didn't know how to respond to his God talk or his wish for Fredonia's help.

"Why does it bother you when I talk about God?"

Simmering anger bubbled in her chest. "I'll tell you why, John Riley. This God of yours wrecked my life, and he's done nothing for me. He's taken everyone important to me and everything I needed. I don't believe in him anymore, and I don't want him doing anything for me."

She turned to the window, trying to swallow her anger. "I went to church with Grandmother Miggs, and I believed. I sang "Jesus Loves Me," and I said my prayers every night. I prayed the prayers the Sunday School teacher said to pray. I believed God watched over me, but the last couple of decades prove he doesn't. If he's real, he's got some explaining to do."

"I'm sorry, Cadence."

"For what?"

"I'm sorry for the hurts you carry, but *people* hurt you—their sin. God loves you, Cadence, and he created you for a purpose."

Cadence tried to bite back angry words, but white-hot rage overwhelmed her. She turned to John Riley, her eyes fierce, anger crackling in her voice. "Listen to me, John Riley Blackburn, you and God and everybody else can get off my back."

She turned to the window wishing she knew her way back to town. She would force him to pull over and let her out of this miserable truck. John Riley turned onto a side road and blew out a soft breath.

"Oh, Cadence," he said in a whisper. He parked and grabbed a bundle to take inside.

When he disappeared inside the house, Cadence sobbed.

The afternoon passed in chilly silence. Cadence stayed in the pickup, and John Riley smiled at her each time he got out. Anger overwhelmed her, but she knew he wasn't to blame.

Her phone buzzed.

—**Checking in.**

—**You ok?**

—**Miss you. L**

Cadence stared at the text. What would happen if she told the truth?

I'm not okay, Laura. I lied to you, and I'm about to steal a lot of money. This hunky preacher is on my last nerve, and I'm angry. I'm mad because some people live their lives without everything falling apart. I'm a big mess, Laura, if you want to know.

John Riley returned to the pickup before she sent the text—she would answer Laura later.

"You're angry at me for telling you the truth," he said in a low voice. "Truth is important to me, Cadence, so I will always tell the truth. It bothers me when people aren't honest."

Her stomach sank—a familiar feeling. Truth wasn't her strong point —obviously.

"What are you talking about?"

"I'm talking about truth. It made you angry when I said people hurt you, not God, but I need to tell you the truth."

Cadence shook her head. "Stop."

"Okay. But there's more."

She turned to him, the tone of his voice setting off alarm bells. "What?"

He pulled the truck to the side of the road. He kept his hands on the wheel—his eyes straight ahead. "There's no Cadence Audley."

Cadence stared at him, her mind froze, and fear churned in her chest.

Think. Think. Think. What will I say? Taylor's appearance was terrible, but this is a nightmare.

She plastered on a sugary sweet smile, "Why, Pastor Blackburn, what do you mean? I'm right here." Her stomach threatened to betray her. If he didn't start driving, she would hop out for fresh air.

"You know what I mean," his voice low.

She blew out several breaths to still her queasy stomach, and tears burned. She bit the inside of her lip. No weakness.

How in the world does he know? What did I say to give myself away? Not good.

Cadence's shoulders tensed, but she refused to speak. A man who valued truth wouldn't believe anything she said.

"Cadence?"

She shook her head and pressed her lips together. He turned in his seat, but she faced the window, pretending he hadn't dropped a bomb in her lap.

"You need to tell me who you are."

She held her hands and squeezed her fingers. She wanted to spill her life story to John Riley. Tell him who she was and why she deceived people. Tell him about Taylor's threats. Tell him life on the run and creating new lives exhausted her. She wanted to find safety and acceptance and home. She wanted to tell the truth but seeing the disappointment in his blue eyes stopped her.

The ugly truth about her crime and her attempts to clean things up and live a decent life sounded shallow.

I am pathetic. Taylor Nash is the only person alive who knows me, and she doesn't like me. There's no hope for someone like me.

Telling John Riley the truth was out of the question, but what if he told Fredonia? What if he dug around and found out what she had done?

I'll catch a plane home and leave an apology note for Fredonia. Laura needs me at the café, and I've been away too long. Besides, I'm good at disappearing.

Her decision made, she turned and smiled. "So what *did* happen to your daddy, John Riley? I'm not the only one with secrets."

"You eavesdropped?"

Cadence wanted to look away, but she bluffed—no weakness.

"I didn't eavesdrop. Fredonia sent me to invite you to lunch, and the judge has a loud voice."

"Judge Crum uses information to better himself while he lies and cheats and pushes his agenda. He uses people to get what he wants then tosses them aside without caring who he hurts. If you want to believe a man like him, you're not the person I thought you were." He buckled his seat belt and pulled the truck onto the road.

"No, John Riley, I'm not the person you thought I was. Isn't that why you pulled the truck over for this little chat?"

John Riley held the steering wheel, his jaw set. She hit her target. *You hurt me, and I hurt you—the law of the jungle, Mr. Preacher.* But her shoulders slumped, and her heart ached. *Why am I so sad?*

CHAPTER 38

Norris Creek, Kentucky, November 1963

Ida Bealle jumped at the baby's cry and hurried upstairs. If she didn't move fast enough, the tiny bundle raged. "Momma's here, Fredonia," she crooned and scooped her daughter out of the crib. A smile spread across her face, and she kissed the baby's pink cheeks. "I have a daughter."

The baby blinked, and Ida Bealle laughed. "Your daddy and I waited so long for you, sweetheart." The baby filled their home with joy. Cracks in her heart healed as she mothered Fredonia. Grief and pain slipped away.

"Your daddy insists he'll call you Freddie." She wrinkled her nose and planted another kiss on the baby's head. "Pretty soon everyone around here will call you 'Freddie,' but for now you're my sweet little Fredonia."

Ida Bealle could stare at her baby for hours. The baby's downy hair and button nose mesmerized her. But Fredonia needed a bottle right now if the look on her scrunched-up face meant anything.

A knock at the door interrupted Ida Bealle's bottle preparations. A girl stood at the screen, peering in the living room. "You needin' help with that baby?"

"Not yet, but it's hard to say what I'll need when she's crawling. Who are you?"

"Olivene Endicott, but folks call me Ollie. Me and my aunt moved into the white house in the holler—the little one back from the road."

Ida Bealle tried to place her—she seemed familiar.

"Come in, Olivene."

"Ollie."

The girl sat down on the couch; her eyes followed Ida Bealle and the baby.

"You like babies, Ollie?"

The girl shook her head. "Not particular 'bout all babies, but my aunt said yours is a purty one. She said I should see if I can help ya now and then. Says new babies is hard."

"They are, but this one is exceptional."

"Can I hold her?"

"Let me grab her bottle, and you can feed her if you like."

Ollie nodded, her eyes never leaving the baby. Ida Bealle sat her blanket-wrapped daughter in the girl's arms, and Ollie closed her eyes, pulling the baby close. She sighed and patted the baby and pressed her nose on the baby's tiny head, inhaling.

Ida Bealle frowned. "Let's get her fed, shall we?"

The girl's eyes popped open, and she took a deep breath. Ollie put the bottle in Fredonia's mouth and giggled as the baby sucked it down.

A strange feeling niggled in the back of Ida Bealle's mind.

"She's a tiny one fer sure." Ollie laughed. She rubbed the baby's fingers, a smile spread across her face, and her eyes shone. "Can I peek at her feet?"

"Let's keep her wrapped up. There's a chill in the air." The girl's request made Ida Bealle defensive. Examining the baby was personal —an odd request from a stranger.

The girl's smile faded. "My aunt says if ya want, I can come by a couple days a week and help you with washing or sweeping up— whatever you want."

"What about school, Ollie?"

"Nah. I don't bother with goin' to school. I can read and figure some."

"What a shame, Ollie! You seem like a smart girl. Do you have plans for the future?"

The girl glanced up from the baby, "Me? Nah, I'm not smart—jest normal, and I got no plans. I'm staying right here." She cuddled the baby; a huge smile spread across her face.

CHAPTER 39

John Riley wanted to wear his counselor hat and help her see her worth, help her work through her hurts and find Jesus. Her name was false, but her pain was real. When he mentioned her lie, she lashed out. He wished he could fix everything and pull her in his arms, kiss her tears away.

You are in deep trouble, man. I wish Preacher Bud were here. Tell me to snap out of it.

"Wanna tell me? I'm a good listener."

She shook her head and turned away.

Okay. Silent treatment.

He prayed as he drove: *Lord? I know I'm crazy, but I'm falling fast and hard. Help. I need wisdom. Tell me to grow up and quit acting like a schoolboy. I can't fall for someone I don't even know, can I? Someone who says she doesn't believe in God anymore isn't the girl for me.*

Should he tell her he checked out Taylor online? He found pictures of a young woman with curly red hair and freckles scattered across her nose. Her kids—also red-headed—smiled at her. A man leaned down with a grin. He overheard Cadence call her trash, but the woman online wasn't trashy.

I know not everything online is true. Yet here I sit in my truck with a woman I'm falling for, and I don't even know her name. You know who she is, God. Help me—give me the words.

After his engagement fiasco, he had shut his heart and quit searching for a wife. He lived a busy, full life serving God, and he was happy. But this dark-haired beauty had thrown him into a tailspin.

I have no idea what you're doing or why she affects me so much. Why did you bring her here? What's your plan?

"Why are we driving in circles?" Cadence asked.

He tapped the steering wheel with his index finger. "Hmm?"

"We went past this cabin half an hour ago."

"We did?" he peeked out the window. "You sure?"

"I'm not sure about anything, John Riley. I have no idea where we are, but I'm positive we drove past this blue-and-green quilt before."

"Hmmm . . ." he glanced out the window. "Hamp and Letha Harliss's place. I imagine Miss Letha made the quilt." He smiled. "Missed my turn back there." He pulled into a driveway and turned the truck in the opposite direction. "Speaking of turning things around, why don't you tell me what's going on?"

She crossed her arms and turned away.

"I don't know who you are, Cadence, but God knows. I know something's wrong. You're running for a reason. Let me help."

"You can't help, John Riley," she whispered. "No one can help me."

"I disagree, but I want you to understand something. This town and these people are important. I won't let you hurt them."

"Will you tell Fredonia?"

"Not yet, but I'm deciding. Since you won't tell me who you are, I wonder why you're here. Why would a beautiful girl like you leave her home and come somewhere like this with someone she doesn't know? It doesn't add up, Miss Audley." He turned and smiled. He didn't enjoy this, but he didn't appreciate her playing him for a fool either.

They pulled into the spot next to the pink Cadillac. He helped her out of the pickup, and his heart raced when he looked into her brown eyes. He resisted the urge to pull her into his arms. She whispered, "Leave me alone, John Riley. I'll leave soon; let it go, please."

He leaned in close enough to kiss her. He smiled but knew the following sentence might ruin their tenuous friendship. She wasn't preacher's wife material—she didn't believe in God. He didn't want to hurt her, but her lies could destroy him and his people. Cadence's eyes made him weak. "Why is Taylor Nash trash?"

The color drained from her face, and she ran to the house. He stood for a moment, deciding if his question was worth the despair on her face. Too much confusion and hurt—not enough truth. He ran his fingers through his hair and sighed.

What's your plan, God?

Cadence hurried to her room, letting the screen door slam. The living room was empty.

"Why did you ask, John Riley?" She knew he wouldn't let the question go, and she couldn't pretend she was okay. Fredonia and Miss Ollie would know, and they would suspect her—not John Riley.

"I mean, he's the preacher," she said. "I'm the outsider." The pain of her losses crashed over her in a wave, and she sobbed. "I want people who love me and somewhere to call home. I don't want to worry about Taylor." She pushed her hand under the pillow—it was still there. She breathed a sigh of relief, pulled the money out, and smelled the bills. Mmmm . . . money. The answer to her problems.

What's in the envelopes? If I can read without damage, I'll see if they mention money. If they do, I'll destroy them.

She shoved the tin under the pillow. Before facing Fredonia and Miss Ollie, she needed a calm mind. She blew out several breaths and pasted on a smile. She could hide her feelings—she could fake anything.

"Fake it 'til you make it, right Audra?" she whispered.

She heard laughter—a reminder that Cadence didn't belong.

Not complicated. I don't fit here, and these people are not my friends.

She pasted on a smile. "Afternoon."

"Cadence, you're back. Everything go okay?"

She nodded, and Miss Ollie raised an eyebrow.

I swear that woman stares into my soul.

Cadence shuddered. If Miss Ollie saw her soul, she was in trouble. The afternoon's conversation made her shiver.

"The thing is, Cadence, God knows."

"You and God and everyone else can get off my back."

She squared her shoulders, pushing the thoughts away. "How can I help?"

"You feeling well?" Miss Ollie asked.

"I'm fine."

"You were shiverin' a minute ago."

"You can rest 'til supper is ready," Fredonia said.

"No. I'm fine." Cadence pasted on another smile.

Miss Ollie pushed a bowl across the table. "Potatoes need peelin'."

Cadence peeled the potatoes as if her life depended on it.

If I can get through these days and keep everything quiet, I'll go back to Deercrest with the money and rid my life of Taylor.

When she went back to Deercrest, life as Cadence, the boring would resume. Saturday thrift store excursions, Friday night dates with Thatcher, and her job at the Muddy Cup Café. Coming here was a mistake, but she would go home with the answer to her problems.

So maybe this God thing is real. See? He gave me money to pay Taylor.

Was God looking out for her by bringing her here? John Riley would say so.

How can I argue?

She peeled potatoes with a fake cheerful smile and ignored the chatter. She didn't need friendship; she needed to get back to Deercrest with the money.

Miss Ollie pushed several more potatoes across the table. "Peel a few more. John Riley eats like a growing boy."

A band of pressure squeezed Cadence's forehead. The thought of trying to survive the meal in John Riley's presence turned her stomach. If he asked questions or smiled at her with his blue eyes, she'd spill all her secrets.

Endure this meal and the next few days—survive.

She mustered another smile and finished the chore.

She survived the meal and didn't say anything stupid. John Riley acted like himself—not like someone who had dropped a bomb on her.

"Will we see you often, Miss Freddie?" John Riley asked.

"I doubt it. I'm glad I came, but there's nothing here for me."

A look passed over Miss Ollie's face.

Awww, I almost feel sorry for her.

"Nothing here for you, Miss Freddie? Oww." John Riley held his hand on his heart in mock pain. "You're gonna make me and Miss Ollie cry."

"You know Norris Creek always holds a special place in my heart, but it's not home anymore."

John Riley sighed and shook his head; he winked at Cadence. His eyes twinkled. "I guess I'll fend off Judge Crum all by myself."

"I'll fend him off with a shovel!" Miss Ollie yelled.

"What happened at the meeting?" Fredonia asked.

"A lot of yelling and threats. The board told him no."

"Who yelled and threatened?"

John Riley raised his eyebrows. "You don't know?"

"Judge Crum. Who else?" Miss Ollie snorted. "Why does he want this old place anyway?"

"Why does Judge Crum want *anything*, Miss Ollie? Pray for him." John Riley said.

"His momma did no one any favors. He's needed a good whoopin' as long as I've known him. Yer Momma loved him, Freddie, but I cain't understand why." Miss Ollie stood to collect their coffee mugs. "Anyone need a refill? Otherwise, I'll wash up and go home. I'm beat."

"Same here, Miss Ollie. I'll drop you off on my way home." John Riley stood and stretched. "You gotta quit feeding me, ladies. I feel like a stuffed pig."

"As long as you don't smell like one!" Ollie hollered from the kitchen.

"Oh, Miss Ollie, what would we do without you?" he said, laughing.

"Starve, Mr. Preacher. That's what."

"You're right, Miss Ollie—we're partners! You feed bellies, and I feed souls!" he hollered back. A snort came from the kitchen, and he laughed. "Miss Cadence, do you have a moment?"

Fredonia winked at Cadence. "What are you waiting for, Miss Cadence?"

Cadence blushed and followed John Riley outside.

Chapter 40

Norris Creek, Kentucky, 1966

Ida Bealle sat in the rocker while the black-and-white puppy chased Fredonia. The little girl screamed and giggled when the puppy knocked her down and licked her face. Ida Bealle moved to help her, but Ollie raced for the baby, pulling her into a hug.

"I okay, Mommy!" Fredonia called. Ida Bealle smiled and waved. The sun hit the toddler's blond curls like an angel in an old painting. Her chubby cheeks, pink from exercise, increased her angelic look. Her blond curls streamed behind her while she ran, and her laughs and shrieks filled Ida Bealle's heart.

What would I do without my baby? She rocked and knit a pink sweater, needles flying as she stitched.

Bud stepped out of the church and hollered, "Freddie!"

Fredonia turned and ran, holding out her hands. He picked the baby up, swinging her high in the air. Ida Bealle loved Fredonia's shrieks and Bud's deep laughter. Their joy filled the space between the church and the parsonage.

"Again, Daddy!" she yelled, and Bud swung her around. Ida Bealle imprinted the memory on her heart. Seeing her gentle, loving Bud become a father to Fredonia—or "Freddie," as he insisted—melted her heart. The little girl captured his heart, and as far as Ida Bealle could tell, he didn't complain.

"Let's get Mommy!" Bud yelled, and they raced onto the porch and grabbed her.

"You'll get my yarn dirty!" she protested.

Bud kissed her, then grabbed Fredonia and sandwiched the little girl between them. Her parents kissed each of her cheeks, and the little girl shrieked.

Ollie stepped onto the porch. "Freddie needs a nap."

"Thank you, Ollie. I'll take care of it." She turned back to kiss the little girl, but Ollie stood on the steps, frowning. "Ollie?"

Ollie shook her head and walked away.

"Bye, Miss Ollie!" Fredonia yelled. Ollie turned and waved at the baby; her smile transformed her face.

Ida Bealle sniffed the delicious baby and covered her face in kisses. "I'm gonna eat you all up like a spoonful of sugar!" She tickled Fredonia and laughed when the baby laughed.

"Do I smell cookies?" Bud sniffed the air.

"Yes, I made spritz for the children after school from the recipe Momma sent."

"Bad day?" He leaned down and kissed her.

"No, Bud. I don't have bad days anymore." She squeezed the baby and smiled at Bud. "The kids got used to stopping by, and Fredonia likes playing with them. Wilbur Crum can eat a dozen, though."

"That boy," Bud muttered. "His momma better get a tighter rein on him. One of these days, someone won't take his shenanigans lightly."

"I'm not worried about Wilbur right now, but you two need lunch, and this little lady needs a nap." She poked the baby's tummy with each word and grinned at Fredonia's giggles. "Come. I tried a new recipe from the box."

Bud groaned. "After all these years, I'm surprised there's one you haven't made. Let's hope it's not from Mrs. Ray."

Ida Bealle laughed. "I promised you I'd never cook another Mrs. Ray recipe again. Her salmon salad was enough of a surprise for a lifetime. We have beans and cornbread with kilt lettuce for lunch."

"Thank you, Mrs. Horne—it sounds delicious," Bud said and planted a kiss on her mouth.

CHAPTER 41

Cadence found John Riley leaning on the porch, staring at the church where a dim light shone. The cool breeze calmed her spirit, and she wished to stay here—right on this porch. This town and these people charmed her. She wanted John Riley to kiss her and to find a safe landing in him. She rocked in Miss Ida Bealle's chair while she waited for John Riley's speech.

I hurt so many people with my lies—people who care about me. I run from my mistakes, and I tell lies. I made up a whole new me. John Riley's out here helping people because he loves them, while I find ways to steal from people who trust me.

I don't want to lie and steal. Grandmother would feel so ashamed of me. She taught me better than this. I blamed Mom for leaving me, Grandmother for dying, Taylor for using me. But I'm not a victim. What if I face what I've done? If God exists, will he forgive me? I'm in such a giant mess, and I'm so scared.

Cadence sighed and cleared her throat. A cold knot of fear twisted in her belly, and she worried what John Riley might do. She hated her lies, but she couldn't tell the truth. She wanted to pray but brushed the temptation aside. She told John Riley that God needed to get off her back—not fair to pray now.

John Riley sat in the chair across from her. She rocked to calm herself and waited for him to scream or threaten and call her names. She knew how to deal with name-calling and threats. But this quiet man across from her unnerved her. "Well?" she said.

He sighed. "The problem is that you refuse to tell me who you are."

"I can't."

"Can't? Or *won't*?"

She wanted to tell John Riley about her miserable childhood and search for belonging, about Taylor's demands—forcing her to run; explain why she lied; tell him she loved this little town and wanted to make a home in Norris Creek; let him know how her stomach fluttered at his grin and to ask for his help. But truth meant jail, losing her reputation, her job at the café, and her friends Laura and Thatcher. Without an income there would be no cottage. Truth meant condemnation, loss, and grief. Truth meant that John Riley and Norris Creek would turn on her.

"Miss Cadence?"

She shook her head and clamped her lips shut even though her wildly beating heart said, *Tell him. Tell him. Tell him.*

If John Riley knew, he would call the authorities in Wisconsin and tell the truth about her. She wasn't ready to face the consequences. Cadence was part of her—the good part.

"Why can't you leave it alone?" she whispered, playing with a thread on her pant leg.

He ran his fingers through his hair. The sadness in his eyes twisted her heart.

"I can't, Miss Cadence. I'm glad you came, and I'm thankful you helped Miss Freddie. But I will protect her and Miss Ollie and the town. This community is strong and fierce, but some of us are vulnerable. It's my job to protect my church flock, and I will protect them until I die—no matter how beautiful the wolf appears. I don't know when you will stop the lies, but I pray for you to find the truth before it's too late. God is truth, Cadence. I know you want him to leave you alone, but he won't. He has a plan for your life, but first you have to tell the truth about who you are—and whatever you've done. Will you, please? If you can't tell me, tell whoever you wronged."

He walked to his pickup and turned when he opened the door, "You have a couple more days here. It will go better for you if you tell Miss Freddie yourself. If you don't, I will, and I can't promise what will happen. Please let Miss Ollie know I'm ready to give her a ride home."

A wave of sadness threatened to drown her. She wanted to run after John Riley and throw herself at his feet, but tears and groveling wouldn't get Taylor off her back or help her get back to Deercrest. She would look weak and foolish, so she squared her shoulders and swallowed the lump in her throat.

A car pulled into the driveway. Judge Crum got out, and she turned to hurry in.

"Wait a minute, little lady!" he called. "I need to ask you a favor!"

He stepped onto the porch and crowded her. She smelled alcohol on his breath and took a step back; her heart pounded.

"When you and Freddie are on your way back to Wesconsin, you put in a good word or two for me. Talk her into sellin' me this place." His speech slurred.

"I'm her employee, Judge Crum," she stammered. "I can't tell her anything."

The judge took another step forward. She tripped on the rocker and fell; her heart pounded, and she whimpered. Judge Crum leaned over and grabbed her arm, digging his fingers into her skin. She turned her nose away from his sour breath, frozen as he towered over her. "Please, stop!" She screamed, her voice high and shaky.

"You will tell her for me; not tell—*convince*. Do we understand each other?"

Cadence tried to calm her heart but wanted to scream for John Riley.

Can't he see this? Handsome preachers don't rescue wolves. Isn't that what he called me?

She turned to the front window. *Why don't they hear me? Where is everyone?*

The little girl deep inside panicked, the little girl who was never rescued, whose mother drove away; the little girl who searched for her grandmother after school. Her breath came in short gasps, and the judge tightened his grip, leaning closer. Tears pooled in her eyes when no one came.

I'm not worth saving.

John Riley slammed his hands on the steering wheel, unable to explain his frustration.

Does it matter what her name is? Why do I care?

He blew out a breath. The problem wasn't her name or identity. The problem was his crush on a stranger he had known for less than a week. He acted like a boy—not a grown man or a respectable preacher. He knew better than letting his heart run away so fast. Not wise, not like him at all—especially since Holly.

Why did Cadence travel with Fredonia when they were strangers? What was she hiding? Miss Freddie and Miss Ollie were safe, but he didn't lie or tolerate liars. If he told himself the truth, Cadence leaving Norris Creek tangled his emotions. He wanted her here—with him.

It didn't matter what her name was or why she had come here or what she did back home. He wanted to hold her and kiss away her hurts. He wanted to heal her pain and give her a safe place to land.

"John Riley, you are a fool," he said.

A car pulled into the yard and parked near the street—someone for Fredonia. He stared into the night in front of his truck and glanced at his watch.

What's keeping Miss Ollie?

He blew out another frustrated breath and glanced at the house. He heard an odd noise and stepped out of the pickup.

Cadence's voice drifted across the yard, "Please—let go of me!"

"Not until you say yes," Judge Crum said.

John Riley sprinted to the porch and bounded up the steps. "Judge, what's going on?"

The judge shot him a warning stare.

"None of your business, Preacher," he sneered. "The little lady and I have business."

John Riley stepped onto the porch when Judge Crum dragged Cadence into a dark corner. Judge Crum smelled of whiskey and something John Riley didn't recognize. Cadence whimpered; her terrified eyes broke John Riley's heart. He took another step.

"Step back, Blackburn. I'm still talking." He pulled Cadence farther into the corner.

"Take your hands off of Miss Audley, Judge." John Riley moved near the judge.

Judge Crum gripped Cadence's arm, and she stared at John Riley, her eyes begging for help. Her fear undid him, and he lunged for the judge's arm. Cadence slipped into the corner when the judge turned on John Riley.

He swung his fist and missed. Cadence screamed.

The porch light came on, and Miss Ollie stood in the door with a shotgun.

"What in tarnation?" Her voice was fierce. "Wilbur Crum, why are you swinging at my preacher?" Miss Ollie gazed around the porch and settled on Cadence.

"I was talking to her," the judge replied, nodding toward Cadence, "and this fool attacked me."

Miss Ollie stared at the three and sniffed the air.

"You're drunk—get on home. Don't you ever threaten my preacher." She pointed the gun at the judge, her eyes blazing. "Off the porch. Go home. Git."

Judge Crum stared at Ollie for a moment, then turned, wobbling on the steps and muttering threats.

Miss Ollie lowered the gun, and Fredonia stepped out. "What happened?"

Cadence stood in the shadows, hugging herself and shivering.

"Hey, Cadence." John Riley stepped to her and gently touched her shoulder. "You okay?"

She shook her head and blew out a breath, grimacing.

"Here. Sit." He helped Cadence to Miss Ida's chair and wrapped a blanket around her shoulders. "Did he hurt you?"

She shook her head; tears filled her eyes. "He grabbed my arm, but it didn't hurt—scared me. I didn't expect it."

"The old fool's drunk." Miss Ollie said, standing near the door, shotgun still in hand. "He's plumb lucky we don't keep bullets in Preacher Bud's gun."

"What did he say?" Fredonia asked.

"He wanted me to promise I'd talk you into selling him the house."

"I don't understand. We said 'no,'" Fredonia said.

"He feels he owns this whole valley and the mountain too. I told you he needs a shovel to the head," Miss Ollie said.

"Miss Ollie, you best not threaten the judge. What he did tonight is wrong, and we will address it, but you can't threaten an officer of the court." Anger coursed through John Riley. When he heard Cadence yell, he had run to rescue her. He tried to calm Miss Ollie, but he struggled. He too wanted to hit the judge with a shovel or talk with Preacher Bud's shotgun.

"John Riley, you get Miss Ollie home, and I'll get Cadence in bed." Fredonia took Cadence's hand. "Come. I'm so sorry. Not a good way to end a visit. I hope you won't let this color your memories because Norris Creek has many fine people."

"And one full-o'-hisself judge," Miss Ollie muttered.

"Yes," Fredonia said, guiding Cadence.

Ready, Miss Ollie?" John Riley asked. "Cadence, are you okay?"

Cadence nodded, but her red-rimmed eyes did a number on his heart.

CHAPTER 42

Norris Creek, Kentucky, 1967

Ida Bealle wrote a letter to Momma while Fredonia sat at her feet and played with blocks. A quiet knock interrupted her mid-sentence. "Wilbur Crum, you need a snack?" she asked the boy peeking through the screen.

He nodded. His red-rimmed eyes gave away his sadness. She smiled at the boy; her heart squeezed at his dejected face. "I didn't bake today, but come in. I'll see if Preacher Bud left any in the cookie jar."

He followed and plopped into a chair, swinging his feet back and forth.

"School good?"

He nodded.

"Like your teacher? Miss Bethy's a nice lady, huh?"

He nodded.

"Oh, good. Preacher Bud left two in the jar. Milk?"

He nodded.

"Cat got your tongue, Wilbur Crum?" She smiled and sat across the table. His unusual silence worried her. He always talked a mile a minute, usually over her while she taught Sunday school.

She patted his arm, but he winced and pulled away.

"Wilbur, are you okay?"

He tugged at his sleeves and turned and wiped a tear on his arm. Ida Bealle wanted this tough little boy to trust her, so she changed the subject.

"If you need Preacher Bud or me, we're here for you. You come by any time you need to talk . . . or not talk."

He nodded, and a hint of a smile turned up the corner of his mouth. He wiped the crumbs from his lips and bolted through the house to the door. "Thanks, Miss Ida Bealle."

Ida Bealle stood in the doorway as he ran down the street to Little Ivy. She wanted to find out who had hurt him and decide how to handle it. She pulled Fredonia close and kissed her cheek, praying that her little girl always knew love.

CHAPTER 43

Cadence lay in bed and sobbed, unable to sleep. The judge had scared her, but John Riley's dash to rescue her kept her awake. No one ever rescued her. She always dealt with people like Judge Crum—people who threatened and used others. She didn't cry over the judge; she cried because John Riley had rescued her. For the first time in her life, someone found her worthy of saving, and bittersweet tears flowed.

Leaving Norris Creek—and John Riley—hurt but getting Taylor off her back was worth the pain. Taylor threatened to expose all the secrets Audra hid.

When Cadence heard Fredonia's bedroom door shut, she pulled the tin from under her pillow.

"Here goes," she whispered and grabbed the envelopes. They'd leave in two days—time to decide.

If the letters mentioned the money—destroy. If not, the money was hers.

She glanced at the brittle envelopes—no dates or numbers. She closed her eyes and picked one, sliding her finger under the flap.

Dear Fredonia, December 23, 1963

My precious baby girl. Oh, how your daddy and I love you. You are a gift. I am still in awe of how God dropped you into our home and hearts as he did seven months ago. The night you came to us, your daddy came home drenched and sick. He laid in bed for three days while I took care of you. We hardly believed our blessing.

You were so tiny, and I was afraid I'd break you. We muddled through all right, you and me. We always have.

When your daddy gathered strength, I asked what happened. After the lady disappeared, he searched the whole valley, up the mountain, and Little Ivy. No one knew of a missing baby.

I told your daddy the lady gave you to us and we were keeping you—settled. He was sad, but you are the answer to my prayers—what my heart needed.

Your daddy and I prayed for a baby for more than twenty years, and I was too old. But God knew you needed us, sweet baby girl. Your daddy and I needed you more.

Most days I smile. I don't bake cookies for the neighborhood children, but they don't mind. I let them come on the porch and peek at you. They kiss you and hold your tiny fingers and tell me how beautiful you are, and it's true. You're the most beautiful baby I've ever seen.

Your daddy agrees. I always knew he'd be a good father, but when he holds you and feeds you, I love him more than ever. You have him wrapped around your little fingers. When he's with you, he can't stop smiling.

Don't ever doubt our love for you. You are our daughter, and you are perfect in every way.

And now you're crying in your crib, so I must close. God gave you strong lungs. Even when you're cranky, I smile, dear one. I'm so very thankful.

With love,

Your momma

Ida Bealle Evans Horne

Cadence's mouth fell open, and she gasped. Fredonia had talked about her childhood on the road trip. Fredonia said she was an only child and that because of her mother's age, birth was difficult for her.

"Fredonia doesn't know," Cadence whispered. "Whoa—it's the tin," she whistled.

The paper in the recipe box said, "Fredonia, find my tin. It explains everything." She remembered finding that paper and trying to decipher the meaning but didn't expect a surprise like this. She should stop— leave the tin for someone else. This secret was too big—she carried enough secrets.

But how will I know if the letters mention money?

A flicker of conscience warned her. Stealing the money escalated her crimes. She didn't have time for a conscience. Time to get free from Taylor—nothing else made sense.

Dear Sweetheart, May 23, 1968

For five years you have filled our hearts with joy. You are so very dear to your daddy and me. We live in awe and wonder that God gave you to us.

No one mentions your abrupt arrival anymore; they accept you as our sweet baby girl—and you are. No explanation needed.

We named you Fredonia Mae. I read a book with a heroine named Fredonia and always loved the name. Mae is after your father's grandmother, who helped raise him. She died before I met your father. Bud and I rarely argue, but we disagreed over your name. He says Fredonia is too big a name for such a tiny tyke and insists on calling you Freddie. Freddie is a horrible way to shorten your beautiful name, but it's his Kentucky roots. There are plenty of girls around here named Billy or Johnnie, so you fit right in.

Ollie is coming to celebrate your birthday tonight. Her name is Olivene, but she goes by Ollie. See what I mean about names around here? She's a dear young girl and loves helping me care for you. She moved to Norris Creek after you came. You were still very tiny. She cried the first time she held you. Can you believe it? I've never seen a teenager cry over holding a baby, but she's taken with you.

She helped me entertain you. I must admit that as tickled as I am to be your momma, you do tire an old woman out. Ollie helps so much—

taking you for walks and playing outdoors. She comes over almost every day, and I don't mind. I get chores done while Ollie plays with you. She's a godsend.

If I didn't know better, I'd think you love her more than you love me. You follow her around, chattering and hugging her. Buddy tells me Ollie's spent so much time with you he thinks you're starting to look alike. I laughed and asked him if he and I are starting to look alike after thirty years of marriage!

I don't know when I will give you these letters—ramblings of your old mother.

Happy birthday, Little Fredonia. We love you.

Love,

Momma

Cadence sat with the letter in her hand for several minutes. Her phone light highlighted the line that read, "You're starting to look alike." Did they?

Two more.

"I should stop," she whispered into the dark room, but she picked up the following letter and read.

Dear Baby Girl, May 23, 1973

Ten years. I can't believe what a big girl you are. Your daddy and I are so very blessed. My arms were empty before you came so long ago —a different life. I don't worry about how much older I am than the other parents until I pick you up at school and see the young mothers. I hope I don't embarrass you, sweetheart. I laugh when I realize I have a ten-year-old child and I'm so very old. My laughter is amazement and happiness, like Sarah in the Bible.

I waited so very long for you. Only God and I know the prayers I prayed and the tears I cried.

Your daddy and I do not argue, but we have a long-standing disagreement. He wants to tell you how you came to us, and I do not. What if you feel insecure and unwanted? You are the most wanted child in the history of the world. Your dad says we must tell the truth. He's a man of integrity, and the truth is so essential to him—me too, but this isn't lying—it's loving. When we disagree, he's disappointed. I know the secret is difficult for him, but I'm not sorry; I'm thankful. I told him I prayed and God provided. He always tells me—"God answers prayer." I agree.

I save my egg money in a tin for you. We don't have a lot, and I'm sure you know that. We're blessed compared to many here, but we aren't well off. The church doesn't pay your daddy much, but God always provides. The church voted on whether or not I was allowed chickens in the backyard. (Can you believe it? Everyone else keeps chickens, but they vote to decide if the preacher's wife can have chickens.) Your daddy sells eggs in town once a week, and I set it aside for you. I've added some of the spending money he gives me. I don't know when I'll give it to you or how you'll spend it—your wedding? Our wedding was beautiful, and I wanted you to have a beautiful wedding too. Whenever the time comes, I pray that you will find a man who loves you as your daddy loves me. He's a wonderful man, baby girl.

Love,
Momma

Cadence slid the letter into the envelope. Her conscience niggled—not Miss Ida Bealle's egg money. She warred for a brief moment but made up her mind—to destroy the letters.

She glanced at the last letter and blew out a breath. Too late to respect Miss Ida Bealle's privacy. She opened the flap.

Dear Freddie, May 23, 1981

Your daddy and I agreed we'd tell you how you came to us after your eighteenth birthday. Imagine our surprise when you left us before we told you.

I know you say you are happy with your husband in the north, and I trust you, but I'm so sad you didn't tell us. We wouldn't have stopped you, but we may have asked you to wait a little longer.

I don't know how to tell you the story. Does it matter now? Your daddy doesn't know what to do either. Perhaps he was right when he said you needed to know long ago.

I've kept the egg money for you and added more. You won't need it from what you tell me, but I can't spend it.

We love you. You will always remain our precious baby girl—our miraculous gift from God.

Love,

Momma

Cadence tucked the letter into the envelope, and her mind raced. Miss Ida Bealle's heartfelt letters didn't change her situation.

Taylor demanded the money in two days, and the only money in her possession was Ida Bealle's egg money.

"Fredonia doesn't need it," she whispered. "She lives in a mansion; fifteen thousand dollars doesn't faze Fredonia. For me the money means freedom. It gets Taylor off my back and keeps my secret safe."

She tried to sleep, but John Riley's handsome smile flashed through her mind. She loved this little town and its people. She liked cranky Miss Ollie, who called her a Yankee and didn't trust her because she wanted to protect Fredonia—her baby.

"How will I ride to Wisconsin with Fredonia and keep this secret?" She sat up. "I can't do it."

She held the tin on her lap, hesitating. Audra never hesitated when choosing survival. Audra never cared whom she hurt, but Cadence struggled. Taking the money meant stealing from Miss Ida Bealle and Fredonia and lying to John Riley. It meant she wasn't a small-time thief, and she wasn't any better than a lost kid looking out for number one.

"What's the matter with me? Help," she whispered. "Are you out there, God?" Her heart hammered in her chest.

I love you, Audra.

"God?" she whispered. She lay down, hugging the tin. Her conscience kept her awake.

Stealing the money is wrong.

"I need to get Taylor off my back one last time, please. There's no other way. I won't steal after this time." She fell asleep, wishing her burdens away.

CHAPTER 44

Cadence woke after a fitful night, conflicted. The money in the tin was more than she needed for Taylor. But when she touched the money, her chest tightened and her stomach lurched. She had never wrestled with right and wrong before. She had done whatever was necessary to care for herself.

She ran her hands through her hair. *Can I betray Miss Ida Bealle? Fredonia? John Riley?*

John Riley's blue eyes stilled her heart. His laughter and dazzling smile turned her into a schoolgirl with a hopeless crush. His disapproval played on repeat, his quiet "Who are you?" and the sad shake of his head when she refused to answer.

"Why does it matter who I am, John Riley?" she whispered. "You're a good man. Forget about me. Fredonia and I will leave soon, and you'll never see me again. People like you don't need people like me tangled up in your life."

She stared at the tin next to her pillow. When Fredonia and Miss Ollie went to church, she would destroy the letters and hide the tin in the cellar. But with the church full of people, someone might notice her dragging the ladder through the yard.

Think. How do I get rid of this?

Fredonia knocked. "Joining us this morning, Cadence?" she called.

"No. Not today."

"Breakfast is on the table if you care to join me for coffee before I leave."

"Be right down."

Cadence shoved the tin under her pillow and smoothed the blanket over the bed, whispering a timid prayer as she hurried to breakfast.

Please don't let me give anything away.

Fredonia sat at the table, sipping a steaming mug of coffee. "Morning. Miss Ollie's been busy." The scent of cinnamon and yeast floated through the kitchen. Fredonia held up a saucer with a fat cinnamon roll—thick frosting oozed over the side. "They're delicious."

She glanced at Fredonia and Miss Ollie. The weight of the secret unsettled her.

Miss Ollie stared. "Yer lookin' rough this morning. Better drink two cups of coffee." She snickered and pulled a pan of rolls from the oven.

Fredonia patted the chair next to her. "Come eat."

Miss Ollie frosted the cinnamon rolls, and Cadence studied her profile. *Do they look alike? I don't want this secret.*

She held the mug of coffee, ignoring the cinnamon roll.

I'm going to throw up. How will I get through this and keep Miss Ida Bealle's secret?

Miss Ollie and Fredonia chatted and bantered back and forth. Miss Ollie slung sarcastic comments, and Fredonia laughed and replied with equal sarcasm.

Cadence stared at the mug. Miss Ollie read her soul, and she wanted to keep Miss Ollie from reading her mind today.

Fredonia pushed back from the table. "John Riley called. Asked me to pick up Tansy for church. Her car's actin' up."

When they were alone in the kitchen, Cadence asked, "Did you ever have children, Miss Ollie?"

Miss Ollie iced the rolls, and her hand stilled. She gazed to the door and shook her head. "I never married," she said, her voice low.

Cadence prodded, "Come on, Miss Ollie. People have children without getting married."

Miss Ollie shook her head, and her chin trembled. "Not around these parts, Cadence. Not good Christian girls." A shadow crossed her face.

"You should tell her," Cadence whispered.

Miss Ollie turned and stared at Cadence. She untied the apron and ran from the kitchen. "I'm gonna be late for church."

Cadence peeked around the house for a spot to hide the tin. Miss Ida Bealle's egg money was safe. She had changed last night when she prayed her "help me" prayer. Maybe God had spoken to her, maybe not, but she had changed. No stealing. No betraying Fredonia

I lied about my name and why I came, but I won't ruin my life by stealing Miss Ida Bealle's egg money. Hide this tin, finish helping Fredonia, and get back to Wisconsin, Cadence. Forget about Norris Creek, Kentucky, and Miss Ollie and the handsome preacher. I'll work for Laura and figure out a way to pay Taylor. There's a way.

She remembered the stack of boxes in the closet under the stairs. "Help me choose what's right." She was somber and reflective—the secret heavy.

What changed? Why do I want to live a good life now?

She stood frozen, wanting to do the right thing, but this fit like a shrunken sweater—her chest tight and her arms numb. The sampler leaned against the wall, mocking her. "The truth will set you free."

Time for truth. I've lived a lie far too long.

Leaving the tin behind meant Taylor won. She glanced at her watch. Taylor expected to knock on her door in an hour and gather money.

What will she do when I'm not there?

Yesterday she planned to text Taylor and ask her to pick up the money in a few days—more time. Now? No idea. Taylor's threats carried consequences, and Cadence worried.

She held Ida Bealle's tin, remembering Laura, Thatcher, and her cozy cottage stuffed with vintage treasures. Comfort and safety—as when she lived with Grandmother Miggs. She knew Laura wouldn't understand her mess, and Thatcher couldn't help. He would have to arrest her. Hiring an attorney was out of the question. Legal counsel cost more than Taylor demanded. But she wouldn't take the egg money no matter what—even if Taylor turned her in.

She clutched the tin. Her mind raced.

I wish I were the person my friends think I am—a person John Riley might love. Can you help me, God? I want to do the right thing, but I'm scared. I don't know what will happen.

Tears rolled down her cheeks. She cried for the young girl who watched her mother drive away. She cried for the little girl carted off to foster care when Grandmother Miggs died. She cried for the teenager who fell for a rich girl's manipulation. She cried for all her lies. Then she cried because she was in love with a preacher who needed to stay far away from a girl like her.

What about Miss Ida Bealle? She was a good person who loved God, and people admired her, but she had lied.

Hiding my story doesn't mean I'm evil. If Ida Bealle can do it, I can too. What if God meant the money for me? Another person with lies to hide.

She wrestled. She wanted to leave the money, but she wanted to return to her quiet life in Deercrest. It was impossible to do both.

She thought of John Riley running onto the porch to rescue her from Judge Crum's grasp. She blushed, remembering the intensity in his gaze when he checked on her. Leaving the money meant she was one step closer to the kind of girl John Riley might love.

I can learn. But do preachers marry jailbirds? What will I do?

The weight of secrets and lack of choices numbed her and concentrating was difficult.

"I'm leaving the money," she said out loud in the empty house.

I'll hide the tin, and when she finds it I'll pretend I never saw it. It's the only way.

She ran to the closet and pulled the door open before she changed her mind. She reached for the light chain when the screen door slammed.

No!

Fredonia popped her head around the closet door.

"Forgot my Bible."

Cadence smiled, straining to appear calm.

"Oh! Mother's tin. Where did you find it?" Fredonia grabbed the tin, and a huge smile lit her face. "Why don't you rest while we're at church?"

Cadence's heart sunk—no way to steal Miss Ida's egg money now. "I found it on the ledge up there." Cadence pointed to the shelf at the end of the closet. The lie formed with lightning speed. "I decided to clear these out for you and searched to find what I missed and spied it behind the shelf bracket. Took me a minute to get it down."

True—it did take a minute to get the tin down.

"I'm so glad. Oh, John Riley's joining us for dinner after church. We'll talk about finishing and getting home. Take it easy while I'm gone." She smiled, disappearing around the corner.

Cadence sat on the boxes and sighed. She enjoyed the slower pace and scenery in Norris Creek. Miss Ollie kept them fed with delicious food, and John Riley's handsome face kept her stomach fluttering. Staying here and ignoring Taylor might work, but jobs were scarce. Miss Ollie tormented her, and the idea of living near John Riley twisted her heart.

"Home it is." She said to the empty closet. "Home to jail and life as an outcast." A strangled laugh escaped. "If I don't laugh, I'll cry."

She pulled the chain to turn the light off. "I do not want to be here when Fredonia reads those letters."

Cadence had enjoyed time with Fredonia as they traveled and worked together. She had softened as the days passed. Her accent had thickened each day in Kentucky. Fredonia had relaxed from the stiff, formal woman Cadence met at the mansion, and Cadence wanted to keep her for a friend.

Until she finds out I'm a thief. Wealthy ladies don't want thieves for friends.

Music from the church floated through the window. She wished she had accepted Fredonia's invitation. Sitting through the church service meant more time near John Riley.

The worst part of going home to Deercrest was leaving John Riley behind.

The truth of who she was and all she hid bothered her for the first time. She wished she were innocent and free.

If I weren't a thief, I'd tell you I love you, John Riley.

Sadness crushed her chest, and she gasped. Tears stung her eyes, but she refused to cry. No more time for tears. Time to go home and push Norris Creek and John Riley behind her.

<h1 style="text-align:center">CHAPTER 45</h1>

Norris Creek, Kentucky, 1968
Ida Bealle clutched pink fabric to her chest while re-threading the Singer sewing machine. Between Freddie's fast growth and love of dirt, Ida Bealle kept busy clothing her daughter.

Bud sat across from her. "We need to talk," he said. His voice was steady but severe.

When she let go of the foot pedal, the machine stopped whirring. She crossed her hands in her lap, willing herself calm. She knew what he was about to say.

"Ida Bealle, you've noticed, haven't you?"

She knew for years but refused to admit the truth. She shook her head and pushed the foot pedal, sliding the pink fabric under the needle.

"Ida Bealle," he whispered. He peered under the top of the sewing machine and gazed into her eyes.

"No, Bud, I haven't noticed a thing." She bit her lip and pushed the pedal to the floor. The sewing machine hummed, and the table shook.

She wanted the sound to drown out her husband's words and quiet the pain in her chest.

Bud stepped behind her, rested his hands on her shoulders, and massaged her knots. She leaned her head on his chest and blew out the breath she held.

He leaned down and kissed the top of her head. "Freddie and Ollie have the same nose."

"The same eyes," Ida Bealle whispered.

Bud kissed her hair again. "The same fire in their eyes when they're angry."

"Ollie was the girl I saw at the Christmas pageant," Ida Bealle whispered.

Bud pulled out a chair. He held her hand, tracing circles on her thumb. "You've known all this time?"

She nodded, but her breath hitched when she tried to hide her emotions. "Not at first, Bud. But when I saw Ollie hold Freddie the first time, I knew."

"Honey," he said in his gentle voice.

"I wanted her." The dam weakened; her heart boiled with shame and anger and a desperate fear of losing Freddie.

"We need to tell Ollie, sweetheart." He ran his hands through his thick hair and blew out a sigh. He paced the kitchen while Ida Bealle stared at the pink fabric, willing her tears to stop.

"The truth sets us free, Ida Bealle. Truth. I've staked my entire life and ministry on integrity, honesty, and the truth of God's Word. We can't hide this. You know she's not even ours legally."

Ida Bealle jumped up and pointed. "Don't you ever say she's not ours, Bud Horne! Do you want the truth? The truth is that they gave her to us—gave her. They knocked on our door and handed her over like a loaf of bread. They didn't want her, and we did. It's that simple. Don't you talk about truth and integrity. I'd die for her, and anyone who thinks they're taking Freddie from me might die too." The dam had broken, and emotions spilled. She sobbed, wetting the pink fabric. "How old was she, Bud? Thirteen? Thirteen isn't old enough for mothering." She hiccupped. Her nose ran, and tears poured down her cheeks. "She doesn't deserve a child—I do."

Bud rubbed his face and paced. "Honey, we didn't adopt her. We took her in, but we can't pretend she's ours when we know Ollie's her mother."

"You listen, Bud Horne—I'm her mother, and we will never speak of this again." She folded the pink fabric, unplugged the machine, and ran upstairs. When she passed her new sampler, Ida Bealle gritted her teeth. "The truth will set you free" hung on the wall, mocking her with its delicate flowers and even stitches. Ida Bealle had worked on the flowers and verse for months, but the sight of it made her chest heave. She jerked it off the wall and turned it backward. *I'll hide it in the storm cellar until I get rid of it.*

CHAPTER 46

The clock struck eleven. Taylor would show up at her house in Deercrest within the hour. Fredonia and Miss Ollie would come home from church soon. Her life crumbled beneath her.

She turned off her phone and paced the living room.

I can't fix this mess. I'm powerless. Everyone I care about will discover my lies. Where will I go? Does it matter if I never have a home?

She tried to convince herself that starting over didn't matter, but it did. This town and these people had changed her. She wanted a peaceful, authentic life—not a facade.

She paced and chewed on her lip, wiping sweaty hands on her jeans. *Survive lunch with John Riley and get Fredonia's reaction to the letters out of the way. Pretend I don't know and go home. Rid my life of Taylor —somehow. But all I want is a life with John Riley.*

She clenched her fists. Cadence was a stick in the river tossing and turning, powerless to stop the forces pushing her.

Ask God for help.

Her skin tingled, and she shook her head. She whispered a few quick prayers this week in case God was out there or cared about her.

"God," she whispered in a shaky voice, "I need help. Please." And since she didn't know what words might get God's attention, she added, "Pretty please." Nothing. She sighed and paced. The embroidered sampler she had found in the storm cellar leaned against the wall, mocking her, "The truth will set you free."

She laughed. "The truth is I lie, and I steal. *That* won't set me free." She plopped onto the couch, trying to plan. When they returned from church, the afternoon would pass in a blur—no time for decisions.

She read the words out loud—"the truth." A ludicrous idea crossed her mind, crazy as her idea of staying in Norris Creek and marrying John Riley.

She shook her head. "Think, Cadence. What are my options?"

Tell the truth. Tell the truth. Tell the truth.

"I should call Thatcher."

⁓ e l l ⁓

Taylor knocked on Audra's door. She had planned to play nice and pretend she was happy to see Audra.

Hey, girl. Good to see you. Stopping by to grab that gift.

She pasted on her sugar-sweet smile and knocked again. After three knocks, she peeked through the front window. The house was dark. She walked to the door near the driveway, pasted on her sweet smile, and knocked again.

Nothing.

She pulled out her phone. The chick at the coffee shop had turned over Audra's number without question. Taylor smirked.

People in these hick towns are stupid.

"Hey, I'm here—at the back door." No answer. Taylor tapped her toes.

I can stand here all day or let myself in. I bet her alarm didn't go off this morning.

Taylor twisted the door handle. Locked. She stepped into the backyard. The kitchen window was too high to climb in without anyone seeing her. The basement window on the far side of the air conditioning unit seemed promising. The bushes in the yard might cover enough to squeeze through the window before anyone noticed.

No more nice girl.

Taylor smashed her phone against the locked window and smiled as glass clattered to the cement below. She laid her sweater on the edge of the window and dropped to the basement floor.

Officer Thatcher Stevens stood in the doorway of Cadence's home. The chaos in the room was a sucker punch. Cadence's clean, organized home lay in shambles. He stepped across the threshold, picking his way around glass and overturned furniture. An officer stepped out of the hallway.

"Back here." He led Thatcher to the kitchen. "It seems there was a struggle of some sort, but we can't tell which door they exited."

Thatcher searched the kitchen. Cupboard doors stood open and canisters spilled onto the floor. A puddle of water mixed with flour and sugar from the canisters. A red substance had smeared across the flipped table and chairs in the middle of the kitchen. The red substance splattered everywhere, giving the room an eerie feel.

The officer pointed at the wall. "Loser."

Thatcher stepped close. "Blood?"

The officer shrugged. "Pretty sure it's paint."

"Where's Cadence?" he peeked through the back window. "Is she outside?"

"Cadence?" The officer stared.

"The homeowner? Where is she?"

"No one's here."

Thatcher Stevens never panicked at a crime scene before, but today might be an exception. He took a deep breath, "Find the homeowner. Who called this in?"

"I'll check with dispatch. All I know is we got a call—possible disturbance at this address. Hutchens and I were in the neighborhood. The back door was wide open. No one answered, so we entered when we saw red on the floor."

"Did you search for her?"

"We secured the premises."

"Get Hutchens, and the two of you search every inch of this property. Upstairs, downstairs, basement, garage. I want to know she's not here before I make calls."

The officer disappeared, and Thatcher stood in the kitchen, his heart pounding.

"Cadence, where are you?"

Turning herself in might work. Beat Taylor at her own game. Cadence smiled, imagining Taylor's rage. She was ready to tell the truth and reclaim her identity.

"I'm not scared anymore," she whispered. "No more lying."

Well, a little scared—jail.

She exhaled and started a pep talk for courage. "You can do this. It's Thatcher. Do it."

The screen door slammed, and Cadence jumped. "Where is it?" Miss Ollie demanded.

"What?"

"You know, Cadence—the tin. Give it to me."

"Over there." Cadence shrugged. "Fredonia knows about it; she was happy to see it."

"Where was it?"

"On the shelf in the closet under the stairs."

"No—I searched every day since Ida Bealle died."

"How did you know?"

"Everyone knew. The tin sat in the living room, and everyone heard how Ida Bealle saved egg money for fifty years for Freddie. Why do you think Judge Crum's been nosing 'round here? He thinks she saved more money than she did."

"Why do you want it?"

Miss Ollie turned, and anger flashed. "It's not the money. You weren't supposed to find this—no one was. Ida Bealle and I agreed to keep our secret, but she never destroyed those stupid letters. She said if Freddie found the tin, she'd learn the secret, and if she never did, she trusted God's will. If I knew where she hid it, I'd have taken care of it long ago."

"Well, I found it, so I guess God wanted her to know," Cadence challenged.

Miss Ollie grabbed the tin and pried off the lid; money and papers spilled across the floor.

"What have you done?" Ollie screamed and dropped to the floor, grabbing money. Cadence bent to help, but Ollie pushed her, and a strangled sob escaped. "You've ruined everything."

They jumped when Fredonia said, "Ladies?"

Miss Ollie turned to Fredonia, tears rolling down her face. "The girl was pilfering through this. I tried to take it from her, but she pushed me."

"Cadence?" Fredonia gasped. "What in the world?"

Cadence's mouth gaped. She had searched the tin—no denying it. But push an old woman?

"I . . . I . . ." she stammered.

Fredonia shook her and reached to help Miss Ollie. Ollie turned to Cadence and raised her eyebrows; a slight smile lifted the corner of her lips. "I'll be okay, Freddie. Jest help me to Ida Bealle's chair. I'll sit a spell before I set out dinner."

Freddie frowned and settled Ollie into the chair. She shook her head at Cadence and crossed her arms.

John Riley knocked twice and opened the screen, "I don't smell dinner. We eating sandwiches, Miss Ollie?"

"Ollie took a tumble, John Riley. We're getting her settled." She shook her head when Ollie opened her mouth.

The money from the tin scattered across the room—no letters.

Did Miss Ollie grab them? Where are they?

Ollie sat in the chair, her hand over her heart. If Fredonia and John Riley believed she had pushed an old woman, they would believe any story. Anyone who hurt an old woman was capable of far worse crimes. Cadence hadn't hurt Ollie, but Audra had hurt many people.

"Cadence and I can pick up lunch. No need to cook," John Riley suggested.

Ollie jumped up. "You ain't feedin' us slop from the diner. No. I'm jest fine. Give me a few minutes." She hurried into the kitchen, and John Riley followed.

"Let me help."

Fredonia turned, "Cadence?"

"I did *not* push her, Fredonia."

"I don't understand why she accused you if you didn't."

Cadence shrugged.

Fredonia's lips set in a thin line. She gazed around the room, and her eyebrows rose as she bent to collect the scattered money.

"Ollie?" Fredonia called as she tucked the bills into the tin. "Can you come here, please?"

Miss Ollie hobbled into the room; John Riley followed behind. He smiled at Cadence from behind Miss Ollie. Her heart lurched.

When he knows, he'll never smile at me again.

Cadence stepped away when her phone buzzed, but she ignored it.

"Miss Ollie, do you have any idea why my mother hid this much money in the house?"

"Egg money."

Fredonia frowned. "Egg money?"

"She saved her egg money for you for when you grew up."

Fredonia sat down in the rocker, clutching the tin. "But it's so much. She never told me."

"You ran off with that boy," Miss Ollie said.

Fredonia nodded. "I didn't need this." A tear rolled down her cheek, and she dabbed it with her sleeve.

"She'd saved it for you since you were a baby but didn't know what to do when you left. She kept adding money 'til she died."

Fredonia's eyes narrowed. "Did you know about this, John Riley?"

He nodded. "Yes, ma'am, Miss Freddie. Everyone knew. She said she saved it for your wedding, and then she chuckled."

Fredonia glanced between John Riley and Miss Ollie. "There are thousands of dollars in here." She snapped the lid tight. "I wish she had spent it."

"I 'spect it's why Judge Crum's been nosin' 'round here." Miss Ollie said.

Fredonia covered her eyes and exhaled. "His mother should have done us all a favor and taught him to be a decent human."

"Miss Freddie, I have a safe in the church office. Want me to lock it up 'til you leave?"

Fredonia nodded. "Or until I figure out what she wanted me to do with it. Why wasn't there a note?"

Cadence noticed Miss Ollie's face flush red as she hurried to the kitchen. "Somethin's burnin'!" she hollered.

CHAPTER 47

Norris Creek, Kentucky, 1978

"Is something' burnin' in here, Momma?" Freddie walked into the kitchen and sniffed the air. She reached over her father's arm and grabbed a cupcake as she plopped into a chair. "What were you two talking about?"

Her mom turned away, but Daddy's eyes crinkled when he smiled. "Parent stuff, Freddie. What have you been doing?"

She wiped frosting off the top and licked her finger. "School, homework, the usual. Hey, Miss Ollie wants me to help her at the café next week. She says I can get a job in the kitchen." She munched the cupcake and calculated her potential earnings.

"I'll check it out, sweetie," he said and kissed her cheek. "Your momma needs help with these cupcakes for Sunday school tomorrow. Why don't you grab an apron and help her out? I'm double-checking that the church is clean."

"These are good, Mom. Where'd ya get the recipe?" she swiped another cupcake.

"If you keep eating my cupcakes, Freddie, I'll need to bake another batch." Mom shook her spatula and blew a kiss. "Recipe's in the red box."

Freddie slid the box across the table. A ding or two in the corners and some scuffs on the bottom showed the age. Papers and cards stuck out. As Freddie flipped through the cards, she groaned and screamed at the recipe names. "Mother, who eats this stuff?" she asked, giggling and gagging. "'Tuna and Pea Supreme'?"

"The Ladies' Missionary Society at my home church filled it with recipes when I married your daddy. I can't bear tossing the awful recipes because they were a gift of love when I moved away from my home and family."

"As long as you don't *cook* these!" Freddie said, wrinkling her nose. "Was it hard when you moved here, Mom?"

"A little . . . but I was in love with your daddy."

Freddie made retching sounds and jumped up, "Okay, enough of the lovey-dovey stuff. I have homework." She kissed her parents and bounded up the stairs two at a time, hoping that when she found her true love, he was like Daddy.

Chapter 48

Cadence hoped she found true love someday, but for now, she ignored her feelings for the handsome preacher.

"Walk with me to lock this up?" John Riley asked.

She followed him into the sunshine wishing she was the kind of girl John Riley wanted. If she stayed in this peaceful town, she would sit on Miss Ida's porch and listen to the birds, eat Tansy's donuts, and tolerate Miss Ollie.

Why did she lie? I didn't touch her.

Norris Creek had wormed its way into her heart, but they would consider her worse than a Yankee if they knew.

"Beautiful day the Lord made." He turned and smiled. "Missed you at preaching this morning. Thought you'd try it out at least once—since you're leavin' and all."

"I'm not much for church. You know that."

He shrugged. "A guy can hope, Miss Cadence." He reached in his pocket for the church keys. "Here—do you mind? My hands are full."

She twisted the key in the heavy brass lock.

"Follow me. The safe's on the back wall behind my books."

Behind the books. Original.

While he entered the code for the safe, Cadence turned away. She didn't want any blame if this money disappeared.

Funny since I planned to steal it not long ago.

"All done. I have a question, Miss Cadence." He stepped close, and she smelled his cologne—woodsy with a hint of citrus.

She wanted to inhale and say, "Mmm." Her heart pounded; all her resolve to go back to Wisconsin and forget him slipped away. If she told him the truth, John Riley would never smile at her like this again.

"Would you mind if I called when you get back home?"

"Why?"

"Check on you. I'm worried."

She swallowed disappointment. John Riley wanted to check up on her, not kiss her.

What a stupid fool you are, Cadence!

"I don't know, John Riley. I don't see the point. You're busy here. I'm busy there." She shrugged.

"I see. Well, I'll pray for you then, Cadence."

"Pray for me?" Her disappointment morphed to anger. "For me to be a good little Christian? I don't need your prayers." She swallowed over the lump in her throat—no time for tears or John Riley's prayers.

I need to call Thatcher before I lose my courage.

Thatcher would learn the truth tomorrow, but she wanted to hide her deceptions from John Riley.

I'll never be Cadence. I'll always be Audra, the kid who got herself in trouble. I'm not worth your time. I'll ruin your life.

"You get lost?" a voice shouted from the auditorium.

"Lockin' your money up tight, Miss Freddie."

Fredonia stepped into the office, and Cadence blushed.

How will I ride home in that pink Cadillac without spilling secrets?

Her phone buzzed, and Cadence frowned.

"Something wrong?" Fredonia asked.

"Not sure." She shrugged and hurried through the sanctuary.

She expected calls from Taylor, but the other notifications left her unsettled.

Why had Thatcher called so many times?

Fredonia waited a moment. John Riley's face turned from her—as if he were hiding.

"She's not right for you, John Riley. She's not from around here, and Norris Creek isn't a town that lets strangers in."

"Miss Ida Bealle did fine."

Fredonia nodded, "Yes, the 1940s was a different time. I hate saying this, but she's hiding something. Good or bad? Hurt? I don't know, but I want you to use caution."

John Riley nodded. "Fair enough, Miss Freddie. Thank you."

"Plus, from what I gather, Tansy's got eyes for you."

John Riley smiled. "Oh, Miss Freddie, speaking of, she's not right for me—"

"I hear her donuts are excellent."

"That they are, Miss Freddie."

She waited while he locked the church doors. "We'll leave early Tuesday morning. I'll leave directions with Miss Ollie for the items left behind. You won't have much work before the parsonage is ready for you to move in."

"I'll enjoy living near the church, but it won't be the same without Miss Ida Bealle's furniture. I won't recognize the place."

"They lived there a long time. When Momma came as a new bride in 1940, Norris Creek was different—the world was different." She sighed.

John Riley patted her back. "Hard to let go?"

Fredonia nodded. She didn't often cry over the loss of her parents, but packing up was final. Too real.

"You know you can visit anytime, right?"

Fredonia nodded. "I'll pop in when you least expect it."

"Perfect. I'll hold you to it, Miss Freddie." He smiled, and Fredonia squeezed his hand.

"You're a good man, John Riley."

Cadence's heart pounded. She grunted while she tugged at the stubborn suitcase zipper and bit her lip to stop herself from swearing in Miss Ida Bealle's house.

"Come on!" she screamed at the zipper. She slipped when the zipper broke. Her eyes stung, but she refused to cry. She grabbed the suitcase and threw it across the room. The bag left a long red streak on the wall as it clattered to the floor. When she had called Thatcher, he reported her vandalized cottage and demanded she return for an interview in his office.

"Taylor Nash!" she yelled into the empty room. "You ruined my life, and now you destroyed my home! My home wasn't yours to ruin!" She slid down the wall and sat next to her broken suitcase. Memories of Taylor overwhelmed her—mean looks, taunts, manipulation.

Cadence bit her lip, and angry tears stung her eyes. She buried her face in her hands. She needed to get to Deercrest and clean up her destroyed home. If she survived her interview with Thatcher, she would take care of Taylor Nash—somehow.

Death is too good for you, Taylor.

"It's a mess, Cadence," Thatcher said. "We sopped up the water but left the rest. You can deal with it after we talk. Can you explain why you're in Kentucky and no one knew? I thought you were sick."

"I can't explain over the phone, but I will tell you, Thatcher."

"In my office tomorrow morning." His words clipped—nothing like her Friday night bowling buddy. He wasn't pleased, but she was a trophy winner when it came to disappointing people.

"Cadence?" John Riley stood at the door. "What happened?" He glanced around. "I heard a thump and thought you fell."

"John Riley, will you take me to the airport? Someone broke into my house, and the police officer wants me there for an interview by tomorrow morning —I'm leaving now."

"Whoa. Of course." He reached for her hand and helped her stand. He gathered her clothes from around the room and piled them onto the bed. "This won't survive the trip, Miss Cadence." The broken suitcase dangled from his finger.

Cadence found a late flight and booked the last seat while Fredonia stuffed her clothes into a suitcase with a working zipper. Miss Ollie sat in the corner of the living room staring at Cadence.

Fredonia waved. "I don't know what's going on, Cadence, but you're upset. If the officer said he wants you in Deercrest tomorrow, then you must go. I'll call on you when I get home."

An hour later, John Riley and Cadence hopped into his pickup truck. Cadence glanced at Cici as John Riley backed out of the driveway. She imagined Taylor smashed under the pink beast, but this time the image made her ill.

I'm sick of my lies, the hiding, and running. I don't know how to fix this mess, but I can't live like this anymore.

"Miss Cadence, can I pray for you?"

She nodded, too weary to protest.

"Dear Lord, Miss Cadence needs your care. She's upset and scared because something's wrong at home. I can see she carries heavy burdens. Please surround her with your comfort and peace and help her know she's a beloved soul. Help her know your love and strengthen her for what lies ahead. Your word says she can turn to you anytime and ask for forgiveness and grace. In the precious name of Jesus. Amen."

She stared at him, stunned.

"What?"

"You said I'm a beloved soul."

"Oh, Miss Cadence, you are. Jesus went to the cross and paid for your sins. Mine too." He grinned his schoolboy grin, and her heart skipped a beat. "We all sin. You, me, Miss Freddie, Miss Ollie, Judge Crum."

"Especially Judge Crum," she said, remembering his fingers around her arm.

"That's where you're mistaken. Judge Crum is a sinner, but his sins are no worse than mine."

"What have you done, John Riley?" Cadence stared at the handsome preacher. "You're so religious."

He chuckled, "My goal in life is to point people to God, but I'm not religious, Miss Cadence."

"You're the most religious person I know. You're a preacher, for crying out loud."

"I lied, stole, lusted, and murdered."

Cadence gasped. "You murdered someone?"

"In my heart. I wanted to kill someone. Jesus says it's the same as murder."

"You're a liar?"

"Yes, ma'am. I am. With the Lord's help, I don't lie like I did in the past. I don't steal or cheat anymore, but I did those things, Miss Cadence. I'm a wretch."

She grinned, "I don't believe you're a wretch."

"I am. God called me to preach his Word and share his love. But without his strength . . . without him changing me, I'm a horrible person. I was a horrible person. God did a wonderful work in me when he reached down and pulled me out of my mess. I gummed things up so bad nothin' could fix what I'd done."

Would he understand?

"Brother Bud kept after me. He'd visit me in jail and tell me 'Jesus loves you, John Riley Blackburn. You can keep messing up, but God has a plan for you, and this isn't it.' He was right. Failure and defeat wasn't part of God's plan for me."

"You were in jail?"

"Drinking. I got myself in trouble when I drank."

Cadence shook her head. "I don't believe you."

"Well, it's the gospel truth. My momma gave up on me. I was failing in school. The sheriff blamed me for everything happening around town—most of the trouble was caused by others, but I gave up. I figured that if the sheriff blamed me for all the bad in town, I might as well have fun doing some of it."

Cadence laughed.

"Why, Miss Cadence, I believe you're laughin' at me! I'm shocked." A smile pulled up the corner of his mouth. "I wouldn't pull your leg. Promise."

"What made a difference?"

"Preacher Bud. He'd sit outside my cell and preach. He saw potential in me and loved me through my mess. One day everything he said clicked."

"Then what happened?"

"I told the Lord I'd quit drinking and running around. I said, 'Okay, Lord—I'll do whatever you want but don't ask me to preach."

"Oh, John Riley!" Cadence giggled.

"Yep. The Lord has a sense of humor. He took a bad teenage hillbilly boy and made him a preacher. But I'm thankful he did, Miss Cadence. I'm thankful."

"John Riley?"

"Yes, Miss Cadence?"

"My name's not Cadence."

He nodded and kept his eyes on the road. "I know, Miss Cadence."

CHAPTER 49

"My name is Audra." She turned away. "When I talk to the officer tomorrow, I'll tell him what I've done. He's my friend, but what I say will hurt him. I will hurt everyone—my boss, her kids."

"Does the break-in at your house have anything to do with this?"

"Yes, and I'm scared," she said with a sigh and blew out years of pent-up rage and sadness. Without that anger, she felt like a deflated balloon. "I'll go to jail."

"Jail is hard, but if it's what you have to do to set things right, you'll survive. I'm not disappointed in you."

His words soothed her pain. "You're not?"

"No. I can't hold it against you because I got in trouble with the law when I was younger. Audra is a beautiful name, by the way."

She smiled. "Thank you, John Riley." He reached over and squeezed her hand.

His kindness gave her strength, and hope bubbled in her soul—a tiny bubble, but it was hope.

He parked near the departures sign and hopped out of the truck with her bag. He stepped close, and for a split second she hoped he would kiss her, but he stepped back and nodded.

"Miss Audra, you go in there tomorrow and confess whatever you need to say. I'll pray for you. Can you do me the favor of letting me or Miss Freddie know how things go for you? I'd appreciate it."

"I will." She hurried into the airport terminal before her tears fell.

Audra leaned her head on the airplane window. John Riley told her to pray anytime. If she asked for forgiveness, God would hear her prayer.

Is that true, God? Can I ask you now—after all I've done?

She considered John Riley and his hope for her future and mulled over what he said about Jesus. She knew Grandmother Miggs believed, but Jesus didn't make a difference in her mother's life. Whatever doubts she held in the past, John Riley's simple prayer and assurance had opened her heart. She wanted to believe and already did—a tiny bit.

"Okay, God," she whispered, "I've tried this a few times, and I'm never sure if you're there. But here's the deal. If you're real, I need you. Can you forgive me? For my lies and hiding and stealing—for hurting so many people. I'm tired of hating my mother and Taylor. I'm tired of my anger over Grandmother's death. I don't want revenge. If you help me get through my interview with Thatcher and help me get my house in order, I'll give up wishing for John Riley to care for me. Thanks."

She sighed. John Riley lived his life for God and said he was happy. His demeanor showed an ease and peace that Audra wanted.

"John Riley says you promise to forgive—even someone like me. I know I said you could get off my back, but I didn't mean it. I need you. Please, God—forgive me. Please help me do what's right. Help me follow you."

She smiled and closed her eyes, reveling in peace for the first time since her grandmother had died.

Audra flicked on the light switch, hoping Thatcher's report was an exaggeration. Nope. Slit couch cushions lay on the floor—stuffing oozing out. Overturned bookshelves, scattered books, and glass was scattered across the floor.

She set the suitcase down, picked her way across the room, and hurried to the kitchen, holding her breath.

"Oh, Taylor, what have you done?" Sugar, spices, and flour dried in a red substance spread across her kitchen. Fragments of figurines and dishes crunched under her feet. The kitchen always cheered her—reminded her of Grandmother Miggs. But this was a nightmare, and she didn't know how to restore her home to the peaceful sanctuary she loved.

Scribbled red letters on the walls spelled l-o-s-e-r.

"No, Taylor. I'm not a loser. Jesus is on my side—you can't hurt me anymore."

She flipped off the light and smiled, unable to explain the peace overwhelming her heart.

Audra arrived early for her appointment, and the clerk ushered her into an empty room. She wiped her sweaty palms on her skirt. She tapped her toes, sat up straight, and glanced at the clock, unable to sit still.

Her heart pounded. She blew out a breath and glanced at the clock again.

Thatcher wants me nervous before he talks to me.

She wiped her palms and stared at the cement wall across from the table and willed her heartbeat to slow.

When the door opened, she smiled at Thatcher, but he breezed in without a smile.

"Morning, Cadence. Coffee?" he pushed a cup across the table. The Muddy Cup logo cheered her.

"Laura was surprised to learn you were out of state. She believed you were lying in bed recuperating from some horrible disease. Explain?"

"You know I like vintage things?"

He nodded.

"I found an old recipe box and returned it to a family member. She asked me to help settle her mother's estate, so we drove to Kentucky in her pink Cadillac."

Thatcher held up a hand. "Let's go back to that lady. Who?"

"Fredonia Addison."

Thatcher's eyebrows shot up. "Fredonia Addison took you to Kentucky?"

"Yes. You know her?"

"Yes. The Addisons are well connected here. I've met her once or twice. Go ahead."

"There's not much to tell. I helped clean out her mother's home, and we were returning to Deercrest on Tuesday, but you called."

"Let's get this straight. Where did you find the old recipe box?"

"The antique store downtown. Allie and I searched for the name we found written on the recipe cards."

"And it led you to Fredonia?"

"The recipe box was her mother's. I don't have anything of my mother's or grandmother's, and I thought—"

"You took it to her, and she invited you to clean out the house—got it. What I don't understand is why you left without telling anyone, why you left and let Laura and me assume you were ill."

Lord, help.

Her heart pounded, and she took a breath to calm herself. Thatcher was all business, not her Friday night bowling friend or the guy who taste-tested her freshly canned pickles. He was Officer Stevens, and her story would sever their friendship. A lump in her throat choked her words. She wanted to omit the truth—go back to normal. But she wasn't the same girl who had run from Deercrest. She was a new girl with a new heart. For the first time, she refused to run from the truth.

She leaned across the table and smiled. "My name is Audra March. I helped commit theft, and I've hidden my identity to avoid the consequences."

Thatcher glanced up from the notes he wrote, his pen stilled. "You need to fill in details, Cadence . . . Audra."

She did and smiled. Claiming her identity filled her with joy. As the radio preacher and Miss Ida Bealle's sampler said—the truth set her free.

CHAPTER 50

Norris Creek, Kentucky, August 1979

The cool storm cellar refreshed Ida Bealle. August's heat turned her into a cranky old woman. She had found bushels of pawpaws on the porch this morning, and she needed to make jam before they spoiled. She muttered as she moved clutter, searching for her canning rings.

"You'd think people would ask before they set their produce on my steps. I have other chores this week. What's this?" She turned a frame around and groaned. The long-forgotten "The truth will set you free" embroidery she had hid. She turned it around and pushed it behind a shelf.

"I don't need a sampler to remind me," she muttered, and a twinge of guilt pinched her heart, but not enough guilt to bring that sampler into the house.

"Aha." The box of rings and lids sat on a high shelf.

Freddie must have brought these down. I'd never store them that high.

Ida Bealle craned her neck and found a dark space at the top of the wall. "What in the world? I've lived here forty years and never saw that." She pulled the step stool over and peered inside. She reached in but found cold cement. "Strange."

"Ida Bealle, what are you doing up there?" Bud stood at the bottom of the cellar stairs, grinning.

"Don't stand there smirking. Get over here and give an old woman a hand."

He wrapped his arms around her. "You are a beautiful woman, Mrs. Horne." He wiggled his eyebrows and winked.

"Get on with yourself, Preacher Horne—no time for smoochin'. Someone left two bushels of pawpaws on the porch, and I'm making jam before they spoil." She moved past him, avoiding the playful pat he aimed at her backside. She smiled; thankful the man God gave her long ago still found her beautiful.

Bud loosened his tie and followed her up the stairs. "I'll help for a few minutes. I have a meeting in an hour, but I'll help. We need to talk."

When he said, "We need to talk," his tone told her it was her least favorite subject.

Bud settled at the table and helped peel pawpaws. "Ida Bealle, she needs the information. What about her eighteenth birthday?"

"Sure, Bud—let's ruin her birthday. 'Hey, Freddie, by the way, we aren't your parents. Happy birthday. Let's have cake.' That what you're thinking?" Pressure squeezed her chest, and her stomach twisted. She and Bud saw eye to eye on everything but this—it was always a sore point between them. He deferred to her wishes but mentioned it often. Lately he brought it up all the time.

"Ida Bealle, come on—give me some credit. I won't ruin her birthday."

"How? How would it be, Bud? Because I can't see this conversation going well."

She piled pawpaws onto the table, pretending she didn't hear.

She caught a glimpse of him out of the corner of her eye. Small streaks of gray lined the hair at his temples, and wrinkles etched his gentle face. He carried a few more pounds, but the years had aged him into a handsome man. She loved him with all her heart and thanked God for Bud every day.

Why can't he leave this alone?

"Why does it matter, Bud? We're her parents, and we love her. We've taught her about God. You taught her to ride a bike and shake off skinned knees. I sat with her when she was sick. We helped her with schoolwork and bought her that ridiculous dog we hated. We did that because we are her parents, Bud. Her parents."

"Hear me out, Ida Bealle." He reached for her hand, and his eyes searched hers. "I've let you have it your way, and I agree. We are her parents, and we loved every moment, but it's not the whole story. It's not the truth. Please?"

Ida Bealle dropped into the chair across from him and took several deep breaths. She wiped her eyes with the corner of her apron. "Okay, Bud. I give up." She wanted to argue and fight, but the defeat in his eyes tugged at her heart. He had given in throughout Freddie's entire life. Now she needed to trust him.

"The truth will set you free," he whispered, patting her hand.

"It doesn't feel free, Bud. It feels like a life sentence. What if she's angry and leaves to find the rest of her family? What if we never see her again?" The heaviness in her chest grew, threatening to drag her into a pit of despair.

Bud nodded, "I can't tell you what will happen, but we'll pray for wisdom. We have a little time." He glanced at his watch. "Gotta run." He kissed her and called, "Thank you, sweetheart!" as the screen door slammed shut.

Ida Bealle stared at the pawpaws on the table and blew out a breath. "Free my eye." She stabbed a piece of fruit with her knife, her heart heavy and her eyes filled with tears. Freddie loved pawpaw jam.

I'll use extra brown sugar to spoil my baby girl.

Miss Ida Bealle's Pawpaw Jam

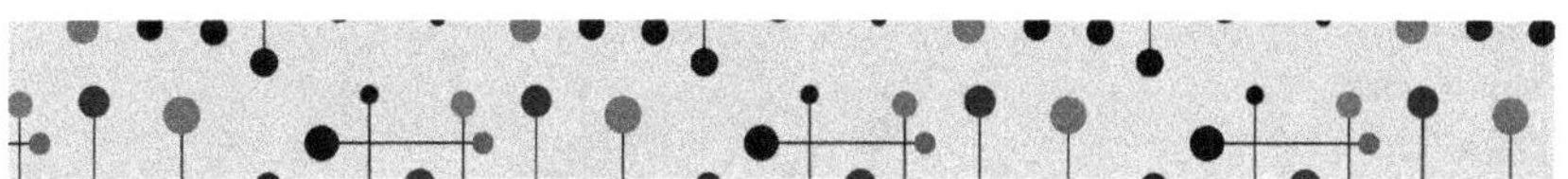

4 c. pawpaw fruit, pureed

½ c. water

½ c. apple cider vinegar

1 c. sugar

½ c. brown sugar

1 tbsp. low sugar pectin or ½ green apple diced fine

1 tsp. cinnamon

1 tsp. vanilla

Heat the pawpaw puree, water, and apple cider vinegar until simmering. Slowly stir in sugar. Continue to simmer for five minutes but stir so it doesn't stick or scorch.

Stir in pectin. Bring to a boil and turn off heat.

Stir in other ingredients.

Water bath can in sterilized jars and process for ten minutes. Check the jar for a good seal after twenty-four hours.

CHAPTER 51

When Audra stepped out of the police station, Laura beeped her horn. Audra leaned in the open window. "I'm sorry, Laura."

Laura waved. "It's all behind us. Get in. I'll take you home. Thatcher said your house is a mess. I'm here to help."

"Who's running the café?"

"Closed for the day. I have a friend with an emergency." Laura smiled.

Audra's heart dropped. "We need to talk."

"Okay."

"I confessed a crime to Thatcher this morning, and my name's not Cadence."

Laura smiled. "Get in, whoever you are."

Audra watched Deercrest pass as Laura drove. The park, the fountain bubbling in the square, and flags flying at businesses twisted her heart. Soon Deercrest would turn on her, and she would move. This time her name was Audra—no more deception.

"I didn't mean to hurt you, Laura," she said, and the story spilled out.

Laura eased the car next to the curb in front of the cottage, and Audra wiped her eyes. Telling the truth to Laura had opened a crack in her heart, and she was helpless to control her emotions. Audra realized her lies hurt too many people. The wall of deception she had raised robbed her of genuine friendship.

"Thanks for the ride, Laura—and for listening." Audra grabbed the door handle and hopped out, avoiding Laura's eyes.

"Hey, where are you going?" Laura called. "The cleaning stuff is in the trunk. Grab it."

Audra gasped. "You'll help me?"

"A little mayhem won't stop me from helping my friend Audra." She emphasized Audra. "Grab this bucket and move it."

"Oh, honey—I'm so sorry." Laura glanced around Audra's living room. "You know who did this? Is this why you left without telling anyone?"

"I know who did it, but I told Thatcher I won't press charges."

Laura laid her hand on her heart. "You should. What if you're not safe?"

"A couple of weeks ago I was different. I dreamed of killing this person. I changed—well, God changed me." Audra shared what she learned about Miss Ida Bealle and Preacher Bud. She shared all she knew about Fredonia's birth and Miss Ollie, who wasn't so terrible after all.

"The other day I didn't know what to do. I planned to do the wrong thing. But I found a sampler Miss Ida Bealle stitched, and the saying pestered me. It said, 'The truth will set you free.' I haven't told the truth for years."

Laura nodded. "I'm thankful, Cad . . . Audra." She rolled her eyes. "It will take me a little while to get used to your name."

"Call me whatever," Audra said, laughing. "It's my fault." She bent and picked up shards of glass.

"Stop. Gloves." Laura pulled a pair of work gloves out of her pocket and tossed them in Audra's direction.

"You'll come back to work at Muddy Cup after you settle everything?" Laura asked, pulling on her gloves.

"You won't fire me?"

"Fire you? You're the best little barista I ever hired. Thatcher came in every day asking about you. I'm pretty sure he missed you—even ordered a latte."

"Thatcher? I can't believe it. He said lattes are floofy." She laughed. "I told him, Laura. He's investigating, and he'll let me know. He wasn't warm fuzzies this morning."

"He's a good guy. I know he'll treat you right. He's fair."

"Yes, but fair means I have to pay for what I did.

Laura smiled. "I like this change—you have a new spark. Even if the worst happens, you'll flourish. You have the Lord, and you're stuck with me too."

Audra laughed and threw another broken figurine into the bucket—the choir boy with the slingshot. "Aww, man—I liked this one."

The walkway through the living room was clear when the doorbell rang.

"No one knows I'm home." Audra frowned and stretched her aching back.

Two Muddy Cup Café employees marched in along with a couple of customers and a neighbor.

"What's going on?"

Laura laughed. "I sent out an SOS."

"And here we are!" her neighbor lady called from the porch.

I don't deserve this.

She plopped onto the destroyed couch and rested her tired feet. The living room was clear of broken things. The empty shelves were wiped clean. The crew moved into the hallway to clean the minimal damage. She planned to join them in the kitchen in a moment. She rubbed her hand over the slit in the couch cushion.

I can't believe I'm not angry.

The trash can in the corner overflowed with treasures—the stuff purchased to recreate her Grandmother's home, the last time she belonged.

A smile spread across her face when understanding filled her heart. She didn't need Grandmother's home to find belonging. She belonged to Jesus, and he accepted her—mess and all.

CHAPTER 52

Norris Creek, Kentucky, May 1980

Ida Bealle paced the kitchen waiting for Bud's return with Freddie. She had worked at the café in town for several months, and Ollie worked there too. Ida Bealle wasn't too worried about Freddie. The café was a reputable establishment—no strange characters hanging around. But Ollie worked during the day, and Freddie worked the evening shift. Ida Bealle wasn't comfortable until her chick was home safe in the nest.

Freddie begged for permission to walk home after work, but five miles in the dark mountains wasn't acceptable for any girl, much less her own. Bud fetched her home every night in his blue truck, but Freddie insisted on walking home when it was light out. Ida Bealle said no, but Bud put his foot down. "She's seventeen, Ida Bealle. You have to let go. It's daylight, and she's a strong girl. It's good for her."

She quit fighting. Bud saw Freddie with a father's heart, but her mother's heart saw Freddie as the little bundle thrust at them in the middle of the night. She still remembered the emotions and protectiveness that engulfed her the moment she laid eyes on the baby.

"You'd keep her a baby if it was up to you, Ida Bealle." He shook his head, but Ida Bealle knew he didn't understand. Freddie was always her baby. Bud might let her grow up, but Ida Bealle struggled.

She wiped the counter of invisible crumbs and swept the immaculate floor. Still no noisy pickup. She rocked on the porch with her knitting, but it was too dark to see the stitches. She sighed and changed position, wrestling the fear crushing her chest.

Something's wrong.

Ida Bealle peered into the dark, willing them home. She had planned to call the sheriff in five minutes when the loud truck rumbled up the lane. The lights turned into the yard, and she willed herself calm before Bud found her upset—again.

The doors slammed, and Freddie laughed at something Bud had said. She bounded onto the porch and kissed Ida Bealle on the cheek. She smelled of grease, onions, and bubble gum. She blew a bubble, and it popped on her nose. "Night, Mom!" she yelled on her way inside.

"Ida Bealle, were you sitting out here worrying again?" Bud's voice was soft. He reached for her hand and massaged her fingers.

"No. I was knitting."

He chuckled, "I don't think you can see a stitch out here." He sat on the porch rail. "We have to let her grow up."

Bud was kind to say we. Bud never worried about Freddie growing up and leaving the nest.

"What if she goes back to her people? Or moves far away?" she whispered.

"Oh, sweetheart. You have to trust God. I will miss her when she leaves—'but God,' right?"

Ida Bealle nodded, and they repeated part of their favorite passage together: "But God, who is rich in mercy, for his great love wherewith he loved us . . ."

"Ephesians 2," Ida Bealle whispered.

"God has equipped her, and she's a responsible young lady, Mrs. Horne. We'll worry about her, but God helped us teach her his ways. We will have a quiet house, but God will provide peace. Should I continue?" his voice teased.

"No, Preacher. I hear your message."

He pulled her to her feet and wrapped his arms around her. He kissed the top of her head and whispered in her hair, "Mrs. Ida Bealle Horne, I love you. You have blessed my life immeasurably, and I'm thankful God gave you to me. He gave us our precious girl too, but you have to pry your fingers off her before she rebels."

She nodded her head. "I don't like it one bit, Bud Horne. And I don't like you right now for sayin' it."

He chuckled, "You're not the first to tell me that after a sermon."

"Remember when Dorothy Faye said you were too loud when you turned Bible pages?" Ida Bealle said.

Bud threw back his head and laughed. The tightness in her chest relaxed in the presence of her husband and his quiet strength.

"We've enjoyed a wonderful life here, haven't we? God is good."

She nodded. She enjoyed life here with Bud and hoped God allowed them many more years together.

A window opened above. "Quiet down there! People are trying to study up here!" Freddie yelled.

"Yes, ma'am," they yelled in unison, and the window slammed shut.

CHAPTER 53

Audra opened the windows in the kitchen to let in the fresh air. A blue jay swooped past on its way to the feeder in the backyard. Her rose bushes bloomed, and a hint of their perfume drifted through the screen. The group of friends spread across the kitchen.

"What is this stuff?" her neighbor asked.

"Paint?"

"It's sticky," Laura said with a sigh. "Grrrrr. Now I'm grumpy."

"I can't thank you enough for your help. We've had a long day." Audra grabbed a cloth and scrubbed red off the chair legs.

She smiled at the group's chatter. They were discussing what type of cleaner to use on the goo when the doorbell rang.

"Pizza's here?" Laura stood from the corner she scrubbed. "They're fast." She hurried through the house.

Audra finished the chair leg and rinsed the cloth. Voices drifted down the hall.

"Cadence . . . Audra!" Laura called. "Someone's here for you!"

Thatcher's here with the decision.

She squared her shoulders and pasted on a smile.

I deserve whatever happens. Thatcher is fair.

She lifted her chin and pasted on a smile, "Thatcher . . . I"

"Evenin', Miss Audra."

"What are you doing here?" She gasped, and her heart pounded as she glanced from Laura to John Riley.

Laura shrugged. "He's not the pizza guy."

"Miss Freddie worried about you after you left, so she bought me a plane ticket and sent me to check on you."

"I'm fine. My friends are helping me clean up. I . . ."

"Are we letting him in, Caden . . . Audra?" Laura held the door open. "It's getting awkward here."

"Oh, yes, I'm sorry. Laura, this is John Riley."

Laura held out her hand. "Pleased to meet you, John Riley. I'm her boss, but she's my friend." Laura nudged Audra. "Come in; I thought you were the pizza guy."

John Riley smiled. "I'm happy to pick one up if you like."

"Nah, it's on the way. I'll leave you two alone."

Audra nodded, and Laura disappeared.

John Riley's kind eyes searched hers. Air whooshed out of her lungs when he held her hand.

"We were so worried about you. You're okay?"

She nodded but wanted to scream, Kiss me already! But he was a preacher, and she was a criminal, and she didn't know how he felt about her. His thumb rubbing circles on her hand told her he wasn't here to say hi, but . . .

"Did Fredonia really send you?"

"She did, but it was after I kept asking her for news. When we didn't hear from you by lunch, she sent me to the airport."

"It was late, and everything was such a mess here, so I turned off the lights and went straight to bed. Then the interview at the police department this morning." She glanced away, ashamed.

"Hey—look at me," John Riley whispered. He tipped her chin up and stroked her cheek. She leaned in, wanting this moment to last forever, wishing for his kiss.

Behind John Riley a throat cleared. Audra jumped back, and her cheeks burned. "Thatcher," she said.

"Evening, Audra." Thatcher nodded to John Riley and waved the folder in his hands. "Can you step outside, please?"

Audra blew out the breath she held and smiled a weak smile at John Riley. She joined Thatcher on the porch, pulling the door shut.

"Who's that?"

"John Riley? He's the friend I met in Kentucky."

"Mmm . . ."

"He's a preacher."

Thatcher raised his eyebrow and scowled. "Will you come to the station for a few minutes? I want to run over some details with you and talking is easier over there. I'll bring you right back."

She wiggled her slippered foot. "Can I grab my shoes?"

Thatcher nodded, and she slipped back inside for sandals. John Riley waited in the living room.

"He needs me at the station for a few minutes."

"Are you in trouble?"

"He didn't say, but I'm sorry to leave when you just got here."

"I'll help the ladies. Don't worry about me. I'll be waiting whenever he brings you back."

His assurances unlocked the piece in her heart that she walled off from everyone else. She fought alone and refused to trust people, but knowing he waited for her cracked her defenses.

"Thank you, John Riley," she whispered.

The only sound on the way to the police station was an occasional squawk from the police radio. Audra sat in the passenger seat, counting her blessings that she didn't ride in the back.

Audra tried to sort the details of her day. When John Riley leaned down to talk to her, his blue eyes reminded her of sea glass. A long-forgotten memory of Mother and Lake Michigan flashed. Mother had spread a blanket on the sand, and they ate peanut butter sandwiches. Audra had found a piece of blue sea glass, and mother laughed and hugged her. She said she wanted to keep it forever because blue sea glass was the prettiest.

Audra closed her eyes, wondering why this memory floated to the surface today but was grateful for a happy memory with her mother.

Thatcher sat across from her at the table where she had spilled her secrets this morning. He opened the folder and pulled out a stack of papers.

"He's a preacher, huh?"

Audra nodded.

"I didn't see you as the type who'd go for a preacher."

"He's not interested in me, Thatcher."

"Oh, I beg to differ, but we have business here."

Audra leaned forward as he spread papers across the table.

"I visited the Boyd family this afternoon. They remembered you—fondly. They seemed surprised to hear of your involvement in the theft. They never suspected you."

Shame flushed her cheeks. "The Boyds took good care of me. I wanted to stay with them."

He pushed a paper across the table. "This is the inventory of the stolen items."

Audra read through the list and pictured Mrs. Boyd wearing the pieces.

Thatcher pointed at the last line, and Audra gasped.

"$10,000?"

He nodded. "This is large enough for felony theft charges, Audra."

The rigid walls around her heart crumbled, walls she had built to keep her from being honest with people——from experiencing pain. She didn't want life behind walls anymore, but the walls seemed insurmountable.

"I know," she whispered. "What do I need to do?"

"They are an extraordinary family. They won't press charges."

Audra stared at Thatcher for several seconds. "What does that mean?"

"I researched the law and consulted with a prosecutor."

"Do I need a lawyer, Thatcher?"

"A lawyer is your right. If you want one, we can't talk anymore."

She stared at him for several moments. "Go ahead."

"First of all, the family won't press charges. Mrs. Boyd said she loved you and always hoped you were well. She said you didn't live with them when this happened?"

Audra nodded.

"She and her husband agreed they don't want you to face charges. The prosecutor said if they don't press charges, he won't prosecute."

She blew out a breath. The twist inside her gut loosened, and the walls around her heart softened. She had held this secret so long that it was part of her identity. It was impossible to believe it had now ended in an instant.

"Furthermore, the prosecutor checked the statute of limitations. He can't prosecute you because it expired three years ago."

Audra's jaw dropped. "Three years? Years?"

Thatcher nodded.

"I carried all this around hiding and lying, and my crime wasn't even a threat anymore?"

"Nope."

She covered her face with her hands and blew out short, deep breaths. "I don't know what to say."

"There's not much to say other than tying up loose ends about the damage to your house. Give me a name, and I'll get the ball rolling."

Audra shook her head. "I can't." Tears pressed against the back of her eyes. Relief and excitement poured over her weary body, and she wanted to shout and cry at the same time.

"They can't hurt you, Audra. It's over."

"No, I mean, I don't want her in trouble. She has kids."

"A mother did this to your house? She's dangerous, Audra. She shouldn't get away with it. We can discover quite a bit with the evidence we collected, but you'll save me some time. Tell me—who did this?"

"Thatcher," she whispered, "I wanted to kill her. But now . . . I . . . can I refuse to say?"

"Yes, but as your friend, I'd like for you to tell me."

Audra thought he emphasized friend. "Can I p . . . pray about it?" she asked, stumbling on pray.

Thatcher's eyebrows shot up, and he grinned. "Looks like the preacher rubbed off on you, Audra."

She smiled. "I got acquainted with God down there, Thatcher."

He nodded. "Well, I can't forbid you from praying. I guess we won't have any more bowling and pizza nights?" He leaned back in his chair and rubbed his chin.

She blushed. "You've been a good friend, Thatcher."

He sat up. "Just a friend?"

She nodded.

"It's okay, Audra. You've been a good friend too—even if you do like those froofy coffees."

She grinned and shook her head. "They're called lattes, Thatcher. Lattes."

He pushed the envelope across the table. "Mrs. Boyd sent this. She said it was left in her files when you moved on. The letter was supposed to move with you, but she forgot about it 'til recently. You can read it later. I'll take you home so I can wrap up my paperwork for the night."

She picked up the envelope, tempted to rip it open, but Thatcher was halfway to the cruiser. Walking home wasted too much time. She needed to see John Riley.

Chapter 54

Norris Creek, Kentucky, May 1981

Ida Bealle settled on the sofa with her knitting while waiting for Bud to bring Freddie home from work. Her needles clacked as she knit, the long scarf pooled in her lap. She loved the feel of the wool yarn as it pulled through her fingers. The shades of blue worked into a striped pattern as she knit. She glanced at the clock and hummed while she worked. The air blew through the screen door, smelling of rain.

"Probably a storm brewin'. I better get upstairs and shut windows." The wind picked up, and dark clouds blew across the sky. She grabbed a sweater and stood on the porch. A storm like this one had blown in eighteen years ago when someone knocked on their door and gave them a baby. She shivered. Freddie had turned eighteen a couple of days ago, and she and Bud had agreed to tell her the story this weekend. Ida Bealle imagined that the news would crush Freddie. She worried about every bit of Bud's plan.

Hoping to see the truck lights before the downpour began, Ida Bealle leaned on the porch rail and waited for the storm. Lights shone at the end of the driveway, and she relaxed.

"Olivene?"

Olivene jumped out, yelling, "She's gone!"

"Who's gone?"

"Freddie!" Olivene raced ahead of Ida Bealle; raindrops pelted as they ran.

"Olivene Endicott, you tell me right now what you're talking about!" Ida Bealle slammed the door shut against the wind.

"Freddie went for her break, and she never came back." Ollie paced back and forth.

Ida Bealle's face drained. "What do you mean?"

"I mean, she went out of the café at her break, and she never came back." Ollie wiped her face and fanned herself as she paced.

"Where's Bud?"

"He came to pick her up, and when I told him, he tore out of there."

Ida Bealle shook her head. "I can't believe this, Ollie. Why didn't you call us or go after her yourself? We let her work there because of you. You're supposed to keep her safe."

"No, Ida Bealle Horne—you're supposed to keep her safe. That's why we gave her to you in the first place."

Ida Bealle gasped. The secret they kept was raw when spoken out loud. She suspected—knew—for years that Ollie was Freddie's birth mother. Now Ollie ripped away Ida Bealle's coping mechanism—denial.

"That's right, Ida Bealle. You were the one supposed to keep her safe and give her a good life. They said I couldn't do it, and they took her from me." Ollie's voice shook as accusations hovered in the air.

"If you think for one second I caused this, Olivene, then you aren't the woman I thought you were. If you plan to accuse me, then you go home right now. Otherwise, sit and quit pacing. You're driving me mad."

Ollie dropped into the chair in the corner and rocked. Ida Bealle sat with her knitting. "We don't even know what happened. I'm sure Bud will be home with her in a few minutes." Her clicking knitting needles soothed her mind, but her heart filled with dread. She tried to choke down the fear engulfing her.

Hours later, Ollie was snoring in the rocker, and Ida Bealle's needles were stilled. When Bud opened the door, they were both startled. Bud shook his head. Ida Bealle raced upstairs to Freddie's room and tore through notebooks and drawers. She hoped to find something—anything—to explain Freddie's disappearance.

Bud stood in the doorway. "I searched everywhere. I didn't know what else to do, so I came home." He gave Ida Bealle a weak smile. "I'm sorry, baby."

"Where is she, Bud? Where is she?" her voice rose a notch with every syllable.

The phone rang, and Ida Bealle dropped the book she held. Bud was already down the stairs, his hand on the receiver. "Freddie, where are you?" He ran his fingers through his hair.

Ida Bealle and Ollie crowded him and eavesdropped.

"No . . . no . . . I'll come to get you . . . no. . . . Oh, Freddie—I'll tell her." Bud hung up the phone.

"Well?" Ollie stood with her hands on her hips.

"She got married."

"What?" The women fired questions at him until he held up his hand.

"I need coffee." He pulled out the grounds and the percolator. Ida Bealle and Ollie waited for him to speak. Ida Bealle's heart thudded in her chest while she stared at her husband.

He poured himself a steaming cup of coffee and sat across from them. He rubbed his bloodshot eyes. "Freddie says she married a man named Phillip Addison, and she's on her way to Wisconsin." He glanced at Ida Bealle and grimaced. "They got married at a justice of the peace in Wolfe County, and they crossed into Ohio. She said she called so we wouldn't worry."

"Worry?" Ida Bealle said. "Why would we worry about our daughter marrying a stranger? Do something, Bud."

"Call the police," Ollie demanded.

Bud shook his head. "They won't do anything. She's marrying age, and she went of her own free will. They're not in Kentucky anymore."

Ida Bealle sat numb. So many questions and not enough answers. She shook her head, her mouth gaping, and tears stung her eyes.

"If you want to sleep on the couch, Ollie, make yourself comfortable," Bud said, and he followed Ida Bealle up the stairs. "We'll figure this out in the morning."

"Ollie," Ida Bealle called. "Who is Phillip Addison?"

"The rich salesman that stops for lunch every Tuesday."

"And you never told us? It sounds like it's not exactly *my* fault she's not safe now, doesn't it?" Ida Bealle stared at Ollie, her lips set in a thin line.

"Come on now, sweetheart," Bud said. He patted her shoulder and nudged her. "Let's not say something we'll regret when the sun comes up."

CHAPTER 55

Norris Creek, Kentucky, April 25, 2015

Ida Bealle rose from her rocker; her joints ached. "John Riley Blackburn, you come here and talk to me!" she called across the lawn.

John Riley waved and ran to the porch, "Mornin' Miss Ida Bealle. You okay?"

Ida Bealle swatted at him. "Go on now, John Riley. I'm not okay. Everything hurts, and I'm old. What about you?"

He leaned against the porch railing and smiled. "I'm fine as frog's hair, Missus Horne."

Ida Bealle chuckled. "Bud used to say that, didn't he? I miss him."

John Riley wrapped his arm around Ida Bealle's shoulders, "Me too. Preacher Bud was one in a million. Did you need me to help you with something?"

"Jest wanted to say good mornin' to you and let you know I love you." She reached up and patted his face. "Bud loved you too, John Riley. It blesses me to see how you're serving the Lord and taking care of the flock. He'd be so proud of you."

John Riley nodded. "I'm thankful for you and Preacher Bud. He taught me all he knew, and God did the rest."

Ida Bealle smiled and pulled his head down to kiss his cheek. "I got a letter from Freddie today. She's busy up there doin' whatever she does." She stared across the yard, remembering Bud and Freddie playing on the church lawn. She watched from the porch, her heart full, filing away the memories. Those days seemed so long ago—a different life.

"Will she come see you soon?"

"Hard to say. Freddie was here for Bud's service and stayed with me a long while, if you remember. I'm afraid Norris Creek isn't her home, but she takes good care of her momma. So do you, son."

John Riley smiled. "I hope you'll call if you need help—no matter what."

"How 'bout you help me eat that cake Olivene baked last night? Come in for a spell." She shuffled to the door, and John Riley followed.

"I never turn down a piece of cake, Miss Ida Bealle—you know that."

"You're a growing boy."

He patted his stomach and laughed. "I need to quit growing."

Ida Bealle chuckled. "'Bout time you found a wife, Preacher Blackburn. Don't you think a good woman would help you serve the Lord?"

"Yes, ma'am, I do, but God hasn't brought her by yet, and my house doesn't have room for anyone else—too small."

Ida Bealle waved around the kitchen." Pretty soon you'll have the parsonage."

"Oh, you stop that. You're gonna live here as long as you wish. We need you a bit longer. No rush on moving out of the parsonage, understood?"

She smiled and sighed, "Bud brought me here as a new bride. Been a lot of living in this house." She glanced around the kitchen, and a tear rolled down her cheek.

John Riley reached over and took her hand. "What's wrong, Miss Ida Bealle?"

"Oh, nothing. I jest miss my people and long for home."

He smiled. "Is God getting your heart ready for your homegoing?"

She nodded.

"We'll miss you when that time comes, but for now, you keep trusting Jesus for your daily strength. And you call me anytime you need a chat. Deal?"

"Yes, Preacher Blackburn," she said, winking. "You're bossy."

John Riley threw back his head, and his laughter filled the small kitchen. He wiped his eyes. "You're a spitfire yourself, Miss Ida Bealle."

She grinned. "Best be getting back to your preacher work over there."

"This is my preacher work; you know that better than anyone. Preacher Bud loved so many people, and if I'm half the preacher he was, I'll thank God for using me."

She squeezed his hand. "Thank you, John Riley. You're a good man. I'm praying for a woman for you."

"You better pray hard for that girl, Miss Ida Bealle. She's in for a heap of trouble, isn't she?"

"And a heap of blessing, John Riley. A heap of blessing." She patted his hand. "I'm mighty tired. I think I'll lie down. Can you see yourself out?"

He nodded, and she shuffled to lie down, hoping Ollie would stop by soon and help her take her shoes off.

Ida Bealle lay down on the couch, propping her head on the armrest, and sighed. She remembered moving to Norris Creek as a new bride and how proud she was watching Bud in the pulpit. She remembered a tiny bundle in a blanket thrust at her and the joy Freddie had brought her barren heart. She regretted the secret, but too many years had passed. Too late for old secrets. She had hidden her egg money tin and the letters in the cubby in the storm cellar. When she mailed her recipe box to Freddie, she tucked in a note and told her to find it. It was as close to telling Freddie as she ever came. Somehow even after so many years, the words froze on Ida Bealle's lips.

She listed her friends and loved ones—many of them already gone on to heaven.

Ida Bealle was tired, so tired. She missed her precious husband, who had loved her so well and spoiled her rotten. Ida Bealle smiled, remembering Bud's smile and playful spirit. "Thank you, God, for blessing me with Bud Horne," she whispered. "Thank you for this life you gave me with Bud and Freddie and all the rest. You've taken care of me for a good long time now, God, but I'm tired. You can take me home whenever you're ready."

Sun shone through the lace curtains and shadows danced around the room. "I'll have to dust those shelves in the morning," she whispered. "I'm so tired." She lay on the couch humming her favorite hymn.

> 'Tis so sweet to trust in Jesus,
> Just to take Him at His word,
> Just to rest upon His promise,
> Just to know, "Thus saith the Lord."
> Jesus, Jesus, how I trust Him!
> How I've proved Him o'er and o'er!
> Jesus, Jesus, precious Jesus!
> O for grace to trust Him more!

Ida Bealle Horne closed her eyes and fell asleep. When she woke, she glimpsed her precious Jesus, and her heart filled with worship.

Audra didn't know how to process the whirlwind twenty-four hours, but for now she was thankful. Her kitchen sparkled, all traces of Taylor's rampage washed away.

Audra whistled. "Wow! Thank you!"

Laura wiped the kitchen windows and removed the last fingerprints. "That's what friends do. But I'm beat, and my kids want their supper." She pulled a rag from her back pocket and dropped the cloth onto a pile. "This kitchen is spotless." She pointed to John Riley. "He did more than everyone combined; he's a hard worker. You should keep him around." She winked at Audra. "Made you blush. I'll let myself out. Nice meeting you, John Riley." She waggled her eyebrows at Audra.

A nervous flutter tickled in her chest. Since Thatcher's call, she had run on adrenaline, and now she wanted to curl up and sleep for days. But, she wanted to talk to John Riley and find out what was inside the envelope.

"Well?" he asked. He sat at the table; his hands folded.

"Do you want a drink? I have coffee, or at least I did before my cupboards got ransacked."

"I'm fine. I'd like to know what happened at the station."

She sat across from him. "I'd invite you to the living room—the couch is more comfortable—but it's not in service at the moment."

He smiled and cleared his throat.

"Right. Well, Thatcher said the family I stole from wouldn't press charges, and the statute of limitations has expired."

"Wonderful news, Audra."

"Then why am I sad? I ran from a lie. I deceived everyone over details that weren't even true. All the emotions I bottled inside me are fighting to get out. I . . ." She shook her head, and a tear trickled down her cheek.

"Hey, you carried this alone . . . for so long. I'm sorry you were alone."

She sighed and took a deep breath, willing her eyes to stay dry. "I lied and stole. I hid who I am. I wanted to kill Taylor for blackmailing me. I didn't care about the Boyds' needs. My whole life feels like a recipe for disaster."

"Your sin caused problems everywhere, but God is bigger than this. He's big enough to help you live a new life," John Riley whispered. "You took the first steps and asked God for forgiveness. You told the truth, and you faced the consequences. What's next?"

"I don't know, but I need to pay the Boyds every penny I stole."

John Riley nodded. "Good start."

"Use my name." She grimaced. "Ugg . . . all my customers, neighbors . . . Fredonia."

"Don't worry about Fredonia, but if Miss Ollie ever finds out . . ." His laugh filled her kitchen. It was a good sound and made her cottage feel like a home.

"Oh, man—Miss Ollie! Phew . . ." She smiled. "I kinda like the old girl."

"Don't ever let her hear you call her old," he said with a wink, and his blue eyes sparkled.

Audra's belly fluttered, and she wished again that she was the type of girl John Riley wanted, that he saw her as someone more than a messed-up girl in need of help.

"Miss Freddie wants to donate Miss Ida Bealle's money for the community center. She said her daddy would have loved the idea."

"There were letters with the money, John Riley. Fredonia's mother is . . ."

"I know."

"How?"

"Preacher Bud told me long ago. It bothered him, and Miss Ida Bealle wouldn't let him tell Miss Freddie, but she swore him to silence years ago. He disagreed, but he loved Miss Ida Bealle somethin' fierce."

"So the perfect Miss Ida Bealle kept secrets?"

"Oh, Miss Ida Bealle wasn't perfect. She was stubborn and intense. She was a beautiful lady, but she was a spitfire."

"Does Fredonia know?"

John Riley shrugged. "It weighed on Preacher Bud, so I doubt Miss Freddie knows. Miss Ida Bealle never spoke of it to me." He sighed. The secrets they held settled around them like a heavy fog.

"Oh, the envelope." Audra hurried through the house, and John Riley followed. Through the screen door the moon shone, flooding her home with soft light.

"Let's sit outside, Miss Audra. Look at that moon."

They settled on the narrow porch, knees touching. Audra held the envelope for a moment, then tore it open. It was a letter and another envelope.

Dearest Audra,

We remember you fondly and are thankful to hear you're well. Don't give any of this another thought. We hold nothing against you.

My apologies that the enclosed letter didn't follow you. I filed the papers when you first came and forgot about the envelope until long after you left.

If you'd like to visit, we'd love to see you again. I always remember you as the sad little girl who came to our home and didn't speak for a month. I wish we could have loved away all your hurts when you were with us. We've prayed for you since you left our home—that you'd know true peace and the One who makes it possible.

Momma Boyd

Audra smiled. "I forgot we called her that." She ran her hands across the other envelope—Grandmother's handwriting. A lump in her throat choked her, and she tried to swallow.

"Do you want privacy?" John Riley whispered.

She shook her head. "Stay, please. She's been gone so long. Grandmother was the last person who loved me and gave me a home. She was the last person who made me feel safe."

Until you, John Riley. The realization hit like a lightning bolt.

She eased the flap open and pulled out the letter and a key.

Dear Audra,

Grandma's sorry to leave you. I planned to watch you grow and protect you. But I'm a sick old woman and won't live long.

Please forgive your mother. I was too hard on her, and your grandfather indulged her. I don't know if that's why she turned out the way she did or not, but it wasn't you. I don't know where she is. I hope you find her, and I hope she's gotten it out of her system and is ready to be a grown-up. I loved her—always did. But I wasn't good at telling her. I wasn't much better at telling you. But oh, how I love you!

You are the best thing to happen to any of us, no matter what your mother did. When Grandpa died and your mom left, it was you and me. You've always made me so proud.

This key is for a safe deposit box at First Federal—small items I wanted to give you when you grew up. I left instructions for you to open it when you turn eighteen. My recipe box is there, my wedding ring and Grandfather's, a few pictures, and the last of my money—$5,000. You spend the money however you choose.

I hope you remember I love you and I'm proud of you. You'll forever be Grandma's baby girl no matter how old you've grown.

Eat some gingerbread cake for me and remember our talks.

Love,
Grandmother

A wave of grief crashed, overwhelming Audra, and she held the letter over her heart, sobbing. John Riley wrapped his arm around her and pulled her to his side.

When the grief had passed, Audra sniffled and wiped her eyes. "Sometimes I wondered if she loved me. She was stern and quiet. But I remember the gingerbread cake and the talks, and I held on to that."

"Do you want to find your mom?" he asked.

Audra shook her head. "No. I don't want to know why she didn't choose me."

John Riley nodded. "I understand that."

"Did you ever search for your daddy?" Audra asked.

"No," he said. "Same reason, I guess. I don't know where he went or what happened. God will fill in the blanks someday. I don't hate him anymore."

Audra nodded. The moonlight reflected in John Riley's dazzling blue eyes.

I can get lost in those eyes.

The weight of her past lifted from her shoulders. She was light and happy and her new faith filled her with confidence and bravery.

She leaned on him. He smelled of Pine-sol instead of his usual cologne. She smiled, thankful for his energy and help. She took a deep breath to clear her mind.

John Riley cared for people and devoted his life to needs—spiritual and physical. She had watched him over the past days as he hauled gifts to his mountain folks. She had watched as he shared his faith and prayed with people one moment and washed dishes the next. He had scrubbed her filthy kitchen without complaint. He didn't judge her for her deception or her past. He accepted her and cared enough to point her to the One who gave her peace. He was a treasure, and she couldn't let him leave for Norris Creek . . . at least not before she told him her feelings.

"I'm not a criminal anymore, John Riley."

"No, ma'am. You are not." He scooted toward her and took her hand.

"Do you think we . . . ? I mean, do you think you . . .?"

He interrupted, "Yes, Miss Audra." He leaned in for a kiss. His gentle lips answered her questions and gave her all she had wished for

—home.

He leaned his forehead on hers and whispered, "Miss Audra, I'm glad I met you." His eyes twinkled, and he winked. "I'm lookin' forward to gettin' to know you better. Can we figure out how this long-distance thing works?"

Audra nodded. "At least until I pay the Boyds back."

"Then what, Miss Audra?" he whispered, his lips next to hers.

She shrugged, "Then you'll get tired of me and decide you want to get to know Tansy better."

His laughter filled her yard. "I'll never get tired of you, Miss Audra."

He wrapped his arm around her, and she rested on his shoulder. The porch lamp bathed them in soft light, and the breeze swirled the perfume of her antique roses. Fireflies twinkled in the air, adding to her delight.

John Riley pulled her hand to his lips and kissed her fingers. "You're home now, Miss Audra."

She held her breath, willing herself to memorize every detail of this perfect moment. As long as she lived, she remembered the night her broken pieces became whole, the night John Riley's heart became her home.

MRS. RAY'S THRIFTY SALAD

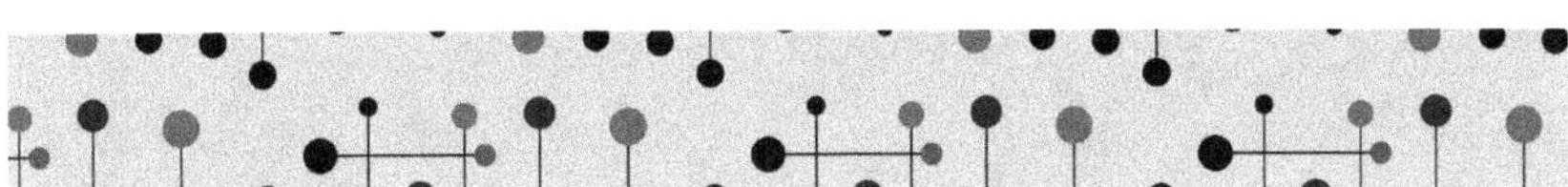

1 package lime gelatin
1 c. hot water
½ c. cold water
¼ tsp. salt
½ c. mayonnaise
2 tbsp. lemon juice
1 c. diced cooked carrots
1 c. cooked peas
1 c. cooked ham, cubed
Tomato Slices

1. Dissolve gelatin in hot water. Stir in cold water, salt, and mayonnaise. Whip with beaters until frothy.

2. Pour into mold and refrigerate fifteen to twenty minutes.

3. Layer the following ingredients in your gelatin mold, one ingredient at a time: Carrots, peas, ham, tomato slices.

4. Pour frothy gelatin over the layers and refrigerate four hours.

5. Unmold onto a bed of lettuce leaves and garnish with radish slices.

**May substitute hard-boiled egg slices for any vegetable or ham. Either way is delicious.

Epilogue

*C*hristmas Eve, *Turkey Creek Baptist Church*

"When will it be time to eat?" one of the blonde Preece girls tugged at Audra's skirt.

She hurried around the church kitchen and set out napkins and cups. She flipped on the industrial-sized coffee brewer and listened to the children running around the basement, costumes flapping behind them. Squeals of excitement were interrupted by Sunday School teachers calling, "Quiet!"

"Soon—now go back to your teacher." She shooed the little girl out of the kitchen and peeked out at the commotion. Children huddled in the corner, reciting their lines while Tansy Spurlock lined up shepherds and straightened their turbans. She rolled her eyes at Audra over the head of one of the Endicott boys.

Christmas pageants stretched the limits of her patience, but she loved them—the familiar Bible passages and sweet children, listening to the melody of carols filling the decorated church, the gifts they passed out to the children. She might complain or roll her eyes and sigh with her friend Tansy, but she wouldn't have it any other way. The Christmas pageant at Turkey Creek Baptist Church was the highlight of her year.

The notes of "Silent Night" drifted downstairs. John Riley's deep voice led the congregation. "Children!" she called. A smile spread across her face as children ran to line up behind her.

The noisy congregation milled around the basement munching on cookies. Audra watched John Riley carry their newborn son while he walked around greeting his congregation. He patted someone on the back, kissed a grandmother's cheek, spoke with one man or another. Children ran to him, pulling on his suit coat. She watched him lean down and smile at a little boy.

John Riley was such a good preacher and a wonderful daddy. He kissed Baby Bud's cheek and wrapped the blanket more tightly, and her heart squeezed at the joy on his face.

He motioned for her to join him and slipped his arm around her. "Good job, Mrs. Blackburn," he whispered in her ear. He handed Baby Bud to Miss Ollie, and Audra followed him to the Christmas tree.

The Ladies' Missionary Society wrapped donated gifts for every child and left them in a pile. John Riley and Audra talked with the children for a moment, prayed, and hugged each one.

The gift pile had dwindled when a familiar woman stepped out from a dark corner. She held her arms out, and Audra reached for a hug.

Freddie waved her away. "Give me that baby." Freddie's eyes sparkled as she stepped over packages and Christmas wrap and grabbed the baby from Miss Ollie.

She snuggled him, smothering his head with kisses. She rested her nose on his tiny head and glanced up with a grin, "Newborn . . . mmm, the best smell in the world." She rocked the baby back and forth. "He's beautiful."

Ollie frowned. "Hey, I was holdin' him. John Riley won't turn him loose, and we just got comfortable. Give him back."

Freddie shook her head, "No way. I'm hogging him the whole time I'm here. Sorry I missed the program—my plane was late."

"We didn't know you were coming," Audra said.

"Surprise." Freddie smiled, reaching out her hand and giving Audra a half hug. She gazed at the baby and smiled. "Good job, little momma." She kissed the baby's head again.

John Riley rested his arm on Audra's shoulders and pulled her to his side. "Hey, Miss Freddie—I'm responsible for some of that baby's beauty."

Freddie laughed. "Okay, Preacher Blackburn, but Audra did all the work. I'm so happy for you."

Ollie's eyes sparkled, and her gruff demeanor disappeared when Fredonia exclaimed over Baby Bud. Bud curled up his fist and let out a wail, and Audra swooped in to grab him, perching the baby on her shoulder while patting his bottom.

"I have another surprise," Freddie said. "I'm moving back to Norris Creek." The commotion in the basement stilled—everyone listened.

Ollie gasped and wiped a tear away.

"Wonderful news. What brought on this decision, Miss Freddie?" John Riley asked.

Fredonia glanced around and waved. "This is home, John Riley. Besides, my mother here is getting older, and I'd like to spend some time with her." She patted Ollie's knee.

Audra held her breath and stared at John Riley, her eyes wide. He mouthed, "Uh-oh."

Miss Ollie froze, and her face paled.

John Riley cleared his throat, "Um . . . when did you? How . . . ?"

Freddie laughed. "Everyone knew but me, huh? It's okay. Momma's note said the tin explained everything, but there was only money—no answers. I considered what she meant but pushed it out of my mind for a while. But when I returned to Deercrest, every time I looked in the mirror, I saw Ollie. I remembered confusing tidbits from my childhood and searched for my birth announcement." She glanced at Miss Ollie. "There are no births in Norris Creek on the day I was born. I searched for all my friends and found their birth announcements in the paper. A bit odd they didn't announce the preacher's baby, don't you think?"

Ollie turned red. Audra felt a flash of sympathy but turned back to Fredonia.

"The announcement in my baby book doesn't say what time I was born or how much I weighed. Momma kept meticulous records . . . why would she leave that out?" Freddie gazed around the circle, "She wouldn't leave that out, would she, Ollie?"

Ollie shook her head.

"I found interesting information in their medical records. My parents' blood type and mine are an impossibility." Freddie paused and glanced around. "I checked with my doctor. They're not my parents."

Miss Ollie's face flushed.

Fredonia smiled. "I don't know why you didn't tell me or why it took me almost sixty years to figure it out, but we have years of catching up." She reached and hugged Miss Ollie. Miss Ollie gripped Freddie's neck, and to Audra's surprise, Ollie burst into tears.

Audra pulled John Riley away, giving the women privacy. The silent church members let out the breaths they had held, and parents gathered children and shooed them out the door. Their gaze drifted toward Ollie and Fredonia as they left.

"Come here with that baby and sit down," Freddie said, patting the chair next to her.

"What about your beautiful home?" Audra asked.

Freddie shook her head, "I was foolish to stay all this time. Momma and Daddy needed me at home, but I was so stubborn. I wanted to honor Phillip's wishes, but over the decades I stayed because I didn't want her to win." Tears shone in her eyes. "I was stupid."

She smiled and reached for Baby Bud. "This little boy needs his Grammy Freddie, and I need all of you. Unless I'm not welcome here."

Ollie growled, "Unless you're not welcome here? That's the stupidest thing I ever heard." She marched to the kitchen. Dishes clanked in the sink, and cupboard doors slammed.

John Riley threw back his head, and his contagious laughter filled the room. Audra and Freddie laughed too.

Freddie patted Bud's back and smiled. "Well, that's settled. Merry Christmas—the prodigal's come home."

Audra thought she heard angels singing "Hallelujah," but maybe it was her joy. Two and a half years ago she had visited Norris Creek as Cadence with murder in her heart, carrying heavy baggage filled with lies. She was lonely and afraid. "But God, who is rich in mercy," filled the empty corners of her heart and forgave her when she believed. Her road home was twisted and lonely, but God changed her. Now she lived in the truth of who God said she was—no more deception. He had given Audra an extraordinary husband, a beautiful baby, and a cozy home in an old parsonage. She knew friends in every holler, and worthwhile projects filled her days. She was safe and whole. And now two grammies loved her Baby Bud.

"John Riley . . ."

"Hmmm . . ."

"Know what I found in Miss Ida Bealle's recipe box?"

John Riley frowned. "Okay, I'm sorry. I hid that 'Salmon Salad Surprise' recipe under the other cards. I can't eat it."

"No, silly." She swatted him. "The recipe for joy."

He leaned down and kissed her, and then she did hear an angel sing.

"Mommy's coming, baby!" she called, her heart overflowing, full of joy.

A LETTER TO MY READERS

Dear Reader,

Thank you for reading my first novel, The Road Home.

I promised my mom I would publish my first book by the age of twelve, and while I'm several years past that (ahem—we won't discuss quite how many that is), I'm almost as excited to finish this book as I was when I worked on stories as a girl.

Learning to write a novel is hard work, but I've enjoyed every moment. Several years ago I was running errands when an old pink Cadillac with three laughing women in the front seat passed me. I smiled at their happiness and wished I had a camera. I made up stories about their adventures and decided to add a pink Cadillac in my novel.

My sister and I enjoy returning items and documents we find at thrift stores—that part of the story is fact. I've returned property records from the 1930s, a junior high diploma from the 1940s, and an old German textbook to a family whose grandmother taught at a one-room schoolhouse in Iowa. If someone had messaged me offering to return something from my family, I would sing the "Hallelujah" chorus.

My grandmother grew up in a tiny Appalachian Kentucky town in the 1920s and 1930s. She lived in a small cabin out of town in coal mining country. Her family lived a hard life, but I've heard stories of endurance and creativity that inspire me.

We visited her hometown in April 2021, and I met cousins who still live there. They showed us the town, and I learned about my roots. History and stories are important to my family, and I enjoyed experiencing a connection to my grandmother.

I've lived in Wisconsin most of my life. My parents grew up in different parts of the United States, so I didn't think I said Wisconsin words, but I do use "ope" now and then.

Some of my favorite vintage items made an appearance in The Road Home. If you would like to peek, visit my website and click on my Pinterest board for The Road Home.

I imagine you want to know if the crazy cat ladies story is fact or fiction. Leave a comment on my blog with your guess, and I'll tell you if you're right.

Thank you for joining me on my journey to The Road Home. Come along for the ride and meet my next cast of characters. Sign up for my newsletter at www.malissachapin.com and be the first to find out where my next novel will take you.

If you enjoyed my first novel, please help me out by leaving a review.

Malissa Chapin

ACKNOWLEDGMENTS

A thank you~

To my parents, Charles and Eva Bonner, thank you for raising me in the admonition of the Lord. I love you.

To my sisters and brother, Rebekah Kotlar, Rachel Hershberger, and John Bonner, who brainstormed with me and read all my ramblings. You helped me, challenged me, and cheered for me—over and over. I love you.

To the men at my house, for putting up with my endless hours at the computer and questions and book chatter. Thanks for detouring to Inez, Kentucky, in the RV so I could see where my Grandma Bonner grew up. I love you.

To Alissa Schwalbach and Christina Lyon for encouraging me before I started and telling me I could do this. Your friendship means everything to me.

To my Sunday school class ladies who shared the best crime and villain suggestions. It cracks me up that you helped me plot the devious parts. I appreciate you and I'm thankful for all the ladies' nights. Your friendship is an important part of my life. I appreciate your support.

To my cousin Tonya Young for helping me with Kentucky details. I've enjoyed getting to know you and I'm thankful for your input and correction when something wasn't right. It was so fun to meet you, but I'm not eating whistlepig.

To Miranda Pautz for helping name Cici and for helping me to understand how it felt to grow up without family guidance and support. You inspire me.

To my alpha readers: Karla Bolender, Laurie Griepentrog, Ashley Hawley, Rachel Hershberger, Jackie Koll, Rebekah Kotlar, Christina Lyon, Christy Reeder, Crystal Thornton, Xanthe Vanderputt, Angela Wix, and Tonya Young. You supported, encouraged, challenged, and corrected me and made this novel better. You are amazing.

To all of my readers, thank you. You're the best.

ABOUT THE AUTHOR

Malissa Chapin grew up reading books, making up stories, and vowing to publish a book before turning twelve. She's a few years late for her goal but still devours books and makes up stories.

Malissa loves creating with words, yarn, fabric, and watercolors and lives in Wisconsin with her family and a crazy cat.

Visit her website:
www.malissachapin.com to join her mailing list and be the first to hear about new releases.

Murder Goes Solo A Piper Haydn Piano Mystery by Malissa Chapin

Coming Soon

Unwrapping 5 Names of God for Christmas by Malissa Chapin

Available on Amazon